CAPTIVE PRINCE

The Captive Prince Trilogy

CAPTIVE PRINCE
PRINCE'S GAMBIT
KINGS RISING

CAPTIVE PRINCE

C. S. PACAT

BERKLEY

NEW YORK

BERKLEY
An imprint of Penguin Random House LLC
penguinrandomhouse.com

Library of Congress Cataloging-in-Publication Data

Pacat, C. S.
Captive prince / C. S. Pacat.—Berkley trade paperback edition.
p. cm.
ISBN 978-0-425-27426-2
1. Princes—Fiction.   2. Monarchy—Fiction.   3. War stories.   I. Title.
PS3616.A323C37 2015
813'.6—dc23
2014035472

Berkley trade paperback edition / April 2015

Printed in the United States of America
25th Printing

Map design by Guy Holt, guyholt.com.au

Captive Prince is dedicated to
all the original readers and supporters of the story.
Your encouragement and enthusiasm
is what made this book possible.

Thank you all so much.

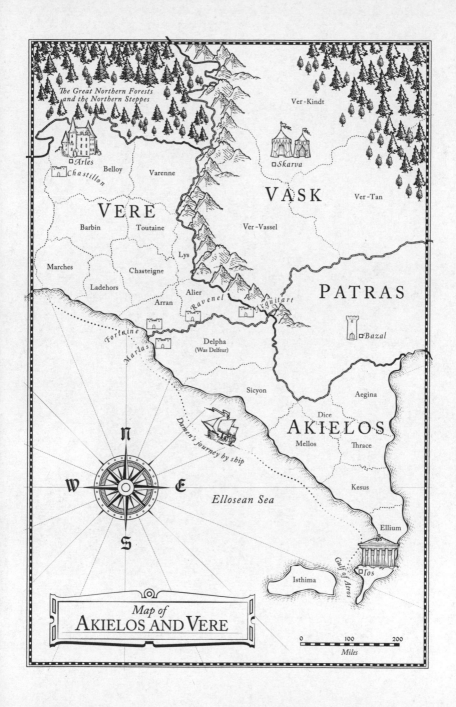

The Great Northern Forests
and the Northern Steppes

Ver-Kindt

Arles
Chastillon
Belloy
Varenne

Skarva

VASK

VERE

Ver-Tan

Barbin
Toutaine

Ver-Vassel

Lys

Marches

Chasteigne

Ladehors

Arran

Alier

Ravenel

Arquitart

PATRAS

Fortaine

Marlas

Delpha
(Was Delfeur)

Bazal

Sicyon

Aegina

Dice

AKIELOS

Damen's Journey by ship

Mellos

Thrace

N

Kesus

W

E

Ellosean Sea

Ellium

S

Ios

Isthima

Gulf of Atros

Map of
AKIELOS AND VERE

0   100   200
Miles

CHARACTERS

AKIELOS
THEOMEDES, King of Akielos

DAMIANOS (Damen), son and heir to Theomedes

KASTOR, illegitimate son of Theomedes and Damen's half brother

JOKASTE, a lady of the Akielon court

ADRASTUS, Keeper of the Royal Slaves

LYKAIOS, a female slave in the household of Damianos

ERASMUS, a male slave

VERE
THE REGENT of Vere

LAURENT, the heir to the throne of Vere

RADEL, overseer of the Prince's household

GUION, a member of the Veretian Council and Ambassador to Akielos

AUDIN, a member of the Veretian Council
HERODE, a member of the Veretian Council
JEURRE, a member of the Veretian Council
CHELAUT, a member of the Veretian Council

NICAISE, a pet

GOVART, a former member of the King's Guard

JORD, a member of the Prince's Guard
ORLANT, a member of the Prince's Guard

VANNES, a courtier
TALIK, her pet

ESTIENNE, a courtier

BERENGER, a courtier
ANCEL, his pet

Patras
TORGEIR, King of Patras
TORVELD, younger brother of Torgeir and Ambassador to Vere

From the Past
ALERON, former King of Vere and Laurent's father
AUGUSTE, former heir to the throne of Vere and Laurent's
    older brother

PROLOGUE

"WE HEAR THAT your Prince," said Lady Jokaste, "keeps his own harem. These slaves will please any traditionalist, but I have asked Adrastus to prepare something special in addition, a personal gift for your Prince from the King. A gem in the rough, as it were."

"His Majesty has already been so generous," said Councillor Guion, Ambassador of Vere.

They strolled the length of the viewing gallery. Guion had dined on mouth-watering spiced meats wrapped in grape leaves, the noonday heat fanned away from his reclining form by attentive slaves. He felt generously willing to admit that this barbaric country had its charms. The food was rustic, but the slaves were impeccable: faultlessly obedient and trained to efface and anticipate, nothing like the spoiled pets at the court of Vere.

The gallery was decorated by two dozen slaves on display.

All were either naked or barely clad in transparent silks. Around their necks the slaves wore gold collars decorated with rubies and tanzanite, and on their wrists golden wrist-cuffs. These were purely ornamental. The slaves knelt in demonstration of their willing submissiveness.

They were to be a gift from the new King of Akielos to the Regent of Vere—a highly generous gift. The gold alone was worth a small fortune, while the slaves were surely some of the finest in Akielos. Privately, Guion had already ear-marked one of the palace slaves for his personal use, a demure youth with a beautifully slender waist and heavily lashed dark eyes.

As they reached the far end of the gallery, Adrastus, the Keeper of the Royal Slaves, bowed sharply, the heels of his laced brown leather boots drawing together.

"Ah. Here we are," said Lady Jokaste, smiling.

They proceeded into an antechamber, and Guion's eyes widened.

Bound and under heavy guard was a male slave unlike any Guion had ever seen.

Powerfully muscled and physically imposing, he was not wearing the trinket-chains that adorned the other slaves in the gallery. His restraints were real. His wrists were lashed behind his back, and his legs and torso were bound with thick cords. Despite this, the force of his body looked only barely contained. His dark eyes flashed furiously above the gag, and if you looked closely at the expensive cords that bound his torso and legs, you could see the red weals where he had fought, hard, against his restraints.

Guion's pulse sped up, an almost panicked reaction. A gem in the rough? This slave was more like a wild animal, nothing like the twenty-four tame kittens who lined the hall. The sheer power of his body was barely held in check.

Guion looked at Adrastus, who was hanging back, as though the slave's presence made him nervous.

"Are all the new slaves bound?" asked Guion, trying to regain his composure.

"No, just him. He, that is—" Adrastus hesitated.

"Yes?"

"He isn't used to being handled," said Adrastus, with an uneasy sideways look at Lady Jokaste. "He hasn't been trained."

"The Prince, we hear, enjoys a challenge," said Lady Jokaste.

Guion tried to quell his reaction as he turned his gaze back to the slave. It was highly questionable whether this barbarous gift would appeal to the Prince, whose feelings towards the savage inhabitants of Akielos lacked warmth, to say the least.

"Does he have a name?" asked Guion.

"Your Prince is, of course, free to name him whatever he likes," said Lady Jokaste. "But I believe it would greatly please the King if he were to call him 'Damen.'" Her eyes glittered.

"*Lady Jokaste,*" said Adrastus, seemingly in objection, though of course that was impossible.

Guion looked from one to the other of them. He saw that he was expected to make some comment.

"'That is certainly—an interesting choice of name," said Guion. In fact he was appalled.

"The King thinks so," said Lady Jokaste, stretching her lips slightly.

◆ ◆ ◆

They killed his slave Lykaios with the quick slice of a sword across her throat. She was a palace slave, untrained in combat and so sweetly obedient that, had he commanded it of her, she would have knelt and bared her own throat for the stroke. She was not given a chance to obey or resist. She folded soundlessly, her pale limbs lying quite still on the white marble. Beneath her, blood began slowly to spread out over the marble floor.

"Seize him!" said one of the soldiers who poured into the room, a man with lank brown hair. Damen might have allowed it simply out of shock, but it was in that instant that two of the soldiers lay hands on Lykaios and cut her down.

At the end of the first exchange, three of the soldiers were dead, and Damen had possession of a sword.

The men facing him wavered and held back.

"Who sent you?" said Damen.

The lank-haired soldier said, "The King."

"Father?" He almost lowered his sword.

"Kastor. Your father is dead. Take him."

Fighting came naturally to Damen, whose abilities were born of strength, natural aptitude and relentless practice. But these men had been sent against him by one who knew all of that very well, and further, was not stinting in his judgement of how many soldiers it would take to overcome a man of Damen's calibre. Overwhelmed by numbers, Damen could only last so long before he was taken, his arms twisted behind his back, a sword at his throat.

He had then, naively, expected to be killed. Instead he was beaten, restrained and—when he fought free, doing a gratifying amount of damage for one who had no weapon—beaten again.

"Get him out of here," said the lank-haired soldier, wiping the back of his hand across the thin line of blood at his temple.

He was thrown into a cell. His mind, which ran along straight and candid lines, could not make sense of what was happening.

"Take me to see my brother," he demanded, and the soldiers laughed, and one kicked him in the stomach.

"Your brother's the one who gave the order," one of them sneered.

"You're lying. Kastor's no traitor."

But the door of his cell slammed shut, and doubt raised its head for the first time.

He had been naive, a small voice began to whisper, he hadn't anticipated, he hadn't seen; or perhaps he had refused to see, giving no credence to the dark rumours that seemed to disrespect the honour with which a son should treat the final days of a sick and dying father.

In the morning they came for him, and understanding now all that had occurred, and wishing to meet his captor with courage and bitter pride, he allowed his arms to be lashed behind his back, submitting to rough handling and moving forward when he was propelled by a hard shove between the shoulders.

When he realised where he was being taken, he began to struggle again, violently.

◆ ◆ ◆

The room was simply carved in white marble. The floor, also marble, sloped faintly, terminating at an unobtrusive carved runnel. From the ceiling hung a pair of shackles, to which Damen, forcefully resisting, was chained against his will, his arms pulled up above his head.

These were the slave baths.

Damen jerked against the restraints. They didn't budge. His wrists were already bruised. On this side of the water, a miscellany of cushions and towels were arranged in an appealing tumble. Coloured glass bottles in a variety of shapes, containing a variety of oils, glimmered like jewels amid the cushions.

The water was scented, milky, and decorated with slowly drowning rose petals. All the niceties. This could not be happening. Damen felt a surge in his chest; fury, outrage, and somewhere buried beneath these, a new emotion that twisted and roiled in his belly.

One of the soldiers immobilised him in a practised hold from behind. The other began to strip him.

His garments were unpinned and drawn off swiftly. His sandals were cut from his feet. The burn of humiliation hot as steam across his cheeks, Damen stood shackled, naked, the moist warmth of the baths curling up against his skin.

The soldiers withdrew to the archway, where a figure dismissed them, his chiselled face handsome, and familiar.

Adrastus was the Keeper of the Royal Slaves. His was a prestigious position that had been bestowed on him by King Theomedes. Damen was hit by a wave of anger so powerful it almost robbed him of vision. When he came back to himself, he saw the way Adrastus was considering him.

"You wouldn't dare lay a hand on me," said Damen.

"I'm under orders," said Adrastus, though he was holding back.

"I'll kill you," said Damen.

"Maybe a—a woman—" said Adrastus, backing up a step and whispering into the ear of one of the attendants, who bowed and left the room.

A slave entered a few moments later. Hand-picked, she matched all that was known of Damen's tastes. Her skin was as white as the marble of the baths, and her yellow hair was simply pinned, exposing the elegant column of her throat. Her breasts were full and swelled beneath the gauze; her pink nipples were faintly visible.

Damen watched her approach with the same wariness with which he would follow the movements of an opponent on the field, though he was no stranger to being serviced by slaves.

Her hand rose to the clasp at her shoulder. She exposed the curve of a breast, a slender waist, the gauze sliding down to her hips, and lower. Her garments dropped to the floor. Then she picked up a water scoop.

Naked, she bathed his body, soaping and rinsing, heedless of the way the water spilled against her own skin and splashed her round breasts. Finally she wet and soaped his hair, washing it thoroughly, finishing by rising up on her toes and tipping one of the smaller tubs of warm water over the back of his head.

Like a dog, he shook it off. He looked around for Adrastus, but the Keeper of the Slaves seemed to have disappeared.

The slave took up one of the coloured vials and poured some of its oil into her palm. Coating her hands, she began to work the stuff into his skin with methodical strokes, applying it everywhere. Her eyes remained downcast, even when her strokes deliberately slowed and she moved against him. Damen's fingers bit into his chains.

"That's enough," said Jokaste, and the slave jerked back from Damen, prostrating herself on the wet marble floor instantly.

Damen, manifestly aroused, weathered Jokaste's calmly appraising gaze.

"I want to see my brother," said Damen.

"You have no brother," said Jokaste. "You have no family. You have no name, rank or position. By now, you should know that much at least."

"Do you expect me to submit to this? To be mastered by—who—Adrastus? I'll tear his throat out."

"Yes. You would. But you won't be serving in the palace."

"Where?" Flatly.

She gazed at him.

Damen said, *"What have you done?"*

"Nothing," she said, "but choose between brothers."

They had last spoken in her rooms in the palace; her hand had pressed to his arm.

She looked like a painting. Her blonde curls were coiled and perfect, and her high smooth brow and classical features were composed. Where Adrastus had held back, her delicate sandals picked their way with calm and sure steps across the wet marble towards him.

He said, "Why keep me alive? What—need—does this satisfy? It's neat enough, except for that. Is it—" He bit down on it; she deliberately misunderstood his words.

"A brother's love? You don't know him at all, do you. What's a death but easy, quick. It's supposed to haunt you forever that the one time he beat you was the one time that mattered."

Damen felt his face changing shape. "—*What*?"

She touched his jaw, unafraid. Her fingers were slender, white and faultlessly elegant.

"I see why you prefer pale skin," she said. "Yours hides the bruising."

◆ ◆ ◆

After they locked him into the gold collar and wrist-cuffs, they painted his face.

There was no taboo in Akielos regarding male nudity, but the paint was the mark of a slave, and it was mortifying. He thought there was no greater humiliation than when he was thrown to the ground in front of Adrastus. Then he saw Adrastus's face, and saw the esurient expression.

"You look . . ." Adrastus gazed at him.

Damen's arms were bound behind his back, and further restraints had restricted his movements to little more than a hobble. Now he was sprawled on the ground at Adrastus's feet. He drew himself up onto his knees, but was prevented from rising further by the restraining grip of his two guards.

"If you did it for a position," said Damen, flat hatred in his voice, "you're a fool. You'll never advance. He can't trust you. You've already betrayed for gain once."

The blow snapped his head to one side. Damen ran his tongue over the inside of his lip and tasted blood.

"I did not give you permission to speak," said Adrastus.

"You hit like a milk-fed catamite," said Damen.

Adrastus took a step back, his face white.

"Gag him," he said, and Damen was struggling again, in vain, against the guards. His jaw was expertly prised open, and a thickly cloth-bound iron bit forced into his mouth and swiftly tied. He could make no more than a muffled sound, but he glared at Adrastus over the gag with defiant eyes.

"You don't understand it yet," said Adrastus, "but you will. You'll come to understand that what they are saying in the palace, in the taverns and in the streets is true. You're a slave. You're worth nothing. *Prince Damianos is dead.*"

CHAPTER ONE

D AMEN CAME BACK to himself in stages, his drugged limbs heavy against the silk cushions, the gold cuffs on his wrists like lead weights. His eyelids raised and lowered. The sounds he heard made no sense at first, the murmur of voices speaking Veretian. Instinct said: Get up.

He gathered himself, pushing up onto his knees.

Veretian voices?

His muddled thoughts, arriving at this conclusion, could make nothing of it at first. His mind was harder than his body to muster. He could not immediately remember anything after his capture, though he knew that time had passed between now and then. He was aware that at some point, he had been drugged. He searched for that memory. Eventually he found it.

He had tried to escape.

He had been transported inside a locked wagon under heavy guard to a house on the edge of the city. He had been pulled from the wagon into a closed courtyard and . . . he remembered bells. The courtyard had filled with the sudden sound of bells, a cacophony of sound from the highest places in the city, carrying in the warm evening air.

Bells at dusk, heralding a new King.

Theomedes is dead. All hail Kastor.

At the sound of the bells, the need to escape had overwhelmed any urge to caution or subterfuge, part of the fury and grief that came upon him in waves. The starting of the horses had given him his opportunity.

But he had been unarmed and surrounded by soldiers, in a closed courtyard. The subsequent handling had not been delicate. They had thrown him into a cell deep in the bowels of the house, after which, they had drugged him. Days had bled into one another.

Of the rest he recalled only brief snatches, including—his stomach sank—the slap and spray of salt water: transportation aboard a ship.

His head was clearing. His head was clearing for the first time in—how long?

How long since his capture? How long since the bells had rung? How long had he allowed this to go on? A surge of will drove Damen from his knees onto his feet. He must protect his household, his people. He took a step.

A chain rattled. The tiled floor slid under his feet, dizzily; his vision swam.

He struck out for support and steadied himself, one

shoulder against the wall. With an effort of will, he did not slide back down it. Holding himself upright, he forced the dizziness back. Where was he? He made his hazy mind take inventory of himself and his surroundings.

He was dressed in the brief garments of an Akielon slave, and from head to toe, he was clean. He supposed this meant he had been tended, though his mind could supply him with no memory of it happening. He retained the gold collar and the gold cuffs on his wrists. His collar was chained to an iron link in the floor by means of a chain and a lock.

Thin hysteria threatened for a moment: he smelled faintly of roses.

As for the room, everywhere he looked his eyes were assaulted with ornamentation. The walls were overrun by decoration. The wooden doors were delicate as a screen and carved with a repeated design that included gaps in the wood; through them you could glimpse shadowy impressions of what lay on the other side. The windows were similarly screened. Even the floor tiles were parti-coloured and arranged in a geometric pattern.

Everything gave the impression of patterns within patterns, the twisty creations of the Veretian mind. It came together then, suddenly—Veretian voices—the humiliating presentation to Councillor Guion, "Are all the new slaves bound?"—the ship—and its destination.

This was Vere.

Damen stared around himself in horror. He was in the heart of enemy territory, hundreds of miles from home.

It didn't make sense. He was breathing, without holes,

and had not suffered the regrettable accident he might have expected. The Veretian people had good reason to hate Prince Damianos of Akielos. Why was he still alive?

The sound of a bolt being thrown back jerked his attention to the door.

Two men strode into the room. Watching them warily, Damen indistinctly recognised the first as a Veretian handler from the ship. The second was a stranger: dark-haired, bearded, wearing Veretian clothing, with silver rings on each of the three joints of every finger.

"This is the slave that is being presented to the Prince?" said the ringed man.

The handler nodded.

"You say he's dangerous. What is he? A prisoner of war? A criminal?"

The handler shrugged a *Who knows?* "Keep him chained."

"Don't be foolish. We can't keep him chained forever." Damen could feel the ringed man's gaze lingering on him. The next words were almost admiring. "Look at him. Even the Prince is going to have his hands full."

"Aboard the ship, when he made trouble, he was drugged," said the handler.

"I see." The man's gaze turned critical. "Gag him and shorten the chain for the Prince's viewing. And arrange an appropriate escort. If he makes trouble, do whatever you have to." He spoke with dismissive words, as though Damen was of minimal importance to him, no more than a task on a checklist.

It was dawning on Damen, through the clearing drug-haze, that his captors did not know the identity of their slave. *A prisoner of war. A criminal.* He let out a careful breath.

He must stay quiet, inconspicuous. Enough presence of mind had returned to him to know that as Prince Damianos he would be unlikely to last a night alive in Vere. Better by far to be thought a nameless slave.

He allowed the handling. He had judged the exits and the quality of the guards in his escort. The quality of the guards was less significant than the quality of the chain around his neck. His arms were lashed behind his back and he was gagged, the collar chain shortened to only nine links, so that even kneeling, his head was bowed, and he could barely look up.

Guards took up position on either side of him, and on either side of the doors, which he faced. He had time then to feel the expectant silence of the room and the tightening string of heartbeats in his chest.

There was a sudden flurry of activity, voices and footsteps approaching.

The Prince's viewing.

The Regent of Vere held the throne for his nephew, the Crown Prince. Damen knew almost nothing about the Prince except that he was the younger of two sons. The older brother and former heir, Damen well knew, was dead.

A scattering of courtiers was entering the room.

The courtiers were nondescript except for one: a young man with an astonishingly lovely face—the kind of face that would have earned a small fortune on the slave-block in Akielos. Damen's attention caught and held.

The young man had yellow hair, blue eyes and very fair skin. The dark blue of his severe, hard-laced clothing was too harsh for his fair colouring, and stood in stark contrast to the overly ornate style of the rooms. Unlike the courtiers who trailed in his wake, he wore no jewellery, not even rings on his fingers.

As he approached, Damen saw that the expression that sat on the lovely face was arrogant and unpleasant. Damen knew the type. Self-absorbed and self-serving, raised to overestimate his own worth and indulge in petty tyrannies over others. Spoilt.

"I hear the King of Akielos has sent me a gift," said the young man, who was Laurent, Prince of Vere.

◆ ◆ ◆

"An Akielon grovelling on its knees. How fitting."

Around him, Damen was aware of the attention of courtiers, gathered to witness the Prince's receipt of his slave. Laurent had stopped dead the moment he had seen Damen, his face turning white, as though in reaction to a slap or an insult. Damen's view, half-truncated by the short chain at his neck, had been enough to see that. But Laurent's expression had shuttered quickly.

That he was only one of a larger consignment of slaves was something Damen had guessed, and the murmurs from the two courtiers nearest him confirmed it, gratingly. Laurent's eyes were passing over him, as though viewing merchandise. Damen felt a muscle slide in his jaw.

Councillor Guion spoke. "He's intended as a pleasure slave, but he isn't trained. Kastor suggested that you might like to break him at your leisure."

"I'm not desperate enough that I need to soil myself with filth," said Laurent.

"Yes, Your Highness."

"Break him on the cross. I believe that will discharge my obligation to the King of Akielos."

"Yes, Your Highness."

He could feel the relief in Councillor Guion. Handlers were quickly motioned to take him away. Damen supposed that he had presented rather a challenge to diplomacy: Kastor's gift blurred the line between munificent and appalling.

The courtiers were making to leave. This mockery was over. He felt the handler bend to the iron link in the floor. They were going to unchain him to take him to the cross. He flexed his fingers, gathering himself, his eyes on the handler, his single opponent.

"Wait," said Laurent.

The handler halted, straightening.

Laurent came forward a few paces to stand in front of Damen, gazing down at him with an unreadable expression.

"I want to speak to him. Remove the gag."

"He's got a mouth on him," warned the handler.

"Your Highness, if I might suggest—" began Councillor Guion.

"Do it."

Damen ran his tongue around the inside of his mouth after the handler released the cloth.

"What's your name, sweetheart?" said Laurent, not quite pleasantly.

He knew better than to answer any question posed in

that saccharine voice. He lifted his eyes to Laurent's. That was a mistake. They gazed at each other.

"Perhaps he's defective," suggested Guion.

Pellucid blue eyes rested on his. Laurent repeated the question slowly in the language of Akielos.

The words came out before he could stop them. "I speak your language better than you speak mine, sweetheart."

His words, carrying only the barest trace of an Akielon accent, were intelligible to all, which earned him a hard blow from the handler. For good measure, a member of the escort pushed his face right down to the floor.

"The King of Akielos says, if it pleases you, call him 'Damen,'" said the handler, and Damen felt his stomach drop.

There were a few shocked murmurs from the courtiers in the chamber; the atmosphere, already prurient, became electric.

"They thought a slave nicknamed for their late Prince would amuse you. It's in poor taste. They are an uncultured society," said Councillor Guion.

This time Laurent's tone didn't change. "I heard that the King of Akielos may marry his mistress, the Lady Jokaste. Is that true?"

"There was no official announcement. But there was talk of the possibility, yes."

"So the country will be ruled by a bastard and a whore," said Laurent. "How appropriate."

Damen felt himself react, even restrained as he was, with a hard jerk aborted by chains. He caught the self-satisfied pleasure on Laurent's face. Laurent's words had been loud enough to carry to every courtier in the room.

"Shall we have him taken to the cross, Your Highness?" said the handler.

"No," said Laurent, "Restrain him here in the harem. After you teach him some manners."

◆ ◆ ◆

The two men entrusted to the task went about it with methodical and matter-of-fact brutality. But they had a natural reluctance to damage Damen totally beyond repair, being that he was the Prince's possession.

Damen was aware of the ringed man issuing a series of instructions, then departing. Keep the slave restrained here in the harem. The Prince's orders. No one is to come in or out of the room. The Prince's orders. Two guards at the door at all times. The Prince's orders. Don't let him off the chain. The Prince's orders.

Though the two men lingered, it seemed that the blows had stopped; Damen pushed himself up slowly to his hands and knees. Gritty tenacity made something of the situation: His head, at least, was now perfectly clear.

Worse than the beating had been the viewing. He had been more shaken by it than he would admit. If the collar-chain had not been so short—so impossibly secure—he might have resisted, despite his earlier resolve. He knew the arrogance of this nation. He knew how the Veretians thought of his people. Barbarian. Slave. Damen had gathered all his good intentions about himself and endured it.

But the Prince—Laurent's particular blend of spoilt arrogance and petty spite—had been unbearable.

"He doesn't look much like a pet," said the taller of the two men.

"You heard. He's a bed slave from Akielos," said the other.

"You think the Prince fucks him?" Sceptically.

"More like the other way around."

"Pretty sweet orders for a bed slave." The taller one's mind stuck on the subject as the other grunted noncommittally in reply. "Think what that'd be like, getting a leg over the Prince."

I imagine it would be a lot like lying down with a poisonous snake, thought Damen, but he kept the thought to himself.

As soon as the men left, Damen reviewed his situation: Getting free was not yet possible. His hands were untied again, and the collar-chain had been lengthened, but it was too thick to separate from the iron link in the floor. Nor could the collar be opened. It was gold, technically a soft metal, but it was also too thick to manipulate, a constant, heavy weight around his neck. It struck him how ridiculous it was to collar a slave with gold. The gold wrist-cuffs were even more foolish. They would be a weapon in a close fight and currency on the journey back to Akielos.

If he stayed alert while pretending to compliance, opportunity would follow. There was enough length in the chain to allow him perhaps three steps of movement in every direction. There was a wooden carafe of water well within reach. He would be able to lie comfortably on the cushions and even relieve himself in a gilt copper pot. He had not been drugged—or bludgeoned all the way to unconsciousness—as had happened in Akielos. Only two guards at the door. An unbolted window.

Freedom was attainable. If not now, then soon.

It must be soon. Time was not on his side: The longer he was kept here, the longer Kastor would have to cement his rule. It was unbearable not to know what was happening in his country, to his supporters, and to his people.

And there was another problem.

No one had yet recognised him, but that didn't mean he was safe from discovery. Akielos and Vere had had few dealings since the decisive battle of Marlas six years ago, but somewhere in Vere there would surely be a person or two who knew his face, having visited his city. Kastor had sent him to the one place where he could expect to be treated worse as a prince than as a slave. Elsewhere, one of his captors, learning his identity, might be convinced to help him, either out of sympathy for his situation, or for the promise of a reward from Damen's supporters in Akielos. Not in Vere. In Vere, he couldn't risk it.

He remembered the words of his father on the eve of the battle of Marlas, warning him to fight, never to trust, because a Veretian would not keep his word. His father had been proven right that day on the battlefield.

He would not think of his father.

It would be best to be well rested. With that in mind, he drank water from the carafe, watching the last of the afternoon light slowly drain from the room. When it was dark, he lay his body, with all its aches, down on the cushions, and, eventually, he slept.

✦ ✦ ✦

And woke. Dragged up, a hand on his collar-chain, until he was on his feet, flanked by two of the faceless, interchange-able guards.

The room was flaring into brightness as a servant lit torches and placed them in the wall brackets. The room was not over-large, and the flickering of the torches transformed its intricate designs into a continuously moving, sinuous play of shape and light.

In the centre of this activity, regarding him with cool blue eyes, was Laurent.

Laurent's severe dark blue clothing fitted him repres-sively, covering him from toe to neck, long-sleeved to his wrists, with no openings that weren't done up with a series of tight intricate ties that looked like they would take about an hour to loosen. The warm light of the torches did nothing to soften the effect.

Damen saw nothing that did not confirm his earlier opin-ion: spoilt, like fruit too long on the vine. Laurent's slightly lidded eyes, the slackness around his mouth, spoke of a night wasted in a dissolute courtier's overindulgence in wine.

"I've been thinking about what to do with you," said Lau-rent. "Break you on a flogging post. Or maybe use you the way Kastor intended you be used. I think that would please me a great deal."

Laurent came forward, until he stood just four paces

away. It was a carefully chosen distance: Damen judged that if he strained the chain to its limit, pulling it taut, they would almost, but not quite, touch.

"Nothing to say? Don't tell me you're shy now that you and I are alone." Laurent's silken tone was neither reassuring nor pleasant.

"I thought you wouldn't soil yourself with a barbarian," said Damen, careful to keep his voice neutral. He was aware of the beat of his heart.

"I wouldn't," said Laurent. "But if I gave you to one of the guards, I might lower myself as far as watching."

Damen felt himself recoil, couldn't keep his reaction off his face.

"You don't like that idea?" said Laurent. "Maybe I can think of a better one. Come here."

Distrust and dislike of Laurent roiled within him, but Damen recalled his situation. In Akielos, he had thrown himself against his restraints, and they had grown ever tighter as a result. Here, he was just a slave, and a chance to escape would come if he did not ruin it with hot-headed pride. He could endure Laurent's juvenile, pin-prick sadism. Damen must get back to Akielos, and that meant that for now, he must do as he was told.

He took a wary step forward.

"No," said Laurent, with satisfaction. "Crawl."

Crawl.

It was as though everything ground to a halt in the face of that single order. The part of Damen's mind that told him he must feign obedience was drowned out by his pride.

But Damen's reaction of scornful disbelief only had time

to register on his face for a split second before he was sent sprawling onto his hands and knees by the guards, after a wordless signal from Laurent. In the next moment, again responding to a signal from Laurent, one of the guards drove his fist into Damen's jaw. Once, then again. And again.

His head rang. Blood from his mouth dripped onto the tile. He stared at it, forcing himself, with an effort of will, not to react. Take it. Opportunity would come later.

He tested his jaw. Not broken.

"You were insolent this afternoon, too. That is a habit that can be cured. With a horse whip." Laurent's gaze tracked over Damen's body. Damen's garments had loosened under the rough hands of the guards, baring his torso. "You have a scar."

He had two, but the one that was now visible lay just below his left collarbone. Damen felt for the first time the stir of real danger, the flicker of his own quickening pulse.

"I—served in the army." It wasn't a lie.

"So Kastor sends a common soldier to rut with a prince. Is that it?"

Damen chose his words carefully, wishing he had his half-brother's facility for falsehood. "Kastor wished to humiliate me. I suppose I—angered him. If he had another purpose in sending me here, I don't know what it is."

"The Bastard King disposes of his waste by tossing it at my feet. Is that supposed to appease me?" said Laurent.

"Would anything?" said a voice behind him.

Laurent turned.

"You find fault in so much, lately."

"Uncle," said Laurent. "I didn't hear you come in."

Uncle? Damen experienced his second shock of the night. If Laurent addressed him as "uncle," this man whose imposing shape filled the doorway was the Regent.

There was no physical resemblance between the Regent and his nephew. The Regent was a commanding man in his forties, bulky, with heavy shoulders. His hair and beard were dark brown, without even the highlights to suggest that a blond of Laurent's fair colouring could have sprung from the same branch of the family tree.

The Regent looked Damen briefly up and down. "The slave appears to have self-inflicted bruising."

"He's mine. I can do with him what I like."

"Not if you intend having him beaten to death. That's not a suitable use for the gift of King Kastor. We have a treaty with Akielos, and I won't see it jeopardised by petty prejudice."

"Petty prejudice," said Laurent.

"I expect you to respect our allies, and the treaty, as do we all."

"I suppose the treaty says that I am to play pet with the dregs of the Akielon army?"

"Don't be childish. Bed who you like. But value the gift of King Kastor. You have already shirked your duty on the border. You will not avoid your responsibilities at court. Find some appropriate use for the slave. That is my order, and I expect you to obey it."

It seemed for a moment as if Laurent would rebel, but he bit down on the reaction and said only, "Yes, uncle."

"Now. Come. Let us put this matter behind us. Thankfully

I was informed of your activities before they progressed far enough to cause serious inconvenience."

"Yes. How lucky that you were informed. I would hate to inconvenience you, uncle."

This was said smoothly, but there was something behind the words.

The Regent answered in a similar tone. "I am glad we are in accord."

Their departure should have been a relief. So should the Regent's intervention with his nephew. But Damen recalled the look in Laurent's blue eyes, and though left alone, with the remainder of the night to rest undisturbed, he could not have said whether the Regent's mercy had improved his situation, or worsened it.

CHAPTER TWO

Thearto "The Regent was here last night?" The man with the
rings on his fingers greeted Damen with no preamble.
When Damen nodded, he frowned, two lines in the centre of
his forehead. "What was the Prince's mood?"

"Delightful," said Damen.

The ringed man gave him a hard stare. He broke from it
to give a brief order to the servant who was clearing away the
remains of Damen's meal. Then he spoke again to Damen.

"I am Radel. I am the Overseer. I have only one thing to
explain to you. They say that in Akielos you attacked your
guards. If you do that here, I will have you drugged as you
were aboard the ship, and have various privileges removed.
Do you understand?"

"Yes."

Another stare, as though this answer was in some way
suspect.

"It is your honour to have joined the Prince's household. Many desire such a position. Whatever your disgrace in your own country, it has brought you to a position of privilege here. You should bow down on your knees in gratitude to the Prince that this is so. Your pride should be put aside, and the petty business of your former life forgotten. You exist only to please the Crown Prince, for whom this country is held in stewardship—who will ascend the throne as King."

"Yes," said Damen, and did his best to look grateful and accepting.

Waking, there had been no confusion as to where he was, unlike yesterday. His memory was very clear. His body had immediately protested Laurent's mistreatment, but Damen, taking a brief inventory, had judged his hurts no worse than those he had occasionally received in the training arena, and put the matter to one side.

As Radel spoke, Damen heard the faraway sound of an unfamiliar stringed instrument playing a Veretian melody. Sound travelled through these doors and windows with their many little apertures.

The irony was that in some ways, Radel's description of his situation as privileged was correct. This was not the rank cell he had inhabited in Akielos, nor was it the drugged, hazily remembered confinement aboard the ship. This room was not a prison room, it was part of the royal pet residences. Damen's meal had been served on a gilt plate intricately modelled with foliage, and when the evening breeze lifted, in through the screened windows came the delicate scent of jasmine and frangipani.

Except that it was a prison. Except that he had a collar and chain around his neck, and was alone, among enemies, many miles from home.

His first privilege was to be blindfolded and taken, complete with escort, to be washed and readied—a ritual he had learned in Akielos. The palace outside of his rooms remained a blindfolded mystery. The sound of the stringed instrument grew briefly louder, then faded into a half-heard echo. Once or twice he heard the low, musical sound of voices. Once, a laugh, soft and lover-like.

As he was taken through the pet residences, Damen remembered that he was not the only Akielon to have been gifted to Vere, and he felt a groundswell of concern for the others. Sheltered Akielon palace slaves would likely be disoriented and vulnerable, never having learned the skills they needed to fend for themselves. Could they even talk to their masters? They were schooled in various languages, but Veretian was not likely to be one of them. Dealings with Vere were limited and, until the arrival of Councillor Guion, largely hostile. The only reason Damen had that language was because his father had insisted that, for a prince, learning the words of an enemy was as important as learning the words of a friend.

The blindfold was removed.

He would never get used to the ornamentation. From its arched ceiling to the depression in which lapped the water of the baths, the room was covered in tiny painted tiles, gleaming in blues, greens and gold. All sound was reduced to hollow echoes and curling steam. A series of curved alcoves for dalliance (currently empty) ringed the walls, by each of them braziers in fantastic shapes. The fretted doors were not wood, but metal. The only instrument of restraint was an incongruous heavy wooden dock. It did not match the rest of the baths at all, and Damen tried not to think that it had been brought here expressly for him. Averting his eyes from it, he found himself looking at the metal intaglio of the door. Figures twined around one another, all male. Their positions were not ambiguous. He shifted his eyes back to the baths.

"They are natural hot springs," Radel explained, as though to a child. "The water comes from a great underground river that is hot."

A great underground river that is hot. Damen said, "In Akielos, we use a system of aqueducts to achieve the same effect."

Radel frowned. "I suppose you think that is very clever." He was already signalling to one of the servants, his manner slightly distracted.

They stripped him and washed him without tying him up, and Damen behaved with admirable docility, resolved to prove that he could be trusted with small freedoms. Perhaps it worked, or perhaps Radel was used to tractable charges—an overseer, not a jailor—for he said, "You will soak. Five minutes."

Curved steps descended into the water. His escort retreated outside; his collar was released from its chain.

Damen immersed himself in the water, enjoying the brief, unexpected sensation of freedom. The water was so hot it was almost on the threshold of tolerance, yet it felt good.

The heat seeped into him, melting the ache of abused limbs and loosening muscles that were locked hard with tension.

Radel had thrown a substance onto the braziers as he left, so that they flared and then smoked. Almost immediately, the room had filled with an over-sweet scent, mingling with the steam. It perfused the senses, and Damen felt himself relax further.

His thoughts, drifting a little, found their way to Laurent.

You have a scar. Damen's fingers slid across his wet chest, reaching his collarbone and then following the line of the faint pale scar, feeling an echo of the uneasiness that had stirred in him last night.

It was Laurent's older brother who had inflicted that scar, six years ago, in battle at Marlas. Auguste, the heir and pride of Vere. Damen recalled his dark golden hair, the starburst blazon of the Crown Prince on his shield splattered over with mud, with blood, dented and almost unrecognisable, like his once-fine filigree armour. He recalled his own desperation in those moments, the scrape of metal against metal, the harsh sounds of breathing that might have been his own, and the feeling of fighting as he never had, all out, for his life.

He pushed the memory to one side, only to have it replaced by another. Darker than the first, and older. Somewhere in the depths of his mind, one fight resonated with another. Damen's fingers dropped below the water line. The other scar Damen carried was lower on his body. Not Auguste. Not on a battlefield.

Kastor had run him through on his thirteenth birthday, during training.

He remembered that day very clearly. He had scored a hit against Kastor for the first time, and when he had pulled off his helm, giddy with triumph, Kastor had smiled and suggested that they swap their wooden practice blades for real swords.

Damen had felt proud. He had thought, I am thirteen and a man, Kastor fights me like a man. Kastor had not held back against him, and he had been so proud of that, even as the blood pushed out from beneath his hands. Now he remembered the black look in Kastor's eyes and thought that he had been wrong about many things.

"Time's up," said Radel.

Damen nodded. He placed his hands on the edge of the baths. The ridiculous golden collar and cuffs still adorned his throat and wrists.

The braziers were now covered, but the lingering scent of the incense was a little dizzying. Damen shook the momentary weakness away and pushed himself up out of the hot baths, streaming water.

Radel was staring at him, wide-eyed. Damen ran a hand through his hair, wringing out the water. Radel's eyes widened. When Damen took a step forward, Radel took an involuntary step back.

"Restrain him," said Radel, a little hoarsely.

"You don't have to—" said Damen.

The wooden dock closed over his wrists. It was heavy and solid, immovable as a boulder or the trunk of a great tree. He rested his forehead against the dock, the wet tendrils of his hair turning the grain dark where they touched the wood.

"I wasn't planning to fight," said Damen.

"I'm glad to hear it," said Radel.

Dried, oiled with scent, the excess oil wiped off with a cloth. No worse than had happened to him in Akielos. The touches of the servants were brisk and perfunctory, even when they handled his genitals. There was no whiff of sensuality in the preparations as there had been when Damen had been touched by the slave with the yellow hair in the Akielon baths. It was not the worst thing that he had been asked to bear.

One of the servants stepped behind him and began to prepare the entrance to his body.

Damen jerked so forcefully that the wood creaked, and behind him he heard the smash of an oil container against the tile and a yelp from one of the servants.

"Hold him down," said Radel, grimly.

They released him from the dock when it was over, and this time his docility was faintly laced with shock, and he was, for a few moments, less aware of what was going on around him. He felt changed by what had just happened to him. No. He was not changed. It was his situation that was changed. He realised that this aspect of his captivity, this danger, despite Laurent's threats, had not previously been real.

"No paint," Radel was telling one of the servants. "The Prince doesn't like it. Jewellery—no. The gold is adequate. Yes, those garments. No, without the embroidery."

The blindfold was tied around his eyes, tight. A moment later, Damen felt ringed fingers on his jawline, lifting it, as though Radel wished simply to admire the picture he made, blindfolded, arms lashed behind his back.

Radel said, "Yes, that will do, I think."

◆ ◆ ◆

This time when the blindfold was lifted, it was on a set of double doors, heavily gilded, that were pushed open.

The room was thronging with courtiers and decked out for an indoor spectacle. Cushioned stands ringed each of the room's four sides. The effect was that of a claustrophobic, silk-draped amphitheatre. There was an air of considerable excitement. Ladies and young lords leaned in and whispered into one another's ears or murmured behind raised hands. Servants attended courtiers, and there was wine and refreshments, and silver trays heaped with sweetmeats and candied fruit. In the centre of the room was a circular depression, with a series of iron links set into the floor. Damen's stomach twisted. His gaze swung back to the courtiers in the stands.

Not just courtiers. Among the more soberly dressed lords and ladies were exotic creatures in brightly coloured silks, showing glimpses of flesh, their beautiful faces daubed with paint. Here was a young woman wearing almost more gold than Damen, two long circling armbands, shaped like snakes. Here, a stunning red-haired youth with a coronet of emeralds and a delicate chain of silver and peridot around his waist. It was as though the courtiers displayed their wealth through their pets, like a noble showering jewels on an already expensive courtesan.

Damen saw an older man in the stands with a young

child beside him, a proprietary arm around the boy, perhaps a father who had brought his son to view a favourite sport. He smelled a sweet scent, familiar from the baths, and saw a lady breathing deeply from a long, thin pipe, curled at one end; her eyes were half-closed as she was fondled by the jewelled pet beside her. All across the stands, hands moved slowly over flesh in a dozen minor acts of debauchery.

This was Vere, voluptuous and decadent, country of honeyed poison. Damen recalled the last night before dawn at Marlas, with the Veretian tents over the river, rich silk pennants lifting in the night air, the sounds of laughter and superiority, and the herald who had spat on the ground in front of his father.

Damen realised he had baulked on the threshold when the chain on his collar yanked him forward. One step. Another. Better to walk than be dragged by the neck.

He didn't know whether to be relieved or disturbed when he was not taken directly to the ring but was instead flung down in front of a seat draped with blue silk and bearing that familiar starburst pattern in gold, mark of the Crown Prince. His chain was cinched to a link in the floor. His view, as he looked up, was of an elegant boot-clad leg.

If Laurent had been drinking to excess last night, nothing in his manner today showed it. He looked fresh, unconcerned and fair, his golden hair bright above clothing of a blue so dark it was almost black. His blue eyes were as innocent as the sky; only if you looked carefully could you see something genuine in them. Such as dislike. Damen would have attributed it to spite—that Laurent intended to make him pay for having overheard the exchange last night with his uncle. But the truth was Laurent had looked at him like that from the first moment he had laid eyes on him.

"You have a cut on your lip. Someone hit you. Oh, that's right, I recall. You stood still and let him. Does it hurt?"

He was worse sober. Damen purposefully relaxed his hands, which, restrained behind his back, had become fists.

"We must have some conversation. You see: I have asked after your health, and now I am reminiscing. I fondly remember our night together. Have you been thinking about me this morning?"

There was no good answer to that question. Damen's mind unexpectedly supplied him with a memory of the baths, the heat of the water, the sweet scent of the incense, the curl of steam. *You have a scar.*

"My uncle interrupted us just as things were getting interesting. It left me curious." Laurent's expression was guileless, but he was systematically turning over stones, searching for weakness. "You did something to make Kastor hate you. What was it?"

"Hate me?" said Damen, looking up, hearing the reaction in his voice, despite his resolution not to engage. Those words worked on him.

"Did you think he sent you to me out of love? What did you do to him? Beat him in a tournament? Or fuck his mistress— what was her name?—Jokaste. Maybe," said Laurent, his eyes widening a little, "you strayed after he fucked you."

That idea revolted him so much, took him so unawares, that he tasted bile in his throat. *"No."*

Laurent's blue eyes gleamed. "So that's it. Kastor mounts his soldiers like horses in the yard. Did you grit your teeth and take it because he was the King, or did you like it? You really," said Laurent, "have no idea how happy that idea makes me. It's perfect: a man who holds you down while he fucks you, with a cock like a bottle and a beard like my uncle's."

Damen realised he had physically drawn back—the chain had pulled taut. There was something obscene about someone with a face like that speaking those words in a conversational voice.

Further unpleasantness was prevented by the approach of a select group of courtiers, to whom Laurent presented an angelic countenance. Damen stiffened when he recognised Councillor Guion, dressed in heavy dark clothing, with his councillor's medallion around his neck. From the brief words that Laurent spoke in greeting, he gathered that the woman with the commanding air was called Vannes, and the man with the peaked nose was Estienne.

"It's so rare to see you at these entertainments, Your Highness," said Vannes.

"I was in the mood to enjoy myself," said Laurent.

"Your new pet is causing quite a stir." Vannes walked around Damen as she spoke. "He's nothing like the slaves that Kastor gifted to your uncle. I wonder if Your Highness has had the chance to see them? They're much more . . ."

"I've seen them."

"You don't sound pleased."

"Kastor sends two dozen slaves trained to worm their way

into the bedchambers of the most powerful members of court. I'm overjoyed."

"What an entirely pleasant sort of espionage," said Vannes, arranging herself comfortably. "But the Regent keeps the slaves on a tight leash, I hear, and has not loaned them out at all. Regardless, I highly doubt we'll see them in the ring. They didn't quite have the—élan."

Estienne sniffed and gathered his pet to him, a delicate flower who looked like he would bruise if you so much as brushed a petal. "Not everyone has your taste for pets who can sweep the ring competitions, Vannes. I, for one, am relieved to hear that all the slaves in Akielos are not like this one. They're not, are they?" This last a little nervously.

"No." Councillor Guion spoke with authority. "None of them are. Among the Akielon nobility, dominance is a sign of status. The slaves are all submissive. I suppose it's intended as a compliment to you, Your Highness, to imply that you can break a slave as strong as this one—"

No. It wasn't. Kastor was amusing himself at everyone's expense. A living hell for his half-brother, and a backhand insult to Vere.

"—as for his provenance, they have arena matches regularly—sword, dagger, and spear—I'd guess he was one of the display fighters. It's truly barbaric. They wear almost nothing during the sword fights, and they fight the wrestling matches nude."

"Like pets," laughed one of the courtiers.

The conversation turned to gossip. Damen heard nothing useful in it, but then, he was having difficulty concentrating.

The ring, with its promise of humiliation and violence, was holding most of his attention. He thought: So the Regent keeps a close watch on his slaves. At least that is something.

"This new alliance with Akielos can't sit easily with you, Your Highness," said Estienne. "Everyone knows how you feel about that country. Their barbaric practices—and of course what happened at Marlas—"

The space around him was suddenly very quiet.

"My uncle is Regent," Laurent said.

"You are twenty-one in spring."

"Then you would do well to be prudent in my presence as well as my uncle's."

"Yes, Your Highness," said Estienne, bowing briefly and moving off to one side, acknowledging it for the dismissal it was.

Something was happening in the ring.

Two male pets had entered and were standing off with slight wariness, in the manner of competitors. One was a brunet, with long-lashed almond eyes. The other, to whom Damen's attention naturally gravitated, was blond, though his hair was not the buttercup yellow of Laurent's, it was darker, a sandy colour, and his eyes weren't blue, they were brown.

Damen felt a shift in the constant, low-grade tension that had been with him since the baths—since he had woken in this place on silk cushions.

In the ring, the pets were being stripped of their clothes.

"Sweetmeat?" said Laurent. He held the confection delicately, between thumb and forefinger, just far enough out of reach that Damen would have to rise up onto his knees in order to eat it from Laurent's fingertips. Damen jerked his head back.

"Stubborn," Laurent remarked mildly, bringing the treat to his own lips instead, and eating it.

A range of equipment was on display alongside the ring: long gilt poles, various restraints, a series of golden balls such as a child might play with, a little pile of silver bells, long whips, the handles decorated with ribbons and tassels. It was obvious that the entertainments in the ring were varied and inventive.

But the one that unfolded in front of him now was simple: rape.

The pets knelt with their arms around one another, and an officiator held a red scarf aloft, then dropped it, fluttering, to the ground.

The pretty picture that the pets made quickly dissolved into a heaving tussle before the sounds of the crowd. Both pets were attractive and both were lightly muscled—neither possessed the build of a wrestler, but they did look marginally stronger than some of the willowy exquisites who curled around their masters in the audience. The brunet was first to gain the advantage, stronger than the blond.

Damen realised what was happening in front of him, as every whisper he had heard in Akielos of the depravities of the Veretian court began unfolding before his eyes.

The brunet was on top, his knee forcing the blond's thighs open. The blond was trying desperately to throw him off, and it wasn't working. The brunet held the blond's arms behind his back and scrabbled, humping ineffectually. And then he was in, smooth as entering a woman, though the blond was struggling. The blond had been—

—prepared—

The blond let out a cry and tried to buck his captor off, but the motion only drove him deeper.

Damen's eyes swung away, but it was almost worse to look at the audience. Lady Vannes's pet sat with flushed cheeks, her mistress's fingers well occupied. To Damen's left, the red-haired boy was unlacing the front of his master's garments and wrapping a hand around what he found there. In Akielos, slaves were discreet; public performances were erotic without being overt, the charms of a slave to be enjoyed in private. The court did not gather to watch two of them fucking. Here, the atmosphere was almost orgiastic. And it was impossible to block out the sounds.

Only Laurent seemed immune. He was probably so jaded that this display did not even cause his pulse to flicker. He sat in a graceful sprawl, one wrist balanced on the armrest of the box seat. At any moment, he might contemplate his nails.

In the ring, the performance was approaching its culmination. And, by now, it was a performance. The pets were adept and playing to their audience. The sounds that the blond was making had changed in quality, and were rhythmic, in time with the thrusts. The brunet was going to ride him to climax. The blond was stubbornly resisting, biting his lip to try and hold himself back, but with every jarring thrust he was driven closer, until his body shivered and gave of itself.

The brunet pulled out and came, messily, all over his back.

Damen knew what was coming, even as the blond's eyes

opened, even as he was helped from the ring by a servant of his master, who fussed over him solicitously, and gifted him with a long diamond earring.

Laurent lifted refined fingers in a prearranged signal to the guard.

Hands clamped down on his shoulders. Damen's chain was detached from his collar, and when he did not spring into the ring like a dog released to the hunt, he was sent there at sword point.

"You kept pestering me to put a pet in the ring," Laurent was saying to Vannes and the other courtiers who had joined him. "I thought it was time I indulged you."

It was nothing like entering the arena in Akielos, where the fight was a show of excellence and the prize was honour. Damen was released from the last of his bonds and stripped of his garments, which were not many. It was impossible that this was happening. He felt again a strange sort of sick dizziness . . . Shaking his head slightly, needing to clear it, he looked up.

And saw his opponent.

Laurent had threatened to have him raped. And here was the man who was going to do it.

There was no way this brute was a pet. Big-boned and heavy-muscled, he outweighed Damen, with a further thick layer of flesh overlying the muscle. He had been chosen for his size, not his looks. His hair was a lank black cap. His chest was a thick pelt of hair that extended all the way down to his exposed groin. His nose was flat and broken; he was clearly no stranger to fights, though it was actually difficult to imagine anyone suicidal enough to punch this man in the nose. He had probably been dragged out of some mercenary company and told: Fight the Akielon, fuck him, and you'll be well rewarded. His eyes were cold as they passed over Damen's body.

All right, he was outweighed. Under normal circumstances, that would not be a cause for anxiety. Wrestling was a trained discipline in Akielos, and one Damen excelled at and enjoyed. But he had had days in harsh confinement, and, yesterday, had endured a beating. His body was tender in places, and his olive skin did not hide all the bruising: Here and there were the telltale signs that would show an opponent where to press down.

He thought about that. He thought about the weeks since his capture in Akielos. He thought about the beatings. He thought about the restraints. His pride was lashing its tail. He would not be raped in front of a room full of courtiers. They wanted to see a barbarian in the ring? Well, the barbarian could fight.

It began, a little sickeningly, as it had begun with the two pets: on their knees, with their arms around one another. The presence of two powerful adult men in the ring released something in the crowd that the pets had not, and the shouted insults, bets and ribald speculation filled the room with noise. Closer, Damen could hear the breath of his mercenary opponent, could smell the rank, masculine smell of the man, over the cloying perfumed roses of his own skin. The red scarf lifted.

The first heave had enough force to break an arm. The man was a mountain, and when Damen matched strength to strength, he found, a little worryingly, that his earlier dizziness was with him still. There was something strange in the way that his limbs felt . . . sluggish . . .

There was no time to think about it. Thumbs were suddenly seeking for his eyes. He twisted. Those parts of the body that were soft and tender, and that, in fair sport, would be avoided, must now be protected at all costs; his opponent was willing to tear, rip and gouge. And Damen's body, otherwise hard and smooth, was newly vulnerable where it was bruised. The man he fought knew it. The pounding blows Damen suffered were all brutally aimed to land on old hurts. His opponent was vicious and formidable, and he had been instructed to do damage.

Despite all this, the first advantage was Damen's. Outweighed and fighting that strange dizziness, he possessed skill that still counted for something. He gained a hold on the man, but when he tried to call on his strength to finish things, he found instead unsteady weakness. The air was suddenly expelled from his lungs after a driving blow to his diaphragm. The man had broken his hold.

He found new leverage. He bore down with all his weight on the man's body and felt him shudder. It took more out of him than it should have. The man's muscles bunched under him, and this time when the hold was broken, Damen felt a burst of pain in his shoulder. He heard his breath go uneven.

Something was wrong. The weakness he felt was not natural. As another wave of dizziness passed over him, he thought suddenly of the over-sweet smell in the baths . . . the incense in the brazier . . . a drug, he realised as his breath heaved. He had inhaled some sort of drug. Not just inhaled, had stewed in it. Nothing had been left to chance. Laurent had acted to make the outcome of this fight certain.

A sudden renewed onslaught came, and he staggered. It took too long to regain himself. He grappled ineffectually; for a few moments neither man could sustain a grip. Sweat on the man's body glistened, making purchase more difficult. Damen's own body had been slightly oiled; the scented slave preparation gave him an ironic, unlooked-for advantage, momentarily protecting his virtue. He thought it was not the moment for stricken laughter. He felt the man's warm breath against his neck.

In the next second he was on his back, pinned, blackness threatening the edge of his vision as the man applied a crushing pressure against his windpipe above the gold collar. He felt the push of the man against him. The sound of the crowd surged. The man was trying to mount.

Thrusting against Damen, the man's breath was now coming in soft grunts. Damen struggled to no avail, not strong enough to break this hold. His thighs were forced apart. No. He sought desperately for some weakness that could be exploited, and found none.

Goal in his sights, the man's attention split between restraint and penetration.

Damen flung the last of his strength at the hold and felt it quaver—enough to shift their positions slightly—enough to find leverage—an arm freed—

He drove his fist sideways, so that the heavy gold cuff on his wrist slammed hard into the man's temple, with the sick sound of an iron bar impacting on flesh and bone. A moment later, Damen followed up, perhaps unnecessarily, with his right fist, and smashed his stunned, swaying opponent into the dirt.

He fell, heavy flesh collapsing, partially across Damen.

Damen somehow pushed away, instinctively inserting distance between himself and the prone man. He coughed, his throat tender. When he found that he had air, he began the slow process of rising to his knees and from there to his feet. Rape was out of the question. The little spectacle with the blond pet had been all performance. Even these jaded courtiers did not expect him to fuck a man who was unconscious.

Except that he could feel, now, the displeasure of the crowd. No one wanted to see an Akielon triumph over a Veretian. Least of all Laurent. The words of Councillor Guion came back to him, almost crazily. *It's in poor taste.*

It was not over. It was not enough to fight through a drug haze and win. There was no way to win. It was already clear that the Regent's diktats did not extend to the entertainments in the ring. And whatever now happened to Damen would happen with the crowd's approbation.

He knew what he had to do. Against every rebelling instinct, he forced himself forward, and dropped to his knees before Laurent.

"I fight in your service, Your Highness." He searched his

memory for Radel's words, and found them. "I exist only to please my Prince. May my victory reflect on your glory."

He knew better than to look up. He spoke as clearly as he could, his words for the onlookers as much as they were for Laurent. He tried to look as deferential as possible. Exhausted and on his knees, he thought that wasn't difficult. If someone hit him right now, he'd fall over.

Laurent extended his right leg slightly, the tip of his well-turned boot presenting itself to Damen.

"Kiss it," Laurent said.

Damen's whole body reacted against that idea. His stomach heaved; his heart, in the cage of his chest, was pounding. One public humiliation substituted for another. But it was easier to kiss a foot than be raped in front of a crowd . . . wasn't it? Damen bent his head and pressed his lips to the smooth leather. He forced himself to do it with unhurried respect, as a vassal might kiss the ring of a liege lord. He kissed just the curve of the toe-tip. In Akielos an eager slave might have continued upward, kissing the arch of Laurent's foot, or, if they were daring, higher, his firm calf muscle.

He heard Councillor Guion: "You've worked miracles. That slave was completely unmanageable aboard the ship."

"Every dog can be brought to heel," said Laurent.

"Magnificent!" A smooth, cultured voice, one Damen didn't know.

"Councillor Audin," said Laurent.

Damen recognised the older man he had glimpsed in the audience earlier. The one who had sat with his son, or nephew.

His clothing, though it was dark like Laurent's, was very fine. Not, of course, as fine as a prince's. But close to it.

"What a victory! Your slave deserves a reward. Let me offer one to him."

"A reward." Laurent, flatly.

"A fight like that—truly magnificent—but with no climax—allow me to offer him a pet, in place of his intended conquest. I think," said Audin, "that we are all eager to see him *really* perform."

Damen's gaze swung around to the pet.

It was not over. *Perform*, he thought, and felt sick.

The young boy was not the man's son. He was a pet, not yet adolescent, with thin limbs and his growth spurt still far in his future. It was obvious that he was petrified of Damen. The little barrel of his chest was rising and falling rapidly. He was, at the oldest, fourteen. He looked more like twelve.

Damen saw his chances of returning to Akielos gutter and die like candle flame, and all the doors to freedom close. Obey. Play by the rules. Kiss the Prince's shoe. Jump through his hoops. He had really thought he would be able to do that.

He gathered the last of his strength to himself and said: "Do whatever you want to me. I'm not going to rape a child."

Laurent's expression flickered.

Objection came from an unexpected quarter.

"I'm not a child." Sulkily. But when Damen looked incredulously at him, the boy promptly went white and looked terrified.

Laurent was looking from Damen to the boy and back

again. Frowning as if something didn't make sense. Or wasn't going his way.

"Why not?" he said, abruptly.

"Why not?" said Damen. *"I don't share your craven habit of hitting only those who cannot hit back, and I take no pleasure in hurting those weaker than myself."* Driven past reason, the words came out in his own language.

Laurent, who could speak his language, stared back at him, and Damen met his eyes and did not regret his words, feeling nothing but loathing.

"Your Highness?" said Audin, confused.

Laurent turned to him eventually. "The slave is saying that if you want the pet unconscious, split in half, or dead of fright, then you will need to make other arrangements. He declines his services."

He pushed up out of the box seat and Damen was almost driven backwards as Laurent strode past, ignoring his slave. Damen heard him say to one of the servants: "Have my horse brought to the north courtyard. I'm going for a ride."

And then it was over—finally, and unexpectedly—it was somehow over. Audin frowned and departed. His pet trotted after him, after an indecipherable look at Damen.

As for Damen, he had no idea what had just happened. In the absence of other orders, his escort had him dressed and prepared to return to the harem. Looking around himself, he saw that the ring was now empty, though he hadn't noticed whether the mercenary had been carried out or had risen and walked out of his own accord. Across the ring was a thin trail of blood. A servant was on his knees mopping at it. Damen was being manoeuvred past a blur of faces. One of them was Lady Vannes, who, unexpectedly, addressed him.

"You look surprised . . . were you hoping to enjoy that boy after all? You had better get used to it. The Prince has a reputation for leaving pets unsatisfied." Her laughter, a low glissando, joined the sounds of voices and entertainment, as across the amphitheatre the courtiers returned, with almost no ripple of interruption, to their afternoon pastime.

CHAPTER THREE

B EFORE THE BLINDFOLD was fixed in place, Damen saw that the men returning him to his room were the same two men who, yesterday, had administered the beating. He didn't know the taller one's name, but he knew from over-heard exchanges that the shorter was called Jord. Two men. It was the smallest escort of his imprisonment, but blind-folded and securely bound, not to mention worn out, he had no way to take advantage of it. The restraints were not taken off until he was once again back in his room, chained by the neck.

The men didn't leave. Jord stood by while the taller man closed the door with himself and Jord on the inside. Damen's first thought was that they had been told to deliver a repeat performance, but then he saw that they were lingering of their own accord, not under orders. That might be worse. He waited.

"So you like a fight," said the taller man. Hearing the

tone, Damen prepared himself for the fact that he might be facing another one. "How many men did it take to collar you in Akielos?"

"More than two," said Damen.

It did not go down well. Not with the taller man, at any rate. Jord took his arm, holding him back.

"Leave it," said Jord. "We're not even supposed to be in here."

Jord, although shorter, was also broader across the shoulders. There was a brief moment of resistance before the taller man left the room. Jord remained, his own speculative attention now on Damen.

"Thank you," said Damen, neutrally.

Jord looked back at him, obviously weighing up whether or not to speak. "I'm no friend of Govart," he said finally. Damen thought at first that Govart was the other guard, but he learned otherwise when Jord said, "You must have a death wish to knock out the Regent's favourite thug."

". . . the Regent's what?" said Damen, feeling his stomach sink.

"Govart. He was thrown out of the King's Guard for being a real son of a bitch. The Regent keeps him around. No idea how the Prince got him in the ring, but that one would do anything to piss off his uncle." And then, seeing Damen's expression: "What, you didn't know who he was?"

No. He hadn't known. Damen's understanding of Laurent rearranged itself, in order that he might despise him more accurately. Apparently—in case a miracle happened and his drugged slave managed to win the ring-fight—Laurent had arranged for himself a consolation prize. Damen had unwittingly earned himself a new enemy. Govart. Not only that, but beating Govart in the ring could be taken as a direct slight by the Regent. Laurent, selecting Damen's opponent with precise malice, would, of course, have known that.

This was Vere, Damen reminded himself. Laurent might talk like he'd been raised on the floor of a brothel, but he had a Veretian courtier's mind, used to deception and double-dealing. And his petty plots were dangerous to someone as much in his power as Damen.

It was mid-morning the next day when Radel entered, here once again to see to Damen's transport to the baths.

"You were successful in the ring and even paid the Prince a respectful obeisance. That is excellent. And I see you haven't struck anyone all morning, well done," Radel said.

Damen digested this compliment. He said, "What was the drug you doused me with before the fight?"

"There was no *drug*," said Radel, sounding a bit appalled.

"There was something," said Damen. "You put it in the braziers."

"That was *chalis*, a refined divertissement. There is nothing sinister about it. The Prince suggested that it might help you relax in the baths."

"And did the Prince also suggest the amount?" said Damen.

"Yes," said Radel. "More than the usual. Since you're quite large. I wouldn't have thought of that. He has a mind for details."

"Yes, I'm learning that," said Damen.

He thought that it would be the same as the previous day: that he was being taken to the baths to be prepared for some new grotesquery. But all that happened was that the handlers bathed him, returned him to his room, and brought him lunch on a platter. The bathing was more pleasant than it had been the day before. No chalis, no handling of intrusive intimacy, and he was given a luxurious body massage, his shoulder checked for any sign of strain or injury, his lingering bruises treated very gently.

As the day waned and nothing whatsoever occurred, Damen realised he felt a sense of anticlimax, almost disappointment, which was absurd. Better to spend the day bored on silk cushions than spend it in the ring. Maybe he just wanted another chance to fight something. Preferably an insufferable yellow-haired princeling.

Nothing happened on the second day, or the third, or the fourth, or the fifth.

The passing of time inside this exquisite prison became its own ordeal; the only thing that interrupted his days was the routine of his meals and the morning bath.

He used the time to learn what he could. The change of guard at his door happened at times that were intentionally irregular. The guards no longer behaved towards him as though he were a piece of furniture, and he learned several of their names; the ring-fight had changed something. No one else broke orders to enter his room without instruction, but once or twice one of the men handling him would speak words to him, though the exchanges were brief. A few words, here and there. It was something he worked on.

He was attended by servants who provided his meals, emptied the copper pot, lit torches, extinguished torches, plumped the cushions, changed them, scrubbed the floor, aired the room, but it was—so far—impossible to build a relationship with any of them. They were more obedient to the order not to speak to him than the guards. Or they were more afraid of Damen. Once, he had gotten as much as startled eye contact and a blush. That had happened when Damen, sitting with a knee drawn up and his head resting against the wall, had taken pity on the servant boy attempting to do his work while cleaving to the door, and said, "It's all right. The chain's very strong."

The abortive attempts he made to get information from Radel met with resistance and a series of patronising lectures.

Govart, said Radel, was not a royally sanctioned thug. Where had Damen gotten that idea? The Regent kept Govart in employ out of some kind of obligation, possibly to Govart's family. Why was Damen asking about Govart? Did he not recall that he was here only to do as he was told? There was no need to ask questions. There was no need to concern himself with the goings-on in the palace. He should put everything out of his mind but the thought that he must please the Prince, who, in ten months, would be King.

By now, Damen had the speech memorised.

◆ ◆ ◆

By the sixth day, the trip to the baths had become routine, and he expected nothing from it. Except that today, the routine varied. His blindfold was removed outside the baths, not in it. Radel's critical gaze was on him, as one surveying merchandise: Was it in fit condition? It was.

Damen felt himself being released from his restraints. Here, outside.

Radel said, briefly, "Today, in the baths, you will serve."

"Serve?" said Damen. That word conjured up the curved alcoves and their purpose, and the etched figures, intertwined.

There was no time to absorb the idea, or to ask questions. Much as he had been propelled into the ring, he was pushed forward into the baths. The guards closed the doors with themselves on the outside, and became half-seen shadows behind the latticed metal.

He wasn't sure what he expected. Perhaps a debauched tableau such as had greeted him in the ring. Perhaps pets sprawled out on every surface, naked and steam-drenched. Perhaps a scene in motion, bodies already moving, soft sounds or splashes in the water.

In fact the baths were empty, except for one person.

As yet untouched by the steam, clothed from toe-tip to neck, and standing in the place where slaves were washed before they entered the soaking bath. When Damen saw who it was, he instinctively lifted a hand to his gold collar, unable to quite believe that he was unrestrained and that they were alone together.

Laurent reclined against the tiled wall, settling his shoulders flat against it. He regarded Damen with a familiar expression of golden-lashed dislike.

"So my slave is bashful in the arena. Don't you fuck boys in Akielos?"

"I'm quite cultured. Before I rape anyone, I first check to see if their voice has broken," said Damen.

Laurent smiled.

"Did you fight at Marlas?"

Damen did not react to the smile, which was not authentic. The conversation was now on a knife edge. He said: "Yes."

"How many did you kill?"

"I don't know."

"Lost count?"

Pleasantly, as one might inquire about the weather.

Laurent said, "The barbarian won't fuck boys. He prefers to wait a few years and then use a sword in place of his cock."

Damen flushed. "It was battle. There was death on both sides."

"Oh, yes. We killed a few of you, too. I would like to have killed more, but my uncle is unaccountably clement with vermin. You've met him."

Laurent resembled one of the etched figures of the intaglio, except that he was done in white and gold, not silver. Damen looked at him and thought: This is the place where you had me drugged.

"Have you waited six days to talk to me about your uncle?" Damen said.

Laurent rearranged himself against the wall into a position that looked even more indolently comfortable than the one before.

"My uncle has ridden to Chastillon. He hunts boar. He likes the chase. He likes the kill, too. It's a day's ride, after which he and his party will stay five nights at the old keep. His subjects know better than to bother him with missives from the palace. I have waited six days so that you and I could be alone."

Those sweet blue eyes gazed at him. It was, when you shook off the sugared tone, a threat.

"Alone, with your men guarding the doors," said Damen.

"Are you going to complain again that you're not allowed to hit back?" said Laurent. The voice sweetened further. "Don't worry, I won't hit you unless I have a good reason."

"Did I seem worried?" said Damen.

"You seemed a little agitated," said Laurent, "in the ring. I liked it best when you were on your hands and knees. Cur. Do you think I will tolerate insolence? By all means, try my patience."

Damen was silent; he could feel the steam now, curling heat against his skin. He could feel, too, the danger. He could hear himself. No soldier would talk this way to a prince. A slave would have been on his hands and knees the second he saw that Laurent was in the room.

"Shall I tell you the part you liked?" said Laurent.

"There was nothing I *liked*."

"You're lying. You liked knocking that man down, and you liked it when he didn't get up. You'd like to hurt me, wouldn't you? Is it very difficult to control yourself? Your little speech about fair play fooled me about as much as your show of obedience. You have worked out, with whatever native intelligence you possess, that it serves your interests to appear both civilised and dutiful. But the one thing you're hot for is a fight."

"Are you here to goad me into one?" said Damen, in a new voice that seemed to rise up from deep within him.

Laurent pushed off the wall.

"I don't roll in the sty with swine," said Laurent, coolly. "I'm here to bathe. Have I said something astonishing? Come here."

It was a moment before Damen found he could obey. The instant he had entered the room, he had weighed the option of physically overpowering Laurent, and dismissed it. He would not make it out of the palace alive if he hurt or killed Vere's Crown Prince. That decision had not come without some regret.

He came to stand two steps away. As well as dislike, he was surprised to find there was something assessing in Laurent's expression, as well as something self-satisfied. He had expected bravado. Certainly there were guards outside the door, and at a sound from their Prince they would likely come bursting in bristling with swords, but there was no guarantee that Damen wouldn't lose his temper and kill Laurent before that happened. Another man might. Another man might think that the inevitable retribution—some sort of public execution, ending with his head on a spike—was worth it for the pleasure of wringing Laurent's neck.

"Strip," said Laurent.

Nudity had never bothered him. He knew by now that it was proscribed among the Veretian nobility. But even if Veretian customs had concerned him, everything that there was to see had been seen, very publicly. He unpinned his garments and let them fall. He was unsure what the point of this was. Unless this feeling was the point.

"Undress me," said Laurent.

The feeling intensified. He ignored it, and stepped forward.

The foreign clothing gave him pause. Laurent extended a coolly peremptory hand, palm up, indicating a starting point. The tight little lacings on the underside of Laurent's wrist continued about halfway up his arm and were of the same dark blue as the garment. Untying them took several minutes; the laces were small, complicated and tight, and he must pull each one individually through its hole, feeling the drag of the tie against the material of the eyelet.

Laurent lowered one arm, trailing laces, and extended the other.

In Akielos, clothing was simple and minimal, with a focus on the aesthetics of the body. By contrast, Veretian clothing was concealing and seemed designed to frustrate and impede, its complexity serving no obvious purpose other than to make disrobing difficult. The methodical ritual of unlacing made Damen wonder, scornfully, if Veretian lovers suspended their passion for a half hour in order to disrobe. Perhaps everything that happened in this country was deliberate and bloodless, including lovemaking. But no, he remembered the carnality of the ring. The pets had dressed differently, offering ease of access, and the red-haired pet had unlaced only that part of his master's clothing that was required for his purpose.

When all the various lacings were untied, he drew the

garment off; it was revealed to be an outer layer only. Beneath it was a simple white shirt, also laced, which had not previously been visible. Shirt, pants, boots. Damen hesitated.

Golden brows arched. "Am I here to wait on the modesty of a servant?"

So he knelt. The boots must be taken off; the pants were next. Damen stepped back when it was done. The shirt (now unlaced) had slipped slightly, exposing a shoulder. Laurent reached behind himself and drew it off. He was wearing nothing else.

Damen's flinty dislike of Laurent forestalled his usual reaction to a well-shaped body. If not for that, he might have experienced a moment of difficulty.

For Laurent was all of a piece: his body had the same impossible grace as his face. He was lighter built than Damen, but his body wasn't boyish. Instead, he possessed the beautifully proportioned musculature of a young man on the new cusp of adulthood, made for athletics or statuary. And he was fair. So fair, skin as fair as a young girl's, smooth and unmarked, with a glimmer of gold trailing down from his navel.

In this over-clothed society, Damen might have expected Laurent to display some self-consciousness, but Laurent seemed as coolly immodest about his nudity as he was about everything else. He stood much like a young god before whom a priest was about to make an offering.

"Wash me."

Damen had never performed a servile task in his life, but he supposed that this one would not overwhelm either his pride or his comprehension. By now he knew the customs of the baths. But he felt a sense of subtle satisfaction from Laurent, and a corresponding internal resistance. It was an uncomfortably intimate form of attendance; he was not restrained, and they were alone, one man serving another.

All the appurtenances had been carefully laid out: a fat-bellied silver pitcher, soft cloths, and bottles of oil and frothy liquid soap, made from clear spun glass, their stoppers capped in silver. The one that Damen picked up depicted a vine heavy with grapes. He felt their contours under his fingers as he unstopped the little bottle with a tug against the resistant suction. He filled the silver pitcher. Laurent presented his back.

Laurent's very fine skin, when Damen poured water over it, was like white pearl. His body under the slick soap was nowhere soft or yielding, but taut like an elegantly sprung bow. Damen supposed that Laurent partook of those refined sports that courtiers sometimes indulged in, and which the other participants would allow him, being their prince, to win.

He continued from shoulders to lower back. The spill of water wet his own chest and thighs, where it ran in rivulets, leaving behind suspended droplets that glimmered and threatened at any moment to trail suddenly downwards. The water was hot when it pulsed up from the ground, and hot when he poured it from the silver pitcher. The air was hot.

He was conscious of it. He was conscious of the rise and fall of his chest, of his breathing, of more than that. He remembered that in Akielos he had been washed by a slave with yellow hair. Her colouring had matched Laurent's so closely they might have been twinned. She had been far less disagreeable. She had closed the distance of inches and pressed her body against his. He remembered her fingers curling around him, her nipples soft as bruised fruit where they pressed into his chest. A pulse beat in his neck.

It was a poor time to lose control of his thoughts. He had now progressed far enough in his undertaking that he encountered curves. They were firm under his hands, and the soap made everything slippery. He looked down, and the washcloth slowed. The hothouse atmosphere of the baths only increased the impression of sensuality, and despite himself, Damen felt the first hardening between his legs.

There was a change in the quality of the air, his desire suddenly tangible in the thick humidity of the room.

"Don't be presumptuous," said Laurent, coldly.

"Too late, sweetheart," said Damen.

Laurent turned, and with calm precision unleashed a backhanded blow that had easily enough force to bloody a mouth, but Damen had had quite enough of being hit, and he caught Laurent's wrist before the blow connected.

They were motionless like that for a moment. Damen looked down into Laurent's face, the fair skin a little heat-flushed, the yellow hair wet at the tips, and under those golden lashes the arctic blue eyes, and when Laurent made a little spasming motion to free himself, he felt his grip on Laurent's wrist tighten.

Damen let his gaze wander downwards—wet from chest to taut abdomen—and further. It was really a very, very nice body, but the cold outrage was genuine. Laurent was not even a little amorous, Damen noted; that part of him, quite as sweetly made as the rest, was quiescent.

He felt the tension hit Laurent's body, though the tone didn't change overmuch from its usual drawl. "But my voice has broken. That was the only prerequisite, wasn't it?"

Damen released his grip, as though burned. A moment later, the blow he had thwarted landed, harder than he could have imagined, smashing across his mouth.

"*Get him out of here,*" said Laurent. It was no louder than his speaking voice, but the doors swung open. Not even out of earshot. Damen felt hands on him as he was pulled roughly backwards.

"Put him on the cross. Wait for me to arrive."

"Your Highness, regarding the slave, the Regent instructed—"

"You can do as I say, or you can go there in his place. Choose. Now."

It was not a choice at all, with the Regent in Chastillon. *I have waited six days so that you and I could be alone.*

There was no further prevarication. "Yes, Your Highness."

◆ ◆ ◆

In a moment of oversight, they forgot the blindfold.

The palace was revealed to be a labyrinth, in which corridors flowed one into another, and every archway framed a different aspect: chambers of different shapes, stairs of patterned marble, courtyards that were tiled or filled with cultivated greenery. Some archways, screened by latticed doors, offered no views, only hints and suggestions. Damen was led from passage to chamber to passage. Once, they moved through a courtyard with two fountains, and he heard the trill of birds.

He remembered, carefully, the route. The guards who accompanied him were the only ones he saw.

He assumed there would be security on the perimeter of the harem, but when they stopped in one of the larger rooms, he realised they had passed the perimeter, and he had not even noticed where it was.

He saw, with a change in his pulse, that the archway at the end of this room framed another courtyard, and that this one was not as well kept as the others, containing detritus and a series of irregular objects, including a few slabs of unworked stone and a wheelbarrow. In one corner, a broken pillar was leaned up against the wall, creating a kind of ladder. This led to the roof. The convoluted roof, with its obscuring curves and overhangs and niches and sculptings. It was, clear as daylight, a path to freedom.

So as not to stare at it like a moonstruck idiot, Damen turned his attention back to the room. There was sawdust on the floor. It was some kind of training area. The ornamentation remained extravagant. Except that the fittings were older and of a slightly rougher quality, it still looked like part of the harem. Probably everything in Vere looked like part of a harem.

The cross, Laurent had said. It stood at the far end of the room. The centre beam was made from the single straight trunk of a very large tree. The cross beam was less thick, but equally sturdy. Around the centre beam was tied a sheaf of quilted padding. A servant was tightening the ties that bound the padding to the beam, and the lacing recalled to mind Laurent's clothing.

The servant began testing the strength of the cross by throwing his weight against it. It didn't budge.

The cross, Laurent had called it. It was a flogging post.

Damen had held his first command at seventeen, and flogging was a part of army discipline. As a commander and a prince, flogging was not something that he had personally experienced, but neither was it something that he disproportionately feared. It was familiar to him as a hard punishment that men, with difficulty, endured.

At the same time, he knew that strong men broke under the lash. Men died under the lash. Though—even at seventeen— death under the lash was not something he would have allowed to happen under his command. If a man was not responsive to good leadership and the rigours of normal discipline—and the fault was not with his superiors—he was turned off. Such a man should not have been taken on in the first place.

Probably, he was not going to die; there was just going to be a great deal of pain. Most of the anger that he felt about this fact he proportioned to himself. He had resisted the provocation to violence exactly because he had known he would end up suffering consequences. And now here he was, for no better reason than that Laurent, possessing a pleasing shape, had left off talking just long enough for Damen's body to forget his disposition.

Damen was strapped to the wooden post face-first with his

arms spread and shackled to the cross section. His legs were untied. There was enough give in the position to squirm; he would not. The guards tugged on his arms, and on the restraints, testing them, positioning his body, even kicking his legs apart. He had to force himself not to struggle against it. It wasn't easy.

He could not have said how much time had passed when Laurent finally entered the room. Enough time for Laurent to dry, and to dress, and to do up all those hundreds of laces.

As Laurent entered, one of the men began testing the lash in his hands, calmly, as they had tested all the equipment. Laurent's face had the hard, strapped-down look of a man resolved on a course of action. He took up a position against the wall in front of Damen. From this vantage, he would not be able to see the impact of the lash, but he would see Damen's face. Damen's stomach turned over.

Damen felt a dull sensation in his wrists and realised that he had begun unconsciously pulling against the restraints. He forced himself to stop.

There was a man at his side with something twined through his fingers. He was lifting it to Damen's face.

"Open your mouth."

Damen accepted the foreign object past his lips in the moment before he realised what it was. It was a piece of wood covered in soft brown leather. It was not like the gags or bits that he had been subjected to throughout his captivity, rather it was the kind that you give a man to bite down on to help him endure pain. The man tied it behind Damen's head.

As the man with the lash moved behind him, he tried to prepare himself.

"How many stripes?" said the man.

"I'm not sure yet," said Laurent. "I'm sure I'll decide eventually. You can begin."

The sound came first: the soft whistle of air, then the crack, lash against flesh, a split second before the jagged pain ripped at him. Damen jerked against the restraints as the lash struck his shoulders, obliterating in that instant his consciousness of anything else. The bright burst of pain was barely given a moment to fade before the second lash hit with brutal force.

The rhythm was ruthlessly efficient. Again and again the lash fell on Damen's back, varying only in the place where it landed, yet that tiny difference grew to have critical importance, his mind clinging to any hope of a fraction less pain, as his muscles bunched and his breathing changed.

Damen found himself reacting not only to the pain but to the rhythm of it, the sick anticipation of the blow, trying to steel himself against it, and reaching a point, as the lash fell again and again across the same welts and marks, when that was no longer possible.

He pressed his forehead to the wood of the post then and just—took it. His body shuddered against the cross. Every nerve and sinew strained, the pain spreading out from his back and consuming all his body, then invading his mind, which was left with no barriers or partitions that could hold against it. He forgot where he was and who was watching him. He was unable to think, or feel anything other than his own pain.

Finally the blows stopped.

Damen took a while to realise it. Someone was untying

the gag and freeing his mouth. After that, Damen became aware of himself in stages, that his chest was heaving and his hair was soaked. He unlocked his muscles and tested his back. The wave of pain that washed over him convinced him that it was much better to be still.

He thought that if his wrists were released from the restraints, he would simply collapse onto his hands and knees in front of Laurent. He fought against the weakness that made him think that. Laurent. His returned awareness of the existence of Laurent arrived at the same moment he realised that Laurent had come forward and was now standing a single pace away, regarding him, his face wiped clean of any expression.

Damen recalled Jokaste pressing cool fingers against his bruised cheek.

"I should have done this to you the day you arrived," said Laurent. "It's exactly what you deserve."

"Why didn't you?" Damen said. A little roughened, the words just came out. There was nothing left to keep them in check. He felt raw, as though a protective outer layer had been stripped away; the problem was that what had been exposed was not weakness but core metal. "You are cold-blooded and honourless. What held back someone like you?" It was the wrong thing to say.

"I'm not sure," said Laurent, in a detached voice. "I was curious what kind of man you were. I see we have stopped too early. Again."

Damen tried to brace himself for another strike, and something in his mind splintered when it did not, immediately, come.

"Your Highness, I'm not certain he'll survive another round."

"I think he will. Why don't we make a wager?" Laurent spoke again in that cold, flat voice. "A gold coin says he lives. If you want to win it from me, you'll have to exert yourself."

Lost to pain, Damen could not have said for how long the man exerted himself, only that he did. When it was over, he was well beyond further impertinence. Blackness was threatening his vision, and it took all he had to keep it back. It was a while before he realised that Laurent had spoken, and even then for the longest time the emotionless voice didn't connect to anything.

"I was on the field at Marlas," said Laurent.

As the words penetrated, Damen felt the world reshape itself around him.

"They wouldn't let me near the front. I never had the chance to face him. I used to wonder what I'd say to him if I did. What I'd do. How dare any one of you speak the word *honour*? I know your kind. A Veretian who treats honourably with an Akielon will be gutted with his own sword. It's your countryman who taught me that. You can thank him for the lesson."

"*Thank who?*" Damen pushed the words out, somehow, past the pain, but he knew. He knew.

"Damianos, the dead Prince of Akielos," said Laurent. "The man who killed my brother."

CHAPTER FOUR

O W," SAID DAMEN through gritted teeth.

"Be still," said the physician.

"You are a clumsy, poking lout," said Damen, in his own language.

"And be quiet. This is a medicinal salve," said the physician.

Damen disliked palace physicians. During the last weeks of his father's illness, the sickroom had thronged with them. They had chanted, muttered pronouncements, thrown divining bones into the air and administered various remedies, but his father had only grown sicker. He felt different about the pragmatic field surgeons who had worked tirelessly alongside the army on campaign. The surgeon who had tended him at Marlas had sewn up his shoulder with a minimum of fuss, restraining his objection to a frown when Damen got on a horse five minutes later.

The Veretian physicians were not of this ilk. It was admonitions not to move and endless instructions and dressings that were continually being changed. This physician wore a gown that reached to the floor and a hat shaped like a loaf of bread. The salve was having absolutely no effect on his back that Damen could discern, though it smelled pleasantly of cinnamon.

It was three days since the lashing. Damen did not clearly remember being taken down off the flogging post and returned to his room. The blurry impressions that he had of the journey reassured him that he had made the trip upright. For the most part.

He did remember being supported by two of the guards, here, in this room, while Radel stared at his back in horror.

"The Prince really . . . did this?"

"Who else?" Damen said.

Radel had stepped forward and slapped Damen across the face; it was a hard slap, and the man wore three rings on each finger.

"What did you do to him?" Radel demanded.

This question had struck Damen as funny. It must have shown on his face, because a second much harder slap followed the first. The sting of it momentarily cleared the blackness that was pressing in on his vision; Damen had taken this further hold on consciousness and held to it. Passing out was not something he had ever done before, but it was a day of firsts, and he was taking no chances.

"Don't let him die yet," was the last thing Laurent had said.

The Prince's word was law. And so, for the small price of

the skin off his back, there were a number of compromises to Damen's imprisonment, including the dubious perquisite of regular pokes from the physician.

A bed replaced the floor cushions, so that he could lie comfortably on his stomach (to protect his back). He was also given blankets and various coloured silk wraps, though he must use them to cover the lower half of his body only (to protect his back). The chain remained, but instead of attaching to his collar it was locked to one golden wrist-cuff (to protect his back). The concern for his back also struck him as funny.

He was bathed frequently, his skin softly sponged with water drawn from a tub. Afterwards, the servants disposed of the water, which, on the first day, was red.

Remarkably, the biggest change was not in the furnishings and routines, it was in the attitude of the servants and the men guarding him. Damen might have expected them to react like Radel, with animosity and outrage. Instead, there was sympathy from the servants. From the guards there was, even more unexpectedly, camaraderie. Where the ring-fight had positioned Damen as a fellow fighter, being pulverised under the Prince's lash had apparently made him one of the fraternity. Even the taller guard, Orlant, who had threatened Damen after the ringfight, seemed to have somewhat warmed to him. Inspecting Damen's back, Orlant had—not without some pride—proclaimed the Prince a cast-iron bitch, and clapped Damen cheerfully on the shoulder, turning him momentarily ashen.

In turn, Damen was careful not to ask any questions that would earn him suspicion. Instead, he embarked on a determined cultural exchange.

Was it true that in Akielos they blinded those who looked on the King's harem? No, it wasn't. Was it true that Akielon women went bare-breasted in summer? Yes, it was. And the wrestling matches were fought naked? Yes. And the slaves also went naked? Yes. Akielos might have a bastard King and a whore Queen, but it sounded like paradise to Orlant. Laughter.

A bastard King and a whore Queen; Laurent's crude apothegm had, Damen discovered, entered common usage.

Damen unlocked his jaw and let it pass. Security was relaxing in small increments, and he now knew a way out of the palace. He tried, objectively, to view this as a fair exchange for a lashing (two lashings, his back reminded him tenderly).

He ignored his back. He focused on anything and everything else.

The men guarding him were the Prince's Guard and had no affiliation with the Regent whatsoever. It surprised Damen how loyal they were to their Prince, and how diligent in his service, airing none of the grudges and complaints that he might have expected, considering Laurent's noxious personality. Laurent's feud with his uncle they took up wholeheartedly; there were deep schisms and rivalries between the Prince's Guard and the Regent's Guard, apparently.

It had to be Laurent's looks that inspired the allegiance of his men, and not Laurent himself. The closest the men got to disrespect was a series of ribald comments regarding Laurent's appearance. Their loyalty apparently did not prohibit the fantasy of fucking the Prince taking on mythic proportions.

Was it true, asked Jord, that in Akielos the male nobility kept female slaves, and the ladies fucked men?

"They don't in Vere?" Damen recalled that, inside the ring and out of it, he had seen only same-sex pairings. His knowledge of Veretian culture did not extend to the practices of intimacy. "Why not?"

"No one of high birth invites the abomination of bastardry," said Jord, matter-of-factly. Female pets were kept by ladies, male pets were kept by lords.

"You mean that men and women—never—"

Never. Not among the nobility. Well, sometimes, if they were perverse. It was taboo. Bastards were a blight, Jord said. Even among the guard, if you screwed women, you kept quiet about it. If you got a woman pregnant and didn't marry her, your career was over. Better to avoid the problem, follow the example of the nobility, and screw men. Jord preferred men. Didn't Damen? You knew what was what, with men. And you could spurt without fear.

Damen was wisely silent. His own preference was for women; it seemed ill-advised to admit this. On the rare occasions when Damen pleased himself with men, he did so because he was attracted to them as men, not because he had any reason to avoid women or substitute for them. Veretians, thought Damen, made things needlessly complicated for themselves.

Here and there, useful information emerged. Pets weren't guarded, which explained the lack of men at the perimeter of the harem. Pets weren't slaves. They came and went as they pleased. Damen was the exception. It meant that once past these guards, it was unlikely he would encounter others.

Here and there, the subject of Laurent was raised.

"Have you . . . ?" said Jord to Damen, with a slowly spreading smile.

"Between the ring-fight and the lashing?" said Damen, sourly. "No."

"They say he's frigid."

Damen stared at him. "What? Why?"

"Well," said Jord, "because he doesn't—"

"I meant why is he so," said Damen, cutting off Jord's prosaic explanation firmly.

"Why is snow cold?" said Jord with a shrug.

Damen frowned and changed the subject. Damen was not interested in Laurent's proclivities. Since the cross, his feelings towards Laurent had solidified from prickling dislike into something hard and implacable.

It was Orlant, finally, who asked the obvious question.

"How'd you end up here, anyway?"

"I wasn't careful," said Damen, "and I made an enemy of the King."

"Kastor? Someone should stick it to that whoreson. Only a country of barbarian scum would put a bastard on the throne," said Orlant. "No offense."

"None taken," said Damen.

◆ ◆ ◆

On the seventh day, the Regent returned from Chastillon.

The first Damen knew of it was the entrance into his room of guards he didn't recognise. They were not wearing the Prince's livery. They had red cloaks, disciplined lines and unfamiliar faces. Their arrival provoked a heated argument between the Prince's physician and a new man, one Damen had never seen before.

"I don't think he should move," said the Prince's physician. Under the loaf of bread, he was frowning.

"The wounds might open."

"They look closed to me," said the other. "He can stand."

"I can stand," Damen agreed. He demonstrated this remarkable ability. He thought he knew what was happening. Only one man other than Laurent had the authority to dismiss the Prince's Guard.

The Regent came into the room in full state, flanked by his red-cloaked Regent's Guard and accompanied by liveried servants and two men of high rank. He dismissed both physicians, who made obeisances and vanished. Then he dismissed the servants and everyone else but the two men who had entered with him. His resulting lack of entourage did not detract from his power. Though technically he only held the throne in stewardship, and was addressed with the same honorific of "Royal Highness" as Laurent, this was a man with the stature and presence of a King.

Damen knelt. He would not make the same mistake with the Regent that he had made with Laurent. He remembered that he had recently slighted the Regent by beating Govart in the ring, which Laurent had arranged. The emotion he felt towards Laurent surfaced briefly; on the ground beside him, the chain from his wrist pooled. If someone had told him, six months ago, that he'd kneel, willingly, for Veretian nobility, he would have laughed in their face.

Damen recognised the two men accompanying the

Regent as Councillor Guion and Councillor Audin. Each wore the same heavy medallion on a thick linked chain: their chain of office.

"Witness with your own eyes," said the Regent.

"This is Kastor's gift to the Prince. The Akielon slave," said Audin, in surprise. A moment later he fished out a square of silk and lifted it to his nose, as if to screen his sensibilities from affront. "What happened to his back? That's barbaric."

It was, thought Damen, the first time he had heard the word *barbaric* used to describe anything other than himself or his country.

"This is what Laurent thinks of our careful negotiations with Akielos," said the Regent. "I ordered him to treat Kastor's gift respectfully. Instead, he had the slave flogged almost to death."

"I knew the Prince was willful. I never thought him this destructive, this wild," said Audin, in a shocked, silk-muffled voice.

"There's nothing wild about it. This is a piece of intentional provocation, aimed at me, and at Akielos. Laurent would like nothing better than for our treaty with Kastor to founder. He mouths platitudes in public, and in private— this."

"You see, Audin," said Guion. "It's as the Regent warned us."

"The flaw is deep in Laurent's nature. I thought he'd outgrow it. Instead, he grows steadily worse. Something must be done to discipline him."

"These actions cannot be supported," agreed Audin. "But

what can be done? You cannot rewrite a man's nature in ten months."

"Laurent disobeyed my order. No one knows that better than the slave. Perhaps we should ask him what should be done with my nephew."

Damen did not imagine he was serious, but the Regent came forward, and stood directly in front of him.

"Look up, slave," the Regent said.

Damen looked up. He saw again the dark hair and the commanding aspect, as well as the slight frown of displeasure that it seemed Laurent habitually elicited from his uncle. Damen remembered thinking that there was no familial resemblance between the Regent and Laurent, but now he saw that this was not quite true. Though his hair was dark, and silvered at the temples, the Regent had blue eyes.

"I hear that you were once a soldier," said the Regent. "If a man disobeyed an order in the Akielon army, how would he punished?"

"He would be publicly flogged and turned off," Damen said.

"A public flogging," said the Regent, turning back to the two men who accompanied him. "That is not possible. But Laurent has grown so unmanageable in recent years, I wonder what would help him. What a shame that soldiers and princes are held to a different accounting."

"Ten months before his ascension . . . is it really a wise time to chastise your nephew?" Audin spoke from behind the silk.

"Shall I let him run wild, wrecking treaties, destroying

lives? Warmongering? This is my fault. I have been too lenient."

"You have my support," said Guion.

Audin was nodding slowly. "The Council will stand behind you when they hear word of this. But perhaps we should discuss these matters elsewhere?"

Damen watched the men depart. Long-term peace with Akielos was obviously something that the Regent was working hard to bring about. The part of Damen that did not wish to raze to the ground the cross, the ring, and the palace containing them, reluctantly acknowledged that goal as admirable.

The physician returned, and fussed, and servants came to make him comfortable, and then departed. And Damen was left alone in his rooms to think about the past.

The battle of Marlas six years ago had ended with twinned, bloody successes for Akielos. An Akielon arrow, a stray lucky arrow on the wind, had taken the Veretian King in the throat. And Damen had killed the Crown Prince, Auguste, in single combat on the northern front.

The battle had turned on Auguste's death. The Veretian forces had quickly fallen into disarray, the death of their prince a staggering, dispiriting blow. Auguste had been a beloved leader, an indomitable fighter and an emblem of Veretian pride: he had rallied his men after the death of the King; he had led the charge that decimated the Akielon northern flank; he had been the point on which wave after wave of Akielon fighters had broken.

"Father, I can beat him," Damen had said, and receiving

his father's blessing, he had ridden out from behind the lines and into the fight of his life.

Damen hadn't known that the younger brother had been on the field. Six years ago, Damen had been nineteen. Laurent would have been—thirteen, fourteen? It was young to fight in a battle like Marlas.

It was too young to inherit. And with the Veretian King dead, and the Crown Prince dead, the King's brother had stepped in as Regent, and his first act had been to call parley, accepting the terms of surrender and ceding to Akielos the disputed lands of Delpha, which the Veretians called Delfeur.

It was the reasonable act of a reasonable man; in person, the Regent seemed similarly levelheaded and sensible, though afflicted with an intolerable nephew.

Damen did not know why his mind was returning to the fact of Laurent's presence on the field that day. There was no fear of discovery. It was six years ago, and Laurent had been a boy, who by his own admission had been nowhere near the front. Even if that were not the case, Marlas had been chaos. Any glimpse of Damen would have been early in the battle, with Damen in full armour, including helm—or if by some miracle he had been seen later, shield and helm lost, by that time Damen had been covered in mud and blood and fighting for his life as they all had been.

But if he were recognised: every man and woman in Vere knew the name of Damianos, prince-killer. Damen had known how dangerous it would be for him if his identity were discovered; he had not known how near to discovery he had come, and by the very person who had the most cause to want him dead. All the more reason why he had to get free of this place.

You have a scar, Laurent had said.

◆ ◆ ◆

"What did you tell the Regent?" Radel demanded. The last time Radel had looked at him like that, he'd lifted his hand and hit Damen, hard. "You heard me. What did you tell him about the lashing?"

"What should I have told him?" Damen gazed back at him calmly.

"What you should have done," said Radel, "is shown loyalty to your Prince. In ten months—"

"—he will be King," said Damen. "Until then, aren't we subject to the rule of his uncle?"

There was a long, cold pause.

"I see it has not taken you long to learn how to make your way here," Radel said.

Damen said, "What has happened?"

"You have been summoned to court," said Radel. "I hope you can walk."

With that, a parade of servants entered the room. The preparations that they began eclipsed any Damen had experienced, including those that had been made before the ring.

He was washed, pampered, primped and perfumed. They carefully skirted his healing back but oiled everywhere else, and the oil they used contained gold pigment, so that his limbs gleamed in the torchlight like those of a golden statue.

A servant approached with a series of three small bowls and a delicate brush, and brought his face close to Damen's, gazing at his features with an expression of concentration, the brush poised. The bowls contained paint for his face. He had not had to suffer the humiliation of paint since Akielos. The servant touched the paint-wet brush tip to skin, gilt paint to line his eyes, and Damen felt the cold thickness of it on his lashes, and cheeks, and lips.

This time Radel did not say, "No jewellery," and four enamelled silver caskets were brought into the room and thrown open. From their gleaming contents, Radel made several selections. The first was a series of fine, near-invisible strings, on which hung tiny rubies spaced at intervals; they were woven into Damen's hair. Then gold for his brow and gold for his waist. Then a leash, snapped onto the collar. The leash was gold, too, a fine gold chain, terminating in a golden rod for his handler, the cat carved at one end holding a garnet in its mouth. Much more of this, and he was going to clank as he walked.

But there was more. There was a final piece; another fine gold chain looped between twin gold devices. Damen didn't recognise what it was until a servant stepped forward and snapped the nipple clamps in place.

He jerked away—too late, besides which it only took a jab to his back to send him to his knees. As his chest rose and fell, the little chain swayed.

"The paint's smudged," said Radel to one of the servants, after assessing Damen's body and face. "There. And there. Reapply it."

"I thought the Prince didn't like paint," said Damen.

"He doesn't," said Radel.

◆ ◆ ◆

It was the custom of the Veretian nobility to dress in sub-dued splendour, distinguishing themselves from the garish brightness of the pets on whom they lavished their greatest displays of wealth. It meant that Damen, cast in gold and escorted through the double doors at the end of a leash, could be mistaken for nothing but what he was. In the crowded chamber, he stood out.

So did Laurent. His bright head was instantly recognis-able. Damen's gaze fixed on him. Left and right, the court-iers were falling silent and stepping back, clearing a path to the throne.

A red carpet stretched from the double doors to the dais, woven with hunting scenes and apple trees and a border of acanthus. The walls were draped in tapestries, where the same rich red predominated. The throne was swathed in the same colour.

Red, red, red. Laurent clashed.

Damen felt his thoughts scattering. Concentration was keeping him upright. His back ached and throbbed.

He forcibly detached his gaze from Laurent, and turned it to the director of whatever public spectacle was now about to unfold. At the end of the long carpet, the Regent sat on the throne. In his left hand, resting across his knee, he held a golden sceptre of office. And behind him, in full robes of state, was the Veretian Council.

The Council was the seat of Veretian power. In the days of King Aleron, the Council's role had been to advise on matters of state. Now the Regent and Council held the nation in stewardship until Laurent's ascension. Comprised of five men and no women, the Council was arrayed in a formidable backdrop on the dais. Damen recognised Audin and Guion. A third man he knew from his extreme age to be Councillor Herode. The others must therefore be Jeurre and Chelaut, though he could not tell one from the other. All five wore their medallions around their necks, the mark of their office.

Also on the dais standing slightly back from the throne, Damen saw Councillor Audin's pet, the child, done up even more garishly than Damen. The only reason Damen outdid him in sheer volume of gilt was because, being several times the little boy's size, he had substantially more skin available to act as canvas.

A herald called out Laurent's name and all of his titles.

Walking forward, Laurent joined Damen and his handler in their approach. Damen was starting to view the carpet as an endurance trial. It was not just the presence of Laurent. The correct series of prostrations before the throne seemed specifically designed to ruin a week's worth of healing. Finally it was done.

Damen knelt, and Laurent bent his knee the appropriate amount.

From the courtiers lining the chamber, Damen heard one or two murmured comments about his back. He supposed that set against the gold paint, it looked rather gruesome. That, he realised suddenly, was the point.

The Regent wanted to discipline his nephew, and, with the Council behind him, had chosen to do it in public.

A public flogging, Damen had said.

"Uncle," said Laurent.

Straightening, Laurent's posture was relaxed and his expression was undisturbed, but there was something subtle in the set of his shoulders that Damen recognised. It was the look of a man settling in for a fight.

"Nephew," said the Regent. "I think you can guess why we are here."

"A slave laid hands on me, and I had him flogged for it." Calmly.

"Twice," said the Regent. "Against my orders. The second time, against the advice that it might lead to his death. Almost, it did."

"He's alive. The advice was incorrect." Again, calmly.

"You were also advised of my order: that in my absence the slave wasn't to be touched," said the Regent. "Search your memory. You'll find that advice was accurate. Yet you ignored it."

"I didn't think you'd mind. I know you are not so subservient towards Akielos that you would want the slave's actions to go unpunished just because he is a gift from Kastor."

The blue-eyed composure was faultless. Laurent, Damen thought with contempt, was good at talking. He wondered if the Regent was regretting doing this in public. But the Regent did not look perturbed, or even surprised. Well, he would be used to dealing with Laurent.

"I can think of several reasons why you should not have a

King's gift beaten almost to death immediately after the signing of a treaty. Not the least because I ordered it. You claim to have administered a just punishment. But the truth is different."

The Regent gestured, and a man stepped forward.

"The Prince offered me a gold coin if I could flog the slave to death."

It was the moment when sympathy palpably swung away from Laurent. Laurent, realising it, opened his mouth to speak, but the Regent cut him off.

"No. You've had your chance to make apologies or give reasonable excuses. You chose instead to show unrepentant arrogance. You do not yet have the right to spit in the face of kings. At your age, your brother was leading armies and bringing glory to his country. What have you achieved in the same time? When you shirked your responsibilities at court, I ignored it. When you refused to do your duty on the border at Delfeur, I let you have your way. But this time your disobedience has threatened an accord between nations. The Council and I have met and agreed we must take action."

The Regent spoke in a voice of unquestioned power that was heard in every corner of the chamber.

"Your lands of Varenne and Marche are forfeit, along with all troops and monies that accompany them. You retain only Acquitart. For the next ten months, you will find your income reduced, and your retinue diminished. You will petition to me directly for any expenses. Be grateful you retain Acquitart and that we have not taken this decree further."

Shock at the sanctions rippled across the assembly. There

was outrage on some faces. But on many others there was something quietly satisfied, and the shock was less. In that moment, it was obvious which of the courtiers comprised the Regent's faction, and which Laurent's. And that Laurent's was smaller.

"Be grateful I retain Acquitart," said Laurent, "which by law you cannot take away and which besides has no accompanying troops and little strategic importance?"

"Do you think it pleases me to discipline my own nephew? No uncle acts with a heavier heart. Shoulder your responsibilities—ride to Delfeur—show me you have even a drop of your brother's blood and I will joyfully restore it all."

"I think there is an old caretaker at Acquitart. Shall I ride to the border with him? We could share armour."

"Don't be facile. If you agreed to fulfil your duty, you would not lack for men."

"Why would I waste my time on the border when, at Kastor's whim, you roll over?"

For the first time, the Regent looked angry. "You claim this is a matter of national pride, but you are unwilling to lift a finger to serve your own country. The truth is that you acted out of petty malice, and now you're smarting at discipline. This is on your own head. Embrace the slave in apology, and we are done."

Embrace the slave?

Anticipation among the gathered courtiers winched tighter.

Damen was urged onto his feet by his handler. Expecting Laurent to baulk at his uncle's order, Damen was startled when, after a lingering look at his uncle, Laurent approached, with soft, obedient grace. He hooked a finger in the chain that stretched across Damen's chest and drew him forward by it. Damen, feeling the sustained pull at twin points, came as he was bid. With cool detachment, Laurent's fingers gathered rubies, inclining Damen's head down far enough to kiss him on the cheek. The kiss was insubstantial: not a single mote of gold paint transferred itself to Laurent's lips in the process.

"You look like a whore." The soft words barely stirred the air by Damen's ear, inaudible to anyone else. Laurent murmured: "Filthy painted slut. Did you spread for my uncle the way you did for Kastor?"

Damen recoiled violently, and gold paint smeared. He was staring at Laurent from two paces away, revolted.

Laurent lifted the back of his hand to his cheek, now streaked with gold, then turned back to the Regent with a wide-eyed expression of injured innocence. "Witness the slave's behaviour for yourself. Uncle, you wrong me cruelly. The slave's punishment on the cross was deserved: you can see for yourself how arrogant and rebellious he is. Why do you punish your own blood when the fault lies with Akielos?"

Move, and counter move. There was a danger in doing something like this publicly. And indeed, there was a slight shift of sympathy within the assembly.

"You claim the slave was at fault and deserved punishment. Very well. He has received it. Now you receive yours. Even you are subject to the rule of Regent and Council. Accept it gracefully."

Laurent lowered his blue eyes, martyring himself. "Yes, uncle."

He was diabolical. Perhaps this was the answer to how he won loyalty from the Prince's Guard; he simply wrapped them around his finger. On the dais, the elderly Councillor Herode was frowning a little and looking at Laurent for the first time with troubled sympathy.

The Regent ended the proceedings, rose, and departed, perhaps for some awaiting entertainment. The councillors left with him. The symmetry of the chamber broke down as courtiers unlocked themselves from their positions on either side of the carpet and began to mingle more freely.

"You may hand me the leash," said a pleasant voice, very close.

Damen looked up into a pair of limpid blue eyes. Beside him, the handler hesitated.

"Why do you delay?" Laurent held out his hand and smiled. "The slave and I have embraced and are joyously reconciled."

The handler passed him the leash. Laurent immediately drew the chain taut.

"Come with me," Laurent said.

CHAPTER FIVE

IT WAS A little too ambitious of Laurent to think that he could extricate himself, easily and discreetly, from a court gathering of which his own censure had been the centrepiece.

Damen, held at the end of a leash, watched as Laurent's progress was thwarted again and again by those who wished to commiserate. There was a press of silk and cambric and solicitude. For Damen, it was not a reprieve, just a delay. He felt at every moment Laurent's hold on the leash, like a promise. Damen felt a tension that wasn't fear. Under different circumstances, without guards or witnesses, he might relish the chance to be alone in a room with Laurent.

Laurent was indeed good at talking. He accepted sympathy gracefully. He put his position rationally. He stopped the flow of talk when it became dangerously critical of his uncle. He said nothing that could be taken as an open slight on the

Regency. Yet no one who talked to him could have any doubt that his uncle was behaving at best misguidedly and at worst treasonously.

But even to Damen, who had no great knowledge of the politics of this court, it was significant that all five councillors had left with the Regent. It was a sign of the Regent's comparative power: he had the full backing of the Council. Laurent's faction, left here griping in the audience chamber, did not like it. They did not have to like it. They could do nothing about it.

This, then, was the time for Laurent to do his best to shore up support, not disappear off somewhere for a private tête-à-tête with his slave.

And yet, despite all of this, they were leaving the audience chamber and moving through a series of interior courtyards large enough to contain trees, geometric greenery, fountains and winding paths. Across the courtyard, glimpses of the continuing revelry could be seen; the trees moved and the lights from the entertainment across the way winked, brightly.

They were not alone. Following at a discreet distance were two guards for Laurent's protection. As always. And the courtyard itself was not empty. More than once they passed couples promenading on the paths, and once Damen saw a pet and courtier twining around one another on a bench, sensuously kissing.

Laurent led them to an arbour, vine-bowered. Beside it was a fountain and a long pool tangled with lilies. Laurent tied Damen's leash to the metalwork of the bower, as he might tie a horse's lead to a post. He had to stand very close to

Damen in order to do it, but gave no sign that he was bothered by the proximity. The tether was nothing more than an insult. Not being a dumb animal, Damen was perfectly capable of untying the leash. What kept him in place was not the thin golden chain casually looped around the metal, it was the liveried guard and the presence of half the court, and a great many men besides that, between him and freedom.

Laurent moved off a few steps. Damen saw him lift a hand to the back of his own neck, as if to release tension. Saw him do nothing for a moment but stand and be quiet and breathe the cool air scented with night flowers. It occurred to Damen for the first time that Laurent might have his own reasons for wanting to escape the attention of the court.

The tension rose, surfacing, as Laurent turned back to him.

"You don't have a very good sense of self-preservation, do you, little pet? Bleating to my uncle was a mistake," said Laurent.

"Because you got your hand slapped?" said Damen.

"Because it's going to anger all those guards you've taken so much trouble cultivating," said Laurent. "They tend to dislike servants who place self-interest above loyalty."

Expecting a direct assault, he was unprepared for one that came at him obliquely, sideways. He set his jaw, let his gaze rake up and down Laurent's form.

"You can't touch your uncle, so you lash out where you can. I'm not afraid of you. If there's something you're going to do to me, do it."

"You poor, misguided animal," said Laurent. "Whatever made you think I came here for you?"

Damen blinked.

"Then again," said Laurent, "maybe I do need you for one thing." He wound the thin chain once around his own wrist, and then, with a sharp jerk, he snapped it. The two ends slithered away from his wrist and dropped, dangling. Laurent took a step backwards. Damen looked at the broken chain in confusion.

"Your Highness," said a voice.

Laurent said, "Councillor Herode."

"Thank you for agreeing to meet with me," began Herode. Then he saw Damen and hesitated. "Forgive me. I . . . assumed you would come alone."

"Forgive you?" said Laurent.

A silence opened up around Laurent's words. In it, their meaning changed. Herode began, "I—" Then he looked at Damen, and his expression grew alarmed. "Is this safe? He's broken his leash. Guard!"

There was the shrill sound of a sword drawn from a sheath. Two swords. The guards pushed their way into the arbour and interposed themselves between Damen and Herode. Of course.

"You've made your point," Herode said, with a wary eye on Damen. "I hadn't seen the slave's rebellious side. You seemed to have him under control in the ring. And the slaves gifted to your uncle are so obedient. If you attend the entertainments later, you'll see that for yourself."

"I've seen them," said Laurent. There was a little silence.

"You know how close I was to your father," said Herode. "Since his death, I have given my loyalty unswervingly to your uncle. I'm concerned that in this case it may have led me to make an error of judgement—"

"If you're concerned that my memory for wrongs against me is longer than ten months," said Laurent, "there's no need for anxiety. I am sure you can persuade me you were genuinely mistaken."

Herode said, "Perhaps we can take a turn in the garden. The slave can avail himself of the garden seat and rest his injuries."

"How thoughtful of you, Councillor," said Laurent. He turned to Damen and said in a melting voice, "Your back must hurt terribly."

"It's fine," said Damen.

"Kneel on the ground then," Laurent said.

A hard grip on his shoulder forced him down; as soon as Damen's knees hit the ground, then a sword was held to his throat to dissuade him from rising. Herode and Laurent were disappearing away together, just one more couple wandering the perfumed garden paths.

◆ ◆ ◆

The revelry across the way began to spill out into the garden, and, steadily, its population increased, and lanterns were hung, and servants began to wander about with refreshments. The place where Damen knelt remained reasonably out of the way, but occasionally courtiers passed him and remarked on him: Look, there is the Prince's barbarian slave.

Frustration curled in him like a lash. He was once again tied up. The guard was less nonchalant about restraining him than Laurent. He was chained to the metal bower by his collar, and this time it was a real chain, not something he could snap.

Little pet, thought Damen with disgust. From Herode's fraught exchange with Laurent he picked the only salient piece of information.

Somewhere inside, not far away, were the other Akielon slaves.

Damen's mind returned to them. His concern for their well-being persisted, but their proximity raised perturbing questions. What was the provenance of these slaves? Were they palace slaves, trained by Adrastus and brought as Damen had been, directly from the capital? Held in solitary confinement aboard the ship, Damen had not yet seen the slaves, nor had they seen him. But if they were palace slaves, handpicked from the best of those who served royalty in Akielos, there was a chance that they would recognise him.

In the unfolding quiet of the courtyard, he heard the soft chime of small bells.

Chained up in an obscure part of the garden away from the courtly entertainments, it was just sheer bad luck that one of the slaves was brought to him.

On the end of a leash, led by a Veretian pet. The slave wore a petite version of Damen's gold collar and wrist-cuffs. The pet was the source of the bells. He was belled like a cat, at his throat. He was wearing a great deal of paint. And he was familiar.

It was Councillor Audin's pet, the child.

Damen cheerlessly supposed that to those susceptible to

little boys, this pet probably had charms in abundance. Under the paint, he had a child's fine clear skin. If his features had been possessed by a girl of the same age, they would have promised, given half a dozen years, a superlatively beautiful young woman. A learned grace disguised, for the most part, the limitations of his undersized child's limbs. Like Damen, he had precious stones woven into his hair, though in his case they were seed pearls, glinting like stars in a tumble of brown curls. His best feature was a pair of amazing blue eyes, unmatched by any Damen had ever seen, except for the ones he had recently been staring into.

The boy's pretty bow lips formed the shape of a kiss, and he spat, right into Damen's face.

"My name is Nicaise," he said. "You're not important enough to slight me. Your master had all his land and money taken away. Even if he hadn't, you're just a slave. The Regent sent me to find the Prince. Where is he?"

"He went back to the audience chamber," Damen said. To say that he was taken aback by Nicaise was an understatement. The lie just came out.

Nicaise stared at him. Then he tugged brutally on the slave's leash. The slave was wrenched forward and almost overbalanced, like a colt on over-long legs. "I'm not going to drag you around all night. Wait here for me." Nicaise tossed the slave's leash onto the ground and turned on his heel, bells chiming.

Damen lifted his hand to his wet face. Instantly, the slave was on his knees beside him, and a soft hand was on his wrist, drawing it back.

"Please, let me. You will smudge the paint."

The slave was looking right at him. Damen saw no recognition in his face. The slave simply lifted the hem of his tunic and used it to dab gently at Damen's cheek.

Damen relaxed. He thought, a little ruefully, that it was probably arrogant of him to have assumed that the slave would know him. He supposed that he looked rather unlike a prince, in gold shackles and gold paint, chained to an arbour in the middle of a Veretian garden.

He also felt sure that this slave was not from the palace in Akielos; Damen would have noticed him. The slave's colouring was eye-catching. His skin was fair, and his curling light brown hair was burnished with gold. He was exactly the type that Damen could have drawn down onto the sheets and spent a very pleasant couple of hours enjoying.

The slave's careful fingers touched his face. Damen felt a moment of obscure guilt for having sent Nicaise off on a wild-goose chase. But he was also glad for this unexpected moment alone with a slave from his homeland.

"What's your name?" said Damen, softly.

"Erasmus."

"Erasmus, it's good to talk to another Akielon."

He meant it. The contrast between this demure, lovely slave and the spiteful Nicaise made him crave the straightforward simplicity of home. At the same time, Damen felt a throb of concern for the Akielon slaves. Their sweet-natured obedience was hardly a blueprint for survival in this court. Damen guessed Erasmus to be about eighteen or nineteen, yet he would be eaten alive by thirteen-year-old Nicaise. Let alone Laurent.

"There was a slave who was kept drugged and bound aboard the ship," Erasmus said, tentatively. From the first, he had spoken Akielon. "They said he was given to the Prince."

Damen nodded slowly, answering the unspoken question. As well as tousled light brown curls, Erasmus had a pair of the most hopelessly artless hazel eyes Damen had ever seen.

"What a charming picture," said a woman's voice.

Jerking back from Damen, Erasmus instantly prostrated himself, pressing his forehead to the ground. Damen stayed where he was. Kneeling and shackled was quite submissive enough.

The woman who had spoken was Vannes. She was strolling the garden paths with two noblemen. One of the men had a pet with him, a red-haired youth whom Damen also faintly recognised from the ring.

"Don't stop on our account," said the redhead, tartly. Damen glanced sideways at Erasmus, who hadn't moved. It was unlikely that Erasmus could speak Veretian.

His master laughed: "Another minute or two, and we might have caught them kissing."

"I wonder if the Prince could be persuaded to have his slave entertain with the others?" said Vannes. "It's not often you get to see a really powerful male perform. It was a shame to pull him out of the ring before he had a chance to mount anyone."

"I'm not sure I'd care to watch him, after what we saw tonight." The master of the redhead spoke.

"I think it's more exciting now that we know he's really dangerous," said the redheaded pet.

"It's a shame his back is ruined, but the front is very nice," said Vannes. "We saw more of it at the ring, of course. As for the danger . . . Councillor Guion suggested that he wasn't trained to perform as a pleasure slave. But training isn't everything. He might have natural talent."

Damen was silent. To react to these courtiers would be madness; the only possible course of action was to stay quiet and hope they would grow bored and drift off; and that was what Damen was determinedly doing, when the one thing happened that was guaranteed to make any situation spectacularly worse.

"Natural talent?" said Laurent.

He strolled into the gathering. The courtiers all bobbed respectfully, and Vannes explained the subject under consideration. Laurent turned to Damen.

"Well?" Laurent said. "Can you couple adequately, or do you just kill things?"

Damen thought that given the choice between the lash and a conversation with Laurent, he might actually choose the lash.

"He's not very talkative," remarked Vannes.

"It comes and goes," said Laurent.

"I'd happily perform with him." It was the pet with the red hair. Ostensibly, he spoke to his master, but the words carried.

"Ancel, no. He could hurt you."

"Would you like that?" said the pet, sliding his arms around his master's neck. Just before he did so, he glanced sideways at Laurent.

"No. I wouldn't." His master frowned.

But it was obvious that Ancel's provocative question had

been aimed not at his master, but at Laurent. The boy was angling for royal attention. Damen was sickened by the idea of some nobleman's boy offering himself up to be hurt on the assumption that it would play to Laurent's tastes. Then he thought of all he knew of Laurent, and only felt sicker, because, of course, the boy's assumptions were probably correct.

"What do you think, Your Highness?" said Ancel.

"I think your master would prefer you intact," said Laurent, dryly.

"You could tie the slave up," said Ancel.

It was a testament to Ancel's lacquered skill that it came out teasing and seductive, rather than what it was, a last attempt of a climber to catch and hold a prince's attention.

It almost didn't work. Laurent seemed unmoved by Ancel's flirtatiousness, even bored by it. He had tossed Damen into the ring, but in the sex-drenched atmosphere of the stands, Laurent's pulse had not even appeared to flicker. He had been singularly immune to the carnality of what the Veretians called "performance," the only courtier without a pet fawning all over him.

They say he's frigid, Jord had said.

"What about something small, while we wait for the main entertainment?" said Vannes. "Surely it's past time for the slave to learn his place?"

Damen saw Laurent absorb those words. Saw him stop and give the idea his full attention, turning the decision over in his mind.

And saw him make it, his mouth curling, his expression hardening.

"Why not?" Laurent said.

"*No*," said Damen, a surge in his chest, half-stymied as he felt hands on him. Fighting in earnest against armed guards, in front of witnesses and in the middle of a crowded court, was an act of self-destruction. But his mind and body rebelled, dragging instinctively at the handling.

A lovers' bench nestled inside the bower, creating two curved semicircles. The courtiers made themselves at ease on it, occupying one side. Vannes suggested wine, and a servant was fetched with a tray. One or two other courtiers wandered over, and Vannes struck up a conversation with one of them about the embassy from Patras, due to arrive in a few days.

Damen was lashed to the seat on the other side, facing them.

There was an air of unreality about what was happening. Ancel's master was delineating the encounter. The slave would be tied up, and Ancel would use his mouth. Vannes protested that it was so rare for the Prince to agree to a performance, they should make the most of it. Ancel's master would not be swayed.

This was really going to happen. Damen gripped the metalwork of the bower, his wrists cuffed to it above his head. He was going to be pleasured for a Veretian audience. He was probably just one of a dozen discreet entertainments that would unfold in this garden.

Damen's eyes fixed on Ancel. He almost told himself that this was not the pet's fault, except that, in large part, it was.

Ancel dropped to his knees and found his way into Damen's slave garments. Damen looked down at him and could not have felt less aroused. Even under the best of circumstances, green-eyed, red-haired Ancel was not his type. He looked about nineteen, and though his was not the obscene youth of Nicaise, his body was delicately boyish. His beauty was in fact polished, self-conscious prettiness.

Pet, thought Damen. The word fit. Ancel pushed his long hair to one side, and began without any formality. He was practised, and manipulated Damen expertly with mouth and hands. Damen wondered if he should feel sympathetic or pleased that Ancel was not going to have his moment of triumph: not even half hard under Ancel's ministrations, Damen doubted he would be able to come for the pleasure of an audience. If there was anything explicit on view, it must be the absence of all desire to be where he was.

There was a faint rustle, and, cool as the water beneath the lily, Laurent came to sit beside him.

"I wonder if we can do better than this," Laurent said. "Stop."

Ancel detached himself from his endeavours and looked up, lips wet.

"You're more likely to win a game if you don't play your whole hand at once," said Laurent. "Start more slowly."

Damen reacted to Laurent's words with inevitable tension. Ancel was close enough for Damen to feel his breath, a hot, focused cloud of heat that rolled in place, a susurration over sensitive skin. "Like this?" Ancel asked. His mouth was an inch from its destination, and his hands slid softly up Damen's thighs. His wet lips parted slightly. Damen, against his will, reacted.

"Like that," said Laurent.

"Shall I . . . ?" said Ancel, leaning forward.

"Don't use your mouth yet," said Laurent. "Just your tongue."

Ancel obeyed. He tongued the head, an elusive touch, barely the suggestion of itself. Not enough pressure. Laurent was watching Damen's face with the same cerebral attention that he might apply to a strategic problem. Ancel's tongue pressed into the slit.

"He likes that. Do it harder," said Laurent.

Damen swore, a single Akielon word. Unable to resist the flickering lures being played across its flesh, his body was awakening and beginning to crave rhythm. Ancel's tongue curled lazily around the head.

"Now lick him. The whole length."

Cool words preceded a long, hot lick, wet from base to tip. Damen could feel his thighs tighten, then, minutely, spread, his breath quickening in his chest. He wanted out of the restraints. There was a metallic sound as he pulled against the cuffs, his hands fists. He turned towards Laurent.

It was a mistake to look at him. Even in the shadows of evening, Damen could see the relaxed arrangement of Laurent's body, the marmoreal perfection of his features, and the detached unconcern with which he gazed at Damen, not bothering to so much as glance down at Ancel's moving head.

If you believed the Prince's Guard, Laurent was the impregnable citadel and took no lovers at all. Right now Laurent gave the impression of a mind somewhat engaged, and a body wholly aloof, untouched by ardour. The ribald fancy of the Prince's Guard held a kernel of plausibility.

On the other hand, the aloof, untouched Laurent was at this moment delivering a precise treatise on cocksucking.

And Ancel obeyed instruction, his mouth doing what it was told. Laurent's commands were leisurely, unhurried, and he had the refined practice of suspending his engagements at the very moment they began to get interesting. Damen was used to taking pleasure where he wished, touching where he wanted, coaxing responses from his partners as he pleased. Frustration peaked as gratification was stymied, relentlessly. Every part of him suffused with thwarted sensation, the cool air over his hot skin, the head in his lap just one part of a whole that included the awareness of where he was and who was sitting beside him.

"Push down on it," Laurent said.

Damen felt the breath release shatteringly from his chest at the first long wet slide, down onto his cock. Ancel couldn't quite take it all, though his throat was exquisitely trained, lacking a gag reflex. Laurent's next order came like a tap on the shoulder, and Ancel drew obediently back up to do no more than suckle the head.

Damen could hear the sound of his own breathing now, even over the clamouring of his flesh. Even without rhythmical attention, diffuse pleasure was beginning to coalesce into something more urgent; he could feel the shift, the orientation of his body towards climax.

Laurent uncrossed his legs, and rose.

"Finish him off," said Laurent, incidentally and without a backwards glance, returning to the other courtiers to make a few remarks about the subject currently under discussion, as though he had no particular need to see out the conclusion now that it was inevitable.

The image of Ancel absorbing his erection was joined in his fragmenting thoughts by the sudden harsh desire to get his hands on Laurent's body and exact revenge—both for his actions and for his airy absence. Orgasm rolled up like flame over a hot surface, stripping out seed that was, professionally, swallowed.

"A little slow in the beginning, but quite a satisfactory climax," said Vannes.

Damen was unshackled from the lovers' seat and pushed back down onto his knees. Laurent was seated opposite, legs crossed. Damen's eyes fixed on him and looked nowhere else; his breathing was still noticeable, and his pulse rapid, but anger produced all the same effects.

The musical sound of bells intruded on the gathering; Nicaise interrupted without any sign of deference to those of higher rank at all.

"I'm here to speak to the Prince," said Nicaise.

Laurent lifted his fingers minutely, and Vannes, Ancel and the others took it as a signal to make a brief obeisance, and depart.

Nicaise came to stand in front of the bench and stared at Laurent with an expression of hostility. Laurent, for his part, was relaxed, one arm spread out over the back of the bench.

"Your uncle wants to see you."

"Does he? Let's make him wait."

One pair of unlikeable blue eyes stared at another. Nicaise sat down. "I don't mind. The longer you wait, the more trouble you'll be in."

"Well, as long as you don't mind," said Laurent. He sounded amused.

Nicaise lifted his chin. "I'm going to tell him you waited on purpose."

"You can if you like. I just assumed he'd guess, but you can save him the effort. Since we're waiting, shall I call for refreshments?" He gestured to the last of the tray-bearing servants, who stopped his retreat and approached. "Do you take wine, or aren't you old enough yet?"

"I'm thirteen. I drink whenever I like." Nicaise scorned the tray, pushing at it so hard it almost overbalanced. "I'm not going to drink with you. We don't need to start pretending politeness."

"Don't we? Very well: I think it is fourteen by now, isn't it?"

Nicaise turned red, under the paint.

"I thought so," said Laurent. "Have you thought about what you're going to do, after? If I know your master's tastes, you have another year, at most. At your age, the body begins to betray itself." And then, reacting to something in the boy's face: "Or has it started already?"

The red grew strident. *That isn't any of your business.*

"You're right, it isn't," said Laurent.

Nicaise opened his mouth, but Laurent continued before he could speak.

"I'll offer for you, if you like. When the time comes. I

wouldn't want you in my bed, but you'd have all the same privileges. You might prefer that. I'd offer."

Nicaise blinked, and then sneered. "With what?"

A breath of amusement from Laurent. "Yes, if I have any land left at all, I may have to sell it to buy bread, never mind pets. We will both have to navigate the next ten months on the tips of our toes."

"I don't need you. He's promised. He's not going to give me up." Nicaise's voice was smug and self-satisfied.

"He gives them all up," said Laurent, "even if you're more enterprising than the others have been."

"He likes me better than the others." A scornful laugh. "You're jealous." And then it was Nicaise's turn to react to something he saw in Laurent's face, and he said, with a horror Damen didn't understand, *"You're going to tell him you want me."*

"Oh," said Laurent. "No. Nicaise . . . no. That would wreck you. I wouldn't do that." Then his voice became almost tired. "Maybe it's better if you think that I would. You have quite a good mind for strategy, to have thought of that. Maybe you will hold him longer than the others." For a moment it seemed as if Laurent would say something else, but in the end he just stood up from the bench and held his hand out to the boy. "Come on. Let's go. You can watch me get told off by my uncle."

CHAPTER SIX

YOUR MASTER SEEMS kind," said Erasmus.

"Kind?" said Damen.

The word was difficult to get his mouth around, grating in his throat as he pushed it out. He looked across in disbelief at Erasmus. Nicaise had trailed off hand in hand with Laurent, leaving Erasmus behind, his leash forgotten on the ground beside him where he knelt. A soft breeze shifted his fair curls, and above them foliage moved like an awning of black silk.

"He cares for your pleasure," explained Erasmus.

It took a moment for those words to attach to their correct meaning, and when they did a breath of helpless laughter was the only possible response. Laurent's precise instructions and their inevitable result had not been intended as a kindness, but rather the opposite. There was no way to explain Laurent's cool, intricate mind to the slave, and Damen didn't try.

"What is it?" said Erasmus.

"Nothing. Tell me. I wished for news of you and the others. How is it for you, so far from home? Are you well treated by your masters? I wondered . . . can you understand their language?"

Erasmus shook his head at the last question. "I—have a little skill with Patran and the northern dialects. Some words are similar." Haltingly, he said a few of them.

Erasmus managed the Veretian well enough; that was not what made Damen frown. The words Erasmus had been able to decipher from what had been said to him were: *Silence. Kneel down. Don't move.*

"Did I misspeak?" said Erasmus, misinterpreting the expression.

"No, you spoke well," Damen said, though his consternation remained. He didn't like the choice of words. He didn't like the idea that Erasmus and the others were rendered doubly powerless by an inability to speak or understand what was being said around them.

"You . . . do not have the manner of a palace slave," offered Erasmus, hesitantly.

That was an understatement. No one from Akielos would mistake Damen for a body slave, he had neither the manner nor the physique. Damen regarded Erasmus thoughtfully, wondering how much to say. "I was not a slave in Akielos. I was sent here by Kastor, as punishment," he said, eventually. There was no point lying about that part of it.

"Punishment," said Erasmus. His gaze dropped to the ground. His whole manner changed.

Damen said, "But you were trained in the palace? How long were you there?" He couldn't account for the fact that he had not seen this slave before.

Erasmus attempted a smile, rallying himself from whatever had disheartened him. "Yes. I— But I never saw the main palace, I was in training silks until I was chosen by the Keeper to come here. And my training in Akielos was very strict. It was thought . . . that is . . ."

"That is?" said Damen.

Erasmus blushed and said in a very soft voice: "In case he found me pleasing, I was being trained for the Prince."

"Were you?" said Damen, with some interest.

"Because of my colouring. You can't see it in this light, but in daylight, my hair is almost blond."

"I can see it in this light," said Damen.

He could hear the approval saturating his own voice. He felt it shift the dynamic between them. He might as well have said, *Good boy.*

Erasmus reacted to the words like a flower inclining towards sunlight. It didn't matter that he and Damen were technically the same rank, Erasmus was trained to respond to strength, to yearn for it and submit to it. His limbs subtly rearranged themselves, a flush spreading on his cheeks, his eyes dropping to the ground. His body became a supplication. The breeze toyed irresistibly with a curl that had tumbled over his forehead.

In the softest little voice he said, "This slave is beneath your attention."

In Akielos, submission was an art, and the slave was the artisan. Now that he was showing his form, you could see that Erasmus was surely the prize pick of the Regent's gift-slaves. Ridiculous, that he was being dragged around by the neck like an unwilling animal. It was like possessing a finely tuned instrument and using it to smash shells open. Misusing it.

He should be in Akielos, where his training would be fêted and prized. But it occurred to Damen that Erasmus might have been lucky in being chosen for the Regent, lucky in never having come to the attention of Prince Damianos. Damen had seen what had happened to the closest of his personal slaves. They had been killed.

He pushed the memory forcibly out of his mind and returned his attention to the slave in front of him.

Damen said, "And is your own master kind?"

"This slave lives to serve," said Erasmus.

It was a formulaic set-phrase and meant nothing. The behaviour of slaves was tightly proscribed, with the result that what was unsaid was often more important than what was said. Damen was already frowning a little when he chanced to look down.

The tunic Erasmus wore had been slightly disordered when he had used it to wipe Damen's cheek, and he'd had no chance to right it. The hem had lifted high enough to expose the top of his thigh. Erasmus, seeing the direction of Damen's gaze, quickly pulled the cloth down to cover himself, stretching it as far as it would go.

"What happened to your leg?" said Damen.

Erasmus had gone ivory white. He didn't want to answer, but would force himself to because he'd been asked a direct question.

"What's wrong?"

Erasmus's voice was barely audible, his hands clutching the hem of his tunic. "I am ashamed."

"Show me," said Damen.

Erasmus's fingers loosened, trembling, and then slowly lifted the fabric. Damen looked at what had been done. At what, three times, had been done.

"The Regent did this? Speak freely."

"No. On the day we arrived, there was a test of obedience. I f-failed."

"This was your punishment for failure?"

"This was the test. I was ordered not to make any sound."

Damen had seen Veretian arrogance and Veretian cruelty. He had suffered Veretian insults, had endured the sting of the lash and the violence of the ring. But he had not known anger until now.

"You didn't fail," said Damen. "That you tried at all proves your courage. What was asked of you was impossible. There's no shame in what happened to you."

Except for the people who had done this. There was shame and disgrace on every one of them, and Damen would hold them to account for what they had done.

Damen said, "Tell me everything that has happened to you since you left Akielos."

Erasmus spoke matter-of-factly. The story was disturbing. The slaves had been transported aboard the ship in cages, below deck. Handlers and sailors alike had taken liberties. One of the women, worried about the lack of access to any usual means of preventing pregnancy, had tried to communicate the problem to her Veretian handlers, not realising that to them illegitimate birth was a horror. The idea that they might be delivering a slave to the Regent with a sailor's bastard growing in her belly caused them to panic. The ship's physic had given her some sort of concoction that induced sweats and nausea. Concerned it would not be enough, her stomach was beaten with rocks. That was before they docked in Vere.

In Vere, the problem was one of neglect. The Regent had not taken any of the slaves to bed. The Regent was a largely absent figure, busy with affairs of state, served by pets of his own choosing. The slaves were left to their handlers and to the vagaries of a bored court. Reading between the lines, Damen could tell that they were treated as animals, their obedience a parlour trick, and the "tests" thought up by the sophisticated court, which the slaves struggled to perform, were in some cases truly sadistic. As in the case of Erasmus. Damen felt sick.

"You must crave freedom more than I do," said Damen. The slave's courage made him feel ashamed.

"Freedom?" said Erasmus, sounding scared for the first time. "Why would I want that? I cannot . . . I am made for a master."

"You were made for better masters than these. You deserve someone who appreciates your worth."

Erasmus flushed and said nothing.

"I promise you," said Damen. "I will find a way to help you."

"I wish—" said Erasmus.

"You wish?"

"I wish I could believe you," said Erasmus. "You talk like a master. But you are a slave, like I am."

Before Damen could reply, there was a sound from the paths, and, as he had done once before, Erasmus prostrated himself, anticipating the arrival of another courtier.

Voices from the path: "Where's the Regent's slave?"

"Back there."

And then, rounding the corner: "There you are." And then: "And look who else they let out."

It was not a courtier. It was not petite, malicious, exquisite Nicaise. It was coarse-featured, broken-nosed Govart.

He spoke to Damen, who had last faced him in the ring in a desperate grapple for purchase and mastery.

Govart casually clasped the back of Erasmus's gold collar and dragged him up by it, as an uncaring owner might heft a dog around. Erasmus, a boy not a dog, choked violently as the collar dug into his tender throat, caught at the join of neck and jaw, just above his Adam's apple.

"Shut up." Govart, irritated by the coughing, slapped him hard across the face.

Damen felt the jerk of restraint as his body hit the limits of his chains, heard the metallic sound before he even realised he'd reacted. "Let him go."

"You want me to?" He shook Erasmus by the collar for

punctuation. Erasmus, who had understood *shut up*, was wet-eyed from the brief choking, but silent. "Don't think I will. Got told to haul him back. No one said I couldn't enjoy myself on the way."

Damen said, "If you want another go around, all you have to do is take a step forward." It would please him a great deal to hurt Govart.

"I'd rather fuck your sweetheart," said Govart. "The way I figure it, I'm owed a fuck."

As he spoke, Govart pushed up the slave tunic, revealing the curves beneath. Erasmus didn't struggle when Govart kicked his ankles apart and lifted his arms up. He let himself be manhandled, and then stayed in position, awkwardly bent over.

The realisation that Govart was going to fuck Erasmus right here in front of him hit with the same sense of unreality that he'd felt when faced with Ancel. It wasn't possible that something like this was going to happen—that this court was so depraved that a mercenary could rape a royal slave a scant distance from the gathered court. There was no one within hearing distance except for the disinterested guard. Erasmus's face, red with humiliation, was turned determinedly away from Damen.

"The way I figure it"—Govart used this phrase again—"your master's the one who fucked us both. He's the one who should really be getting it. But in the dark, one blond's as good as another. Better," said Govart. "Stick your cock in that frigid bitch, he'd freeze it off. This one likes it."

He did something with his hand under the bunched-up tunic. Erasmus made a sound. Damen jerked, and this time the harsh metallic noise suggested loudly that the ancient iron was about to give.

The sound of it shook the guard loose from his post.

"There some problem?"

"He doesn't like me fucking his little slave friend," said Govart. Erasmus, mortifyingly exposed, looked like he was silently breaking down.

"Fuck him somewhere else then," the guard said. Govart smiled. Then he pushed Erasmus hard in the small of the back.

"I will," Govart said. Shoving Erasmus ahead of him, he disappeared along the paths, and there was absolutely nothing Damen could do to stop him.

◆ ◆ ◆

Night turned to morning. The garden entertainments ended. Damen was deposited back in his room, clean and tended and chained and powerless.

◆ ◆ ◆

Laurent's prediction regarding the reaction of the guards—and the servants, and all the members of his retinue—turned out to be stingingly accurate. Laurent's household reacted to collusion with the Regent with anger and enmity. The fragile relationships Damen had managed to build were gone.

It was the worst possible time for a change in attitude. Now, when those relationships might have brought him news or been able in some small way to influence the treatment of the slaves.

He had no thought of his own freedom. There was only the constant pull of concern and of responsibility. To escape alone would be an act of selfishness and betrayal. He could not leave, not if it meant abandoning the others to their fate. And yet, he was totally without power to affect any change in their circumstances.

Erasmus was right. His promise to help was an empty one.

Outside his room, several things were happening. The first was that, in response to the Regent's edicts, the Prince's household was being cut back. Without access to income from his various estates, Laurent's retinue was substantially diminished and his spending curtailed. In the whirlwind of changes, Damen's room was moved from the royal pet residences to somewhere inside Laurent's wing of the palace.

It didn't help him. His new room had the same number of guards, the same pallet, the same silks and cushions, the same iron link in the floor, though this one looked newly installed. Even short of funds, Laurent didn't seem inclined to skimp on security for his Akielon prisoner. Unfortunately.

From snippets of overheard conversation, Damen learned that, elsewhere, the delegation from Patras had arrived to discuss trade with Vere. Patras bordered on Akielos and was a country of similar culture—not traditionally an ally of Vere. The news of talks concerned him. Was the delegation here simply to discuss trade, or was it part of some larger shift in the political landscape?

He had about as much luck finding out the business of

the Patran delegation as he had had in helping the slaves, which was to say none at all.

There had to be something he could do.

There was nothing he could do.

To face his own powerlessness was awful. He had at no point since his capture truly thought of himself as a slave. He had played lip service to the role, at best. He had viewed punishments as no more than minor obstacles, because this situation in his mind was temporary. He had believed that escape was in his future. He still believed that.

He wanted to be free. He wanted to find his way home. He wanted to stand in the capital, raised on its marble pillars, and look out over the greens and blues of mountains and ocean. He wanted to face Kastor, his brother, and ask him, man to man, why he had done what he had done. But life in Akielos went on without Damianos. These slaves had no one else to help them.

And what did it mean, to be a prince, if he did not strive to protect those weaker than himself?

The sun, sinking low in the sky, brought light into his room through the grilled windows.

When Radel entered, Damen begged an audience with the Prince.

◆　◆　◆

Radel, with obvious relish, refused. The Prince, said Radel, did not care to trouble himself with a turncoat Akielon slave. He had more exalted business to attend to. Tonight there was a banquet in honour of the Patran ambassador. Eighteen courses, and the most talented pets entertaining with dance and games and performance. Knowing Patran culture, Damen could only imagine the reaction of the delegation to the more inventive entertainments of the Veretian court, but he stayed silent as Radel described the glory of the table, and the courses in detail, and the wines: mulberry wine and fruit wine and sinopel. Damen was not fit for that company. Damen was not fit to eat the leavings from the table. Radel, having made his point at satisfactory length, left.

Damen waited. He knew that Radel would be obliged to pass on the request.

He had no illusions about his relative importance in Laurent's household, but if nothing else, his inadvertent role in Laurent's power struggle with his uncle meant that his request for an audience would not be ignored. Would probably not be ignored. He settled in, knowing that Laurent would make him wait. Surely not longer than a day or two, he thought.

That was what he thought. And so, when night came, he slept.

◆ ◆ ◆

He woke amid crushed pillows and disturbed silken sheets to find that Laurent's cool blue gaze was on him.

The torches were lit, and the servants who had lit them were withdrawing. Damen moved; silk, skin-warm, slid away completely to pool among the cushions as he pushed himself up. Laurent paid it no attention. Damen recalled that a visit from Laurent had woken him from sleep once before.

It was closer to dawn than sunset. Laurent was dressed in court clothes, having come, presumably, after the eighteenth course and whatever nightly entertainments had followed. Not drunk this time.

Damen had expected a long, excruciating wait. There was slight resistance from the chain as it dragged across the cushions, following his movement. He thought about what he had to do, and why he had to do it.

Very deliberately, he knelt and bowed his head, and lowered his eyes to the floor. For a moment, it was so quiet that he could hear the flames from the torches fluttering in the air.

"This is new," said Laurent.

"There's something I want," said Damen.

"Something you want." The same words, precisely enunciated.

He had known it was not going to be easy. Even with someone else, not this cold, unpleasant prince, it would not be easy.

"You get something in return," said Damen.

He set his jaw as Laurent slowly paced around him, as though simply interested in viewing him from all angles. Laurent stepped mincingly over the chain that lay slack on the ground, completing his tour.

"Are you misguided enough to try to bargain with me? What could you possibly offer that I would want?"

"Obedience," said Damen.

He felt Laurent react to that idea. Subtly but unmistakably, the interest was there. Damen tried not to think too much about what he was offering, what it would mean to keep this promise. He would face that future when he came to it.

"You want me to submit. I'll do it. You want me to publicly earn the punishment that your uncle won't let you mete out? Whatever performance you want from me, you'll have it. I will throw myself on the sword. In exchange for one thing."

"Let me guess. You want me to take off your chains. Or reduce your guard. Or put you in a room where the doors and windows are unbarred. Don't waste your breath."

Damen forced the anger down. It was more important to be clear. "I don't think the slaves in your uncle's care are well treated. Do something about it, and the bargain is made."

"The slaves?" Laurent said, after a slight pause. And then, with renewed drawling scorn: "Am I supposed to believe that you care about their welfare? How exactly would they be treated better in Akielos? It is your barbaric society that forced them into slavery, not mine. I would not have thought it possible to train the will out of a man, but you have managed it. Congratulations. Your show of compassion rings false."

Damen said, "One of the handlers took a heated iron from the fire to test whether the slave would obey an order to stay silent while he used it. I don't know if that is usual practice in this place, but good men don't torture slaves in Akielos. Slaves are trained to obey in all things, but their submission is a pact: They give up free will in exchange for perfect treatment. To abuse someone who cannot resist—isn't that monstrous?"

Damen continued, "Please. They're not like me. They're not soldiers. They haven't killed anyone. They're innocent. They will serve you willingly. And so will I, if you do something to help them."

There was a long silence. Laurent's expression had changed.

Finally, Laurent said, "You overestimate my influence over my uncle."

Damen began to speak, but Laurent cut him off.

"No. I—" Laurent's golden brows had drawn slightly together, as though he had encountered something that did not make sense. "You would really sacrifice your pride over the fate of a handful of slaves?" He had worn the same look on his face at the ring; he was gazing at Damen as though he was searching for an answer to an unexpected problem. "Why?"

Anger and frustration broke free of their bonds.

"Because I am stuck here in this cage, and I have no other way to help them." He heard the rage lash in his voice and tried to force it down, with limited success. His breathing was uneven.

Laurent was staring at him. The little golden frown was etched deeper.

After a moment, Laurent gestured to the guard at the door and Radel was summoned. He arrived presently.

Without taking his eyes off Damen, Laurent said, "Has anyone been in or out of this room?"

"No one but your own staff, Your Highness. As you ordered."

"Which of the staff?"

Radel recited a list of names. Laurent said, "I want to speak to the guards who were watching over the slave in the gardens."

"I'll send for them personally," said Radel, departing on the errand.

"You think this is a trick," said Damen.

He could see from the assessing look on Laurent's face that he was right. The bitter laughter just came out.

"Something amuses you?" said Laurent.

"What would I have to gain from—" Damen broke off. "I don't know how to convince you. You don't do anything without a dozen motives. You lie even to your own uncle. This is a country of deviousness and deception."

"Whereas pure Akielos is free of treachery? The heir dies on the same night as the King, and it is merely coincidence that smiles on Kastor?" said Laurent, silkily. "You should kiss the floor when you beg for my favour."

Of course Laurent would invoke Kastor. They were alike. Damen forcibly reminded himself of why he was here. "I apologise. I spoke out of turn." Grittily.

Laurent said, "If this is a fabrication—if I find you have been moonlighting with emissaries from my uncle—"

"I haven't," said Damen.

The guard took a little longer to rouse than Radel, who presumably never slept, but they arrived reasonably promptly. Dressed in livery and looking alert, rather than, as might be expected, yawning and trailing bed linen.

"I want to know who spoke with the slave the night you watched over him in the gardens," said Laurent. "Nicaise and Vannes I know about."

"That was it," came the answer. "There was no other." And then, as Damen felt a sick sensation in his stomach: "No. Wait."

"Oh?"

"After you left," the guard said, "he got a visit from Govart."

Laurent turned back to Damen, blue eyes like ice.

"No," said Damen, knowing Laurent believed this now to be some scheme of his uncle's. "It's not what you think."

But it was too late.

"Shut him up," said Laurent. "Try not to leave any new marks. He's caused enough trouble for me as it is."

CHAPTER SEVEN

S EEING NO REASON whatsoever to cooperate with that order, Damen stood up.

It had an interesting effect on the guard who brought up short and swung his gaze back to Laurent, seeking further guidance. Radel was also in the room, and at the door stood the two guards who were on watch.

Laurent narrowed his eyes at the problem, but offered no immediate solution.

Damen said, "You could bring in more men."

Behind him were strewn the cushions and rumpled silk sheets, and trailing across the floor was the single chain linked to his wrist-cuff that was no impediment to movement at all.

"You are really courting danger tonight," Laurent said.

"Am I? I thought I was appealing to your better nature.

Order whatever punishment you like from the coward's distance of a chain-length. You and Govart are two of a kind."

It was not Laurent but the guard who reacted, steel flashing out of the sheath. "Watch your mouth."

He was wearing livery, not armour. The threat was negligible. Damen looked at his drawn sword with scorn. "You're no better. You saw what Govart was doing. You did nothing to stop him."

Laurent raised a hand, halting the guard before he could take another angry step forward.

"What was it he was doing?" said Laurent.

The guard stepped back, then shrugged. "Raping one of the slaves."

There was a pause, but if Laurent had any reaction to these words, it didn't show on his face. Laurent transferred his gaze back to Damen and said, pleasantly, "Does that bother you? I recall you being free with your own hands, not so very long ago."

"That was—" Damen flushed. He wanted to deny that he'd done anything of the kind, but he remembered rather unequivocally that he had. "I promise you, Govart did a great deal more than simply enjoy the view."

"To a slave," Laurent said. "The Prince's Guard doesn't interfere with the Regency. Govart can stick his cock into anything of my uncle's he likes."

Damen made a sound of disgust. "With your blessing?"

"Why not?" said Laurent. His voice was honeyed. "He certainly had my blessing to fuck you, but it turned out he'd rather take a blow to the head. Disappointing, but I can't fault his taste. Then again, maybe if you had spread in the ring, Govart wouldn't have been so hot to get inside your friend."

Damen said, "This isn't a scheme of your uncle's. I don't take orders from men like Govart. You're wrong."

"Wrong," said Laurent. "How lucky I am to have servants to point out my shortcomings. What makes you think I will tolerate any of this, even if I believed what you are saying to be true?"

"Because you can end this conversation any time you like."

With so much at stake, Damen was sick of certain kinds of exchanges; the kind Laurent favoured, and enjoyed, and was good at. Wordplay for its own sake; words that built traps. None of it meant anything.

"You're right. I can. Leave us," Laurent said. He was gazing at Damen while he said it, but it was Radel and the guards who bowed and went out.

"Very well. Let us play this out. You're concerned for the well-being of the other slaves? Why hand me that kind of advantage?"

"Advantage?" said Damen.

"When someone doesn't like you very much, it isn't a good idea to let them know that you care about something," said Laurent.

Damen felt himself turn ashen as the threat sank in.

"Would it hurt worse than a lashing for me to cut down someone you care for?" said Laurent.

Damen was silent. *Why do you hate us so much?* he almost said, except that he knew the answer to that question.

"I don't think I need to bring in more men," said Laurent.
"I think all I have to do is tell you to kneel, and you'll do it.
Without me lifting a finger to help anyone."

"You're right," said Damen.

"I can end this any time I like?" said Laurent. "I haven't
even begun."

◆ ◆ ◆

"The Prince's orders," Damen was told the next day, as he
was stripped and re-dressed. And when he asked what these
preparations were for, he was told that tonight he would
serve the Prince at the high table.

Radel, clearly disapproving of the fact that Damen was
being taken into refined company, delivered a peripatetic lec-
ture, striding up and down in Damen's room. Few pets were
invited to serve their masters at the high table. To offer him
this opportunity, the Prince must see something in Damen
that surpassed Radel's understanding. It was pointless to
instruct someone like Damen in the rudiments of polite etiquette, but he should try to keep silent, obey the Prince and
refrain from attacking or molesting anyone.

In Damen's experience, being taken out of his rooms at
Laurent's request did not end well. His three excursions had
comprised the ring, the gardens and the baths, with a subsequent trip to the flogging post.

His back was by now mostly healed, but that was of no
consequence; the next time Laurent struck out, it would not
be directly at him.

Damen had very little power, but there was a crack that

ran right down the middle of this court. If Laurent would not be persuaded, Damen must turn his attention to the Regent's faction.

Out of habit, he observed the security outside of his room. They were on the second floor of the palace, and the passage they walked along had a number of windows fretted by grilles, looking out on an uninviting sheer drop. They also passed a number of armed men, all wearing the livery of the Prince's Guard. Here were the guards that had been absent from the pet residences. A surprising number of men: They could not all be here for his benefit. Did Laurent keep this kind of security about him all the time?

They passed through a pair of ornate bronze doors, and Damen realised that he had been brought into Laurent's own chambers.

Damen's eyes raked the interior derisively. These rooms were everything he would have expected of a princeling pampered lavishly, extravagantly, beyond reason. Decoration overran everything. The tiles were patterned, the walls intricately carved. The vantage was enchanting; this second-floor chamber had a loggia of semicircular arches that hung above gardens. Through an archway the bedchamber could be seen. The bed was swathed in sumptuous curtains, a panoply of luxurious embellishment and carved wood. All that was missing was a rumpled, perfumed trail of clothing strewn across the floor, and a pet lounging on one of the silk-draped surfaces.

There was no such evidence of habitation. In fact, amid the opulence, there were only a few personal effects. Close to Damen was a reclining couch and a book, fanned open, revealing illuminated pages and scrollwork glinting with gold leaf. The leash Damen had worn in the gardens also lay on the couch, as though tossed there casually.

Laurent emerged from the bedchamber. He had not yet closed the delicate band that collared his shirt, and white laces trailed, exposing the hollow of his throat. When he saw that Damen had arrived, he paused beneath the archway.

"Leave us," said Laurent.

He spoke to the handlers who had brought Damen to this chamber. They freed Damen from his restraints and departed.

"Stand up," said Laurent.

Damen stood. He was taller than Laurent, and physically stronger, and wearing no restraints at all. And they were alone together, as they had been last night, as they had been in the baths. But something was different. He realised that at some point he had begun to think of being alone in a room with Laurent as dangerous.

Laurent detached himself from the doorway. As he drew close to Damen, his expression soured, his blue eyes curdled with distaste.

Laurent said, "There is no bargain between us. A prince does not make deals with slaves and insects. Your promises are worth less to me than dirt. Do you understand me?"

"Perfectly," said Damen.

Laurent was staring at him coldly. "Torveld of Patras may be persuaded to request that the slaves go with him to Bazal, as part of the trade deal being negotiated with my uncle."

Damen felt his brow furrow. This information did not make sense.

"If Torveld insists strongly enough, I think my uncle will agree to some sort of—loan—or, more accurately, a permanent arrangement couched as a loan, so that it will not offend our allies in Akielos. It's my understanding that Patran sensibilities regarding the treatment of slaves are similar to your own."

"They are."

"I have spent the afternoon seeding the idea with Torveld. The deal will be finalised tonight. You will accompany me to the entertainments. It is my uncle's custom to conduct business in relaxed surroundings," said Laurent.

"But—" said Damen.

"But?" Icily.

Damen rethought that particular approach.

He turned over the information he'd just been given. Reexamined it. Turned it over again.

"What changed your mind?" Damen said, carefully.

Laurent didn't answer him, just looked at him with hostility. "Don't speak, unless you're asked a question. Don't contradict anything that I say. These are the rules. Break them and I will joyfully leave your countrymen to rot." And then: "Bring me the leash."

The staff to which the leash was affixed had the heavy weight of pure gold. The fragile chain was intact; it had either been repaired or replaced. Damen picked it up, not very quickly.

"I'm not sure I believe anything you've just told me," Damen said.

"Do you have a choice?"

"No."

Laurent had closed the lacings on his shirt, and the picture he now presented was immaculate.

"Well? Put it on," he said, with a touch of impatience. The leash, he meant.

Torveld of Patras was in the palace to negotiate a trade agreement. That much was true. Damen had heard the news from several sources. He remembered Vannes discussing the Patran delegation, several nights ago, in the garden. Patras had a culture similar to that of Akielos; that, also, was true. Perhaps the rest followed. If a consignment of slaves was on offer, Torveld would conceivably bargain for them, knowing their value. It might be true.

Perhaps. Maybe. Might.

Laurent was not feigning any change of heart, or warmth of feeling. His wall of contempt was firmly in place—was even more evident than usual, as though this act of benevolence was forcing all his considerable dislike to the surface. Damen found that the necessity of winning Laurent over to his cause was giving way to the sobering realisation that he had put the fate of the others into the hands of a volatile, malicious man he did not trust and could not predict, nor understand.

He felt no new rush of warmth for Laurent. He was not inclined to believe that cruelty delivered with one hand was redeemed by a caress from the other, if that's even what this was. Nor was he naive enough to think that Laurent was acting out of any altruistic impulse. Laurent was doing this for some twisty reason of his own.

If it was true.

When the leash was affixed, Laurent took hold of the handler's staff and said, "You're my pet. You outrank others. You do not need to submit to the orders of anyone except myself and my uncle. If you blurt out tonight's plans to him, he will be very, very annoyed with me, which you might enjoy, but you won't like my riposte. It's your choice, of course."

Of course.

Laurent paused on the threshold. "One more thing."

They were standing beneath a high arch, which threw shadows on Laurent's face and made it difficult to read. It was a moment before he spoke.

"Be careful of Nicaise, the pet you saw with Councillor Audin. You rejected him in the ring, and that is not a slight he is likely to forget."

"Councillor Audin's pet? The child?" Incredulous.

"Don't underestimate him because of his age. He has experienced things many adults have not, and his mind is no longer that of a child. Though even a child may learn how to manipulate an adult. And you're mistaken: Councillor Audin is not his master. Nicaise is dangerous."

"He's thirteen years old," said Damen, and found himself subjected to Laurent's long-lidded gaze. "Is there anyone at this court who isn't my enemy?"

"Not if I can help it," Laurent said.

◆ ◆ ◆

"So he's tame," said Estienne, and reached out tentatively, as though to pat a wild animal.

It was a question of which part of the animal he was

patting. Damen knocked his hand away. Estienne gave a yelp and snatched his hand back, nursing it against his chest.

"Not that tame," said Laurent.

He didn't reprimand Damen. He didn't seem particularly displeased with barbaric behaviour, as long as it was directed outward. Like a man who enjoys owning an animal who will rake others with its claws but eat peacefully from his own hand, he was giving his pet a great deal of license.

As a result, courtiers kept one eye on Damen, giving him a wide berth. Laurent used that to his advantage, using the propensity of courtiers to fall back in reaction to Damen's presence as a means of extricating himself smoothly from conversation.

The third time this happened, Damen said, "Shall I make a face at the ones you don't like, or is it enough to just look like a barbarian?"

"Shut up," said Laurent, calmly.

It was said that the Empress of Vask kept two leopards tied up by her throne. Damen tried not to feel like one of them.

Before the negotiations, there were to be entertainments; before the entertainments, a banquet; before the banquet, this reception. There were not as many pets as there had been at the ring, but Damen did see one or two familiar faces. Across the room, he saw a flash of red hair, found a pair of emerald eyes; Ancel uncurled himself from his master's arm, pressed fingers to his lips, and blew Damen a kiss.

The Patran delegation, when they arrived, were obvious from the cut of their clothes. Laurent greeted Torveld like an equal, which he was. Almost.

In negotiations of consequence, it was common to send a man of high birth to act as ambassador. Torveld was Prince Torveld, younger brother to King Torgeir of Patras, though in his case, "younger" was relative. Torveld was a handsome man in his forties, close to twice Damen's age. He had a neatly trimmed brown beard in the Patran style, brown hair still largely untouched by grey.

Relations between Akielos and Patras were friendly and extensive, but Prince Torveld and Prince Damianos had never met. Torveld had spent most of the last eighteen years on Patras's northern border in dealings with the Vaskian Empire. Damen knew of him by reputation. Everyone knew of him. He had distinguished himself in the campaigns to the north when Damen was still in swaddling. He was fifth in line to inherit, after the King's litter of three sons and a daughter.

Torveld's brown eyes grew markedly warm and appreciative when he looked at Laurent.

"Torveld," said Laurent. "I'm afraid my uncle is delayed. While we wait, I thought you could join my pet and me for some air on the balcony."

Damen thought Laurent's uncle probably wasn't delayed. He reconciled himself to an evening of listening to Laurent lying a great deal, about everything.

"I'd be delighted," said Torveld, with real pleasure, and gestured for one of his own servants to accompany them also. They strolled together in a small party, Laurent and Torveld in front, and Damen and the servant following a few steps behind.

The balcony had a bench for courtiers to recline on and a shadowed alcove for servants to discreetly retire to. Damen, his proportions suited to battle, was not built to be discreet, but if Laurent insisted on dragging him about by the neck, he could suffer the intrusion or find a balcony with a bigger alcove. It was a warm night, and the air was perfumed with all the beauty of the gardens. Conversation unfolded easily between the two men, who surely had nothing at all in common. But, of course, Laurent was good at talking.

"What news from Akielos?" Laurent asked Torveld, at one point. "You were there recently."

Damen looked at him, startled. Laurent being Laurent, the topic was not an accident. From anyone else, it would have been kindness. He couldn't help his pulse quickening at his first word of home.

"Have you ever visited the capital, at Ios?" asked Torveld. Laurent shook his head. "It's very beautiful. A white palace, built high on the cliffs to command the ocean. On a clear day, you can look out and see Isthima across the water. But it was a dark place when I arrived. The whole of the city was still in mourning for the old King and his son. That terrible business. And there were some factional disputes among the kyroi. The beginnings of conflict, dissent."

"Theomedes united them," said Laurent. "You don't think Kastor can do the same?"

"Perhaps. His legitimacy is an issue. One or two of the kyroi have royal blood running through their veins. Not as much as Kastor, but gotten inside of a marriage bed. That situation breeds discontent."

"What impression did you have of Kastor?" asked Laurent.

"A complicated man," said Torveld. "Born in the shadow of a throne. But he does have many of the qualities needed in a king. Strength. Judiciousness. Ambition."

"Is ambition needed in a king?" said Laurent. "Or is it simply needed to become king?"

After a pause: "I heard those rumours, too. That the death of Damianos was no accident. But I don't credit them. I saw Kastor in his grief. It was genuine. It cannot have been an easy time for him. To have lost so much and gained so much, all in the space of a moment."

"That is the fate of all princes destined for a throne," said Laurent.

Torveld favoured Laurent with another of those long, admiring looks that were starting to come with grating frequency. Damen frowned. Laurent was a nest of scorpions in the body of one person. Torveld looked at him and saw a buttercup.

To hear that Akielos was weakened was as painful as Laurent must have meant it to be. Damen's mind tangled with the thought of factional disputes and dissent. If there was unrest, it would come first from the northern provinces. Sicyon, maybe. And Delpha.

The arrival of a servant, trying not to show that he was out of breath, forestalled whatever Torveld might have said next.

"Your Highness, forgive my interruption. The Regent sends that he is awaiting you inside."

"I've kept you to myself too long," said Laurent.

"I wish we had more time together," said Torveld, showing no inclination to rise.

The Regent's face, when he saw the two princes enter the room together, was a series of unsmiling lines, though his greeting to Torveld was genial, and all the right formalities were exchanged. Torveld's servant bowed and departed. It was what etiquette demanded, but Damen could not follow his example, not unless he was prepared to wrench the leash bodily out of Laurent's hand.

Formalities done, the Regent said, "Could you excuse my nephew and me for a moment?"

His gaze came to rest heavily on Laurent. It was Torveld's turn to withdraw, good-naturedly. Damen assumed that he was to do the same, but he felt Laurent's grip tighten subtly on the leash.

"Nephew. You were not invited to these discussions."

"And yet, here I am. It's very irritating, isn't it?" said Laurent.

The Regent said, "This is serious business between men. It's no time for childish games."

"I seem to recall being told to take on more responsibility," said Laurent. "It happened in public, with a great deal of ceremony. If you don't remember it, check your ledgers. You came out of it richer by two estates and enough revenue to choke every horse in the stables."

"If I thought you were here to take on responsibility, I'd welcome you to the table with open arms. You have no interest in trade negotiations. You've never applied yourself seriously to anything in your life."

"Haven't I? Well, then it's nothing serious, uncle. You have no cause to worry."

Damen saw the Regent's eyes narrow. It was an expression that reminded him of Laurent. But the Regent said only, "I expect appropriate behaviour," before preceding them to the entertainments, displaying far more patience than Laurent deserved. Laurent didn't follow immediately; his gaze stayed on his uncle.

"Your life would be a lot easier if you stopped baiting him," said Damen.

This time coldly, flatly, "I told you to shut up."

CHAPTER EIGHT

EXPECTING A SLAVE'S inconspicuous place on the sidelines, Damen was surprised to find himself seated beside Laurent, albeit with a cool distance of nine inches interposed between them. He wasn't sitting half in his lap, as Ancel was with his master across the way.

Laurent sat consciously well. He was dressed severely as always, though his clothing was very fine, as befitting his rank. No jewellery except for a fine gold circlet on his brow that was mostly hidden by the fall of his golden hair. When they sat, he unclipped Damen's leash, wound it around the handler's rod, then tossed it to one of the attendants, who managed to catch it with only a slight fumble.

The table stretched out. On the other side of Laurent sat Torveld, evidence of a small coup for Laurent. On the other side of Damen was Nicaise. Possibly also evidence of a coup for Laurent. Nicaise was separated from Councillor Audin, who sat elsewhere, close by the Regent; Nicaise didn't seem to have a master anywhere near him.

It seemed like a blunder of etiquette to have Nicaise at the high table, considering the sensibilities of the Patrans. But Nicaise was dressed respectably and wore very little paint. The only flash of pet gaudiness was a long earring in his left ear; twin sapphires dangled, almost brushing his shoulder, too heavy for his young face. In every other way, he could be mistaken for a member of the nobility. No one from Patras would suppose that a child catamite sat at table alongside royalty; Torveld would likely make the same incorrect assumption Damen had made and think that Nicaise was somebody's son or nephew. Despite the earring.

Nicaise also sat well. His beauty at close range was striking. So was his youth. His voice, when he spoke, was unbroken. It had the clear fluting tone of a knife tapped against crystal, without cracks.

"I don't want to sit next to you," said Nicaise. "Fuck off."

Instinctively, Damen looked around to see if anyone from the Patran delegation had heard, but no one had. The first course of meat had arrived, and the food had everyone's attention. Nicaise had picked up a gilt three-pronged fork, but had paused before sampling the dish in order to speak. The fear he'd shown of Damen at the ring seemed to still be there. His knuckles, clenched around the fork, were white.

"It's all right," said Damen. He spoke to the boy as gently as he could. "I'm not going to hurt you."

Nicaise stared back at him. His huge blue eyes were fringed like a whore's, or like a doe's. Around them, the table was a coloured wall of voices and laughter, courtiers caught up in their own amusements, paying them no attention.

"Good," said Nicaise, and stabbed the fork viciously into Damen's thigh under the table.

Even through a layer of cloth, it was enough to make Damen start, and instinctively grab the fork, as three drops of blood welled up.

"Excuse me a moment," Laurent said smoothly, turning from Torveld to face Nicaise.

"I made your pet jump," said Nicaise, smugly.

Not sounding at all displeased: "Yes, you did."

"Whatever you're planning, it's not going to work."

"I think it will, though. Bet you your earring."

"If I win, you wear it," said Nicaise.

Laurent immediately lifted his cup and inclined it towards Nicaise in a little gesture sealing the bet. Damen tried to shake the bizarre impression that they were enjoying themselves.

Nicaise waved an attendant over and asked for a new fork.

Without a master to entertain, Nicaise was left free to prick at Damen. He began with a stream of insults and explicit speculation about Damen's sexual practices, pitched in a voice too quiet for anyone else to hear. When, at length, he saw that Damen was not rising to this bait, he turned his commentary on Damen's owner.

"You think sitting at the high table with him means something? It doesn't. He won't fuck you. He's frigid."

This subject was almost a relief. No matter how crude the boy was, there was nothing he could say about Laurent's proclivities that Damen had not already heard speculated about extensively and in coarse language by bored guards on indoor duty.

"I don't think he *can*. I think it doesn't work, what he has. When I was younger, I used to think he'd had it cut off. What do you think? Have you seen it?"

When he was younger?

Damen said, "He hasn't had it cut off."

Nicaise's eyes narrowed.

Damen said, "How long have you been a pet in this court?"

"Three years," said Nicaise, in the sort of tone that said: You won't last here three minutes.

Damen looked at him and wished he hadn't asked. Whether he had a "child's mind" or not, physically Nicaise had not yet crossed over from child to adolescent. He was still prepubescent. He looked younger than any of the other pets Damen had seen at this court, all of whom had at least passed puberty. Three years.

The Patran delegation continued oblivious. With Torveld, Laurent was on his best behaviour. He had apparently—incredibly—divested himself of malice and washed his mouth out with soap. He talked intelligently about politics and about trade, and if every now and then a little edge glimmered, it came across as wit—not barbed, just enough to say: You see? I can keep up.

Torveld showed less and less inclination to look at anyone else. It was like watching a man smile as he surrendered himself to drown in deep water.

Thankfully, it did not go on too long. In a miracle of

restraint, there were only nine courses, served ribboned and artfully arranged on jewelled plates by attractive pages. The pets themselves "served" not at all. Sitting nestled alongside their owners, some of them were hand-fed, and one or two even brazenly helped themselves, playfully filching choice morsels from their masters, like pampered lapdogs who have learned that whatever they do, their doting owners will find them charming.

"It's a shame I haven't been able to arrange for you to view the slaves," said Laurent, as the pages began to cover the table with sweets.

"You don't need to. We saw palace slaves in Akielos. I don't think I've ever seen slaves of that quality, even in Bazal. And I trust your taste, of course."

"I'm glad," said Laurent.

Damen was aware that beside him, Nicaise had started intently listening.

"I'm sure my uncle will agree to the exchange if you push for it strongly enough," said Laurent.

"If he does, I will owe it to you," said Torveld.

Nicaise got up from the table.

Damen bridged the nine chilly inches at the first opportunity. "What are you doing? You were the one who warned me about Nicaise." He spoke in a low voice.

Laurent went very still; then he deliberately shifted in his seat and leaned in, bringing his lips right to Damen's ear. "I think I'm out of stabbing range, he's got short arms. Or perhaps he'll try to throw a sugarplum? That *is* difficult. If I duck, he'll hit Torveld."

Damen gritted his teeth. "You know what I meant. He heard you. He's going to act. Can't you do something about it?"

"I'm occupied."

"Then let me do something."

"Bleed on him?" said Laurent.

Damen opened his mouth to reply and found his words stopped by the startling touch of Laurent's fingers against his lips, a thumb brushing his jawline. It was the sort of absent touch that any master at the table might give to a pet. But from the shocked reaction that rolled over the courtiers at the table, it was clear that Laurent did not do this sort of thing often. Or ever.

"My pet was feeling neglected," Laurent apologised to Torveld.

"He's the captive Kastor sent you to train?" said Torveld, curiously. "He's—safe?"

"He looks combative, but he's really very docile and adoring," said Laurent, "like a puppy."

"A puppy," said Torveld.

To demonstrate, Laurent picked up a confection of crushed nuts and honey and held it out to Damen as he had at the ring, between thumb and forefinger.

"Sweetmeat?" said Laurent.

In the stretched-out moment that followed, Damen thought explicitly about killing him.

Damen leaned in. It was sickly sweet. He didn't let his lips touch Laurent's fingers. A great many people were looking at them. Laurent washed his fingers fastidiously in the gold washing bowl when he was done, and dried them on a little square cloth of silk.

Torveld stared. In Patras, slaves fed masters—peeling fruit and pouring drinks—not the other way around. It was that way also in Akielos. The conversation recovered from its pause and turned to trivial matters. Around them the creations of sugar and candied spices and glazed pastries in fantastical shapes were slowly being demolished.

Damen looked around for Nicaise, but the boy had gone.

◆ ◆ ◆

In the relaxed end-of-meal lull before the entertainments, Damen was given free rein to wander about, and went to find him. Laurent was occupied, and for the first time there were not two guards looming perpetually over him. He could have walked out. He could have walked right out of the palace doors and from there into the surrounding city of Arles. Except he couldn't leave this place until Torveld's embassy departed with the slaves, which was, of course, the only reason he was off the leash at all.

He didn't make very good progress. The guards might be gone, but Laurent's caress had bought Damen another type of attention.

"I predicted when the Prince brought him to the ring that he was going to become quite popular," Vannes was saying to the noblewoman beside her. "I saw him perform in the gardens, but it was almost a waste of his talents; the Prince wouldn't let him take an active role."

Damen's attempts to excuse himself had no impact on her at all.

"No, don't leave us just yet. Talik wished to meet you,"

Vannes told Damen. She was saying to the noblewoman, "Of course, the idea of one of us keeping males is grotesque. But if one could—don't you think he and Talik would make a good matched pair? Ah. Here she is. We'll give you two a moment together." They were departing.

"I am Talik," the pet declared. Her voice carried the strong accent of Ver-Tan, the eastern province of Vask.

Damen recalled someone saying that Vannes liked pets who could sweep the ring competitions. Talik was almost as tall as Damen, her bare arms well muscled. There was something slightly predatory about her gaze, her wide mouth and the arc of her brows. Damen had assumed that pets, like slaves, were sexually submissive to their masters, as was the custom in Akielos. But he could only guess at the arrangements between Vannes and this woman in bed.

She said, "I think a warrior from Ver-Tan would easily kill a warrior from Akielos."

"I think it would depend on the warrior," he said, carefully.

She appeared to consider him along with his answer, and, eventually, to find both acceptable.

She said, "We are waiting. Ancel will perform. He is popular, 'in fashion.' You've had him." She didn't wait for him to confirm this statement. "How was he?"

Well instructed. Damen's mind supplied the answer, sly as a suggestion murmured in his ear. He frowned at it. He said, "Adequate."

Talik said, "His contract with Lord Berenger ends soon. Ancel will seek a new contract, a high bidder. He wants money, status. He is foolish. Lord Berenger may offer less money, but he is kind, and never puts pets into the ring. Ancel has made many enemies. In the ring, someone will scratch his green eyes out, an 'accident.'"

Damen was drawn in against his will. "That's why he's chasing royal attention? He wants the Prince to"—he tried out the unfamiliar vocabulary—"offer for his contract?"

"The Prince?" said Talik, scornfully. "Everyone knows the Prince does not keep pets."

"None at all?" said Damen.

She said, "You." She looked him up and down. "Perhaps the Prince has a taste for men, not these painted Veretian boys who squeal if you pinch them." Her tone suggested that she approved of this on general principle.

"Nicaise," said Damen, since they were speaking of painted Veretian boys. "I was looking for Nicaise. Have you seen him?"

Talik said, "There."

Across the room, Nicaise had reappeared. He was speaking into the ear of Ancel, who had to bend almost in half to reach the little boy's level. When he was done, Nicaise made straight for Damen.

"Did the Prince send you? You're too late," said Nicaise.

Too late for what? was the reply in any court except this one. He said, "If you've hurt any one of them—"

"You'll what?" Nicaise was smirking. "You won't. You don't have time. The Regent wants to see you. He sent me to tell you. You should hurry. You're keeping him waiting." Another smirk. "He sent me ages ago."

Damen stared at him.

"Well? Off you go," said Nicaise.

It was possibly a lie, but he couldn't risk the offense if it wasn't. He went.

It wasn't a lie. The Regent had summoned him, and when he arrived, the Regent dismissed all those around him, so that Damen was alone at his chair. At the end of the softly lit hall, it was a private audience.

Around them, heavy with food and wine, the noise of the court was warm and loosened. Damen made all the deferences that protocol required. The Regent spoke.

"I suppose it excites a slave to plunder the treasures of a prince. You have taken my nephew?"

Damen stayed very still; he tried not to disturb the air when he breathed. "No, Your Highness."

"The other way around, perhaps."

"No."

"Yet you eat out of his hand. The last time I spoke to you, you wished him flogged. How else do you account for the change?"

You won't like my riposte, Laurent had said.

Damen said, carefully, "I'm in his service. I have that lesson written on my back."

The Regent gazed at him for a while. "I'm almost disappointed, if it's no more than that. Laurent could benefit from a steadying influence, someone close to him with his best interests at heart. A man with sound judgement, who could help guide him without being swayed."

"Swayed?" said Damen.

"My nephew is charming, when he wishes it. His brother

was a true leader; he could inspire extraordinary loyalty from his men. Laurent has a superficial version of his brother's gifts, which he uses to get his own way. If anyone could have a man eating from the hand that struck him, it's my nephew," said the Regent. "Where is your loyalty?"

And Damen understood that he was not being asked a question. He was being given a choice.

He badly wanted to step across the chasm that separated the two factions of this court: On the other side was this man who had long since won his respect. It was grittily painful for him to realise that it was not in his nature to do that— not while Laurent was acting on his behalf. If Laurent was acting on his behalf . . . even if Laurent was acting on his behalf, he had so little stomach for the drawn-out game that was being played tonight. And yet.

"I'm not the man you want," he said. "I don't have influence over him. I'm not close to him. He has no love for Akielos, or its people."

The Regent gave him another long, considering look.

"You are honest. That is pleasing. As for the rest, we will see. That will do for now," said the Regent. "Go and fetch me my nephew. I prefer him not to be left alone with Torveld."

"Yes, Your Highness."

He wasn't sure why it felt like a reprieve, but it did.

A few inquiries made of other servants, and Damen learned that Laurent and Torveld had retreated once again to one of the balconies, escaping the stifling crush inside the palace.

Reaching the balcony, Damen slowed. He could hear the sound of their voices. He looked back at the thronging court chamber; he was out of sight of the Regent. If Laurent and Torveld were discussing trade negotiations, it would be better to delay a little and give them whatever extra time they might need.

"—told my advisors that I was past the age to be distracted by beautiful young men," he heard Torveld say, and it was suddenly eminently clear that they were not discussing trade negotiations.

It was a surprise, but on reflection, it had been happening all night. That a man of Torveld's honourable reputation would choose Laurent as the object of his affections was difficult to swallow, but perhaps Torveld admired reptiles. Curiosity blossomed. There had been no topic that engendered more speculation than this one among courtiers and members of the Prince's Guard alike. Damen paused, and listened.

"And then I met you," said Torveld, "and then I spent an hour in your company."

"More than an hour," said Laurent. "Less than a day. I think you get distracted more easily than you admit."

"And you not at all?"

There was a slight pause in the rhythm of their exchange.

"You . . . have been listening to gossip."

"Is it true, then?"

"That I am—not easily courted? It can't be the worst thing you heard about me."

"By far the worst, from my perspective."

It was said warmly and won a breath of insubstantial amusement from Laurent.

Torveld's voice changed, as though they stood closer together. "I have heard a great deal of gossip about you, but I judge as I find."

Laurent said, in the same intimate voice, "And what do you find?"

Damen stepped forward determinedly.

Hearing his footfall, Torveld started and looked round; in Patras, affairs of the heart—or of the body—were usually private. Laurent, reclined elegantly against the balustrade, did not react at all except to shift his gaze in Damen's direction. They were indeed standing close together. Not quite kissing distance.

"Your Highness, your uncle has sent for you," said Damen.

"Again," said Torveld, a line appearing in the middle of his forehead.

Laurent detached himself. "He's overprotective," he said. The line disappeared when Torveld looked at Laurent.

"You took your time," Laurent murmured as he passed Damen.

He was left alone with Torveld. It was peaceful out here on the balcony. The court sounds were muted, as though they were very distant. Louder and more intimate were the sounds of insects in the gardens below, and the slow back-and-forth of greenery. At some point it occurred to Damen that he was supposed to have lowered his eyes.

Torveld's attention was elsewhere.

"He is a prize," said Torveld warmly. "I'll wager you never thought a prince could be jealous of a slave. Right now I would exchange places with you in a heartbeat."

You don't know him, thought Damen. *You don't know any-thing about him. You've known him one night.*

"I think the entertainment will begin shortly," Damen said.

"Yes, of course," said Torveld, and they followed Laurent back to the court.

◆ ◆ ◆

Damen had, in his life, been required to sit through many spectacles. In Vere "entertainment" had taken on new mean-ing. When Ancel came forward holding a long stick in his hands, Damen readied himself for the kind of performance that would make the Patran delegation faint. Then Ancel touched each end of the stick to the torch in the wall bracket, and they burst into flame.

It was a kind of fire dance in which the stick was thrown and caught, and the flame, tossed and twirled, created sinu-ous shapes, circles and ever-moving patterns. Ancel's red hair created a pleasing aesthetic alongside the red-and-orange fire. And even without the hypnotic movement of the flame, the dance was beguiling, its difficulties made to look effortless, its physicality subtly erotic. Damen looked at Ancel with new respect. This performance required training, discipline and athleticism, which Damen admired. It was the first time that Damen had seen Veretian pets display skill in anything other than wearing clothes or climbing on top of one another.

The mood was relaxed. Damen was back on the leash, being used very possibly as a chaperone. Laurent was acting with the carefully bland manners of one trying politely to manage a difficult suitor. Damen thought with some amusement: boxed in by your own cleverness. As Damen watched, Torveld's servant produced a peach, then a knife, then cut a slice at Torveld's instruction, offering it to Laurent, who blandly accepted. When he had finished the morsel, the servant brought forth a little cloth from his sleeve with a flourish for Laurent to clean his immaculate fingers. The cloth was transparent silk, edged in gold thread. Laurent returned it crumpled.

"I'm enjoying the performance," Damen couldn't resist saying.

"Torveld's servant is better supplied than you are," was all Laurent said.

"I don't have sleeves to carry handkerchiefs in," said Damen. "I wouldn't mind being given a knife."

"Or a fork?" said Laurent.

A ripple of applause and a small commotion forestalled a reply. The flame dance was finished, and something was happening at the far end of the room.

Baulking like a green colt at the rein, Erasmus was being dragged forward by a Veretian handler.

He heard a girl's fluting voice say, "Since you like them so much, I thought we could watch one of the slaves from Akielos perform."

It was Nicaise, here on the small matter of an earring.

Torveld was shaking his head, congenially enough. "Laurent," he said. "You've been swindled by the King of Akielos. That can't be a palace slave. He isn't showing form at all. He can't even sit still. I think Kastor just dressed up some serving boys and shipped them off to you. Although he is pretty," said Torveld. And then, in a slightly different voice, "Very pretty."

He was very pretty. He was exceptional even among slaves chosen to be exceptional, handpicked to be served up to a prince. Except he was clumsy and graceless and showing no sign of training. He had finally dropped to his knees, but he looked like he was staying there only because his limbs had seized up, his hands clenched as though cramped.

"Pretty or not, I can't take two dozen untrained slaves back with me to Bazal," Torveld was saying.

Damen took Nicaise by the wrist. "What have you done?"

"Let go! I haven't done anything," said Nicaise. He rubbed his wrist when Damen released it. To Laurent: "You let him speak to his betters like that?"

"Not to his betters," said Laurent.

Nicaise flushed at that. Ancel was still lazily twirling the fire stick. The flickering of the flames cast an orange light. The heat, when it came near, was surprising. Erasmus had turned white, as though about to vomit in front of everyone.

"Stop this," said Damen to Laurent. "It's cruel. That boy was badly burned. He's afraid of the fire."

"Burned?" said Torveld.

Nicaise said, quickly, "Not burned, branded. He has the scars all over his leg. They're ugly."

Torveld was looking at Erasmus, whose eyes were glassy and showed a kind of stupefied hopelessness. If you knew what he thought he was facing, it was hard to believe he was kneeling down waiting for it.

Torveld said, "Have the fire put out."

The sudden acrid smell of smoke drowned out the Veretian perfumes. The fire was out. Summoned forward, Erasmus managed a slightly better prostration and seemed to calm further in the presence of Laurent, which made little sense until Damen recalled that Erasmus had thought of Laurent as "kind."

Torveld asked Erasmus several questions, which Erasmus answered in Patran with shy but improving form. After that, Torveld's fingers somehow found their way to rest for a moment protectively on the top of Erasmus's head. After that, Torveld asked Erasmus to sit beside him during the trade negotiations.

After that, Erasmus kissed Torveld's toe, then ankle, his curls brushing against Torveld's firm calf muscle.

Damen looked at Laurent, who had simply let all of this unfold before him. He could see what had made Torveld transfer his affections. There was a superficial resemblance between the Prince and the slave. Erasmus's fair skin and burnished hair were the closest thing in the room to Laurent's gold and ivory colouring. But Erasmus had something Laurent lacked: a vulnerability, a need for caring, and a yearning to be mastered that was almost palpable. In Laurent, there was only a patrician coolness, and if the purity of Laurent's profile drew the eye, Damen had the scars on his back to prove that one could look, but not touch.

"You planned this!" said Nicaise, his low voice was a hiss. "You wanted him to see—you tricked me!" In the same voice a lover might have said: How could you! Except there was anger there, too. And spite.

"You had a choice," said Laurent. "You didn't have to show me your claws."

"You tricked me," said Nicaise. "I'm going to tell—"

"Tell him," said Laurent. "All about what I've done and how you helped me. How do you think he'll react? Shall we find out? Let's go together."

Nicaise gave Laurent a look that was desperately, spitefully calculating.

"Oh, will you—enough," said Laurent. "Enough. You're learning. It won't be as easy to do next time."

"I promise you, it won't," said Nicaise venomously, and he left without, Damen noted, giving Laurent his earring.

✦ ✦ ✦

Fed, sated and entertained, the court dispersed and the Council and Regent sat down and began negotiations. When the Regent called for wine, it was Ancel who poured it. And when he was done, Ancel was invited to sit beside the Regent, which he did, very decoratively, with a well-pleased expression on his face.

Damen had to smile. He supposed that he couldn't blame Ancel for ambition. And it wasn't a bad achievement, for an eighteen-year-old boy. There were courtiers aplenty in Damen's homeland who would consider it the height of accomplishment to attain a king's bed. The more so if it was a position of any permanence.

Ancel was not the only one to have gotten what he wanted tonight. Laurent had delivered all Damen had asked for, tied up neatly in a bow. All within the space of a day. If you put everything else aside, you had to admire it for sheer organisational efficiency.

If you did not put everything else aside, you recalled that this was Laurent, and that he had lied and cheated in order to bring this about. You thought about Erasmus, dragged through a night of horrors, and about what it meant for an adult to trick and use a boy who, for all he soundly deserved it, was still only thirteen.

"It's done," said Laurent, who had come to stand beside him.

Laurent seemed, bizarrely, to be in a good mood. He leaned a shoulder rather casually against the wall. His voice was not exactly warm, but nor was the ice edge polished to cut.

"I've arranged for Torveld to meet with you later, to discuss the transportation of the slaves. Did you know that Kastor sent them to us without any handlers from Akielos?"

"I thought you and Torveld would have other plans." It just came out.

Laurent said, "No."

Damen realised that he was pushing at the limits of Laurent's good mood. So he said, not without difficulty, "I don't know why you did any of this, but I think the others will be well treated in Bazal. Thank you."

"You are permanently disgusted by us, aren't you?" said Laurent. And then, before Damen could speak: "Don't answer that question. Something made you smile earlier. What was it?"

"It was nothing. Ancel," said Damen. "He's finally found the royal patronage he was looking for."

Laurent followed his gaze. He calmly appraised the way that Ancel leaned in to pour wine, the way that the Regent's ringed fingers lifted to trace the line of Ancel's cheek.

"No," said Laurent, without much interest. "That's done for appearance's sake only. I think not all the practices of this court would meet with the approval of Torveld's delegation."

"What do you mean?"

Laurent detached his gaze from the Regent and turned it back on Damen, his blue eyes showing neither his usual hostility, nor arrogance, nor contempt, but instead something that Damen could not make out at all.

"I warned you about Nicaise because he is not Councillor Audin's pet. Haven't you guessed yet whose pet he is?" Laurent said, and then, when he didn't answer: "Ancel is too old to interest my uncle."

CHAPTER NINE

H E WAS TAKEN to see Torveld in the early morning, after a long interview with two Patran servants in which he dredged up all the knowledge he had regarding the treatment of slaves. Some of the questions he was asked he had no idea how to answer. Others he was more comfortable with: Were they trained in Patran protocols, and which guests could they be expected to entertain? Yes, they had language and protocol training in Patran, as well as Vaskian, though perhaps not the provincial dialects. And of course they knew all that was needed of Akielos and Isthima. Not Vere, he heard himself saying. No one had ever believed there would be a treaty, or an exchange.

Torveld's rooms resembled Laurent's, though they were smaller. Torveld came out of the bedchamber looking well rested, wearing only pants and an over-robe. It fell straight to the ground on either side of his body, revealing a well-defined chest, lightly haired.

Through the archway Damen could see the tumble of milky limbs on the bed and the burnished head. Just for a moment he remembered Torveld making love to Laurent on the balcony, but the hair was a shade too dark, and curled.

"He's sleeping," said Torveld.

He spoke in a low voice, so as not to disturb Erasmus. He motioned Damen towards a table where they both sat. Torveld's robe settled in folds of heavy silk.

"We have not yet—" Torveld said, and there was a silence. Damen had grown so used to explicit Veretian talk that he waited, in the silence, for Torveld to say what he meant. It took him a moment to realise that this silence said all that was needed, to a Patran. Torveld said, "He is . . . very willing, but I suspect there has been some mistreatment, not only the branding. I brought you here because I wanted to ask you the extent of it. I am concerned that I will inadvertently . . ." Another silence. Torveld's eyes were dark. "I think it would help for me to know."

Damen thought, this is Vere, and there is no delicate Patran way to describe the things that happen here.

"He was being trained as a personal slave for the Prince of Akielos," said Damen. "It's likely that he was a virgin before he arrived in Vere. But not after."

"I see."

"I don't know the extent of it," said Damen.

"You don't need to say more. It's as I thought," said Torveld. "Well, I thank you for your candour, and for your work this morning. I understand it's customary to give pets a gift after they perform a service." Torveld gave him a considering look. "You don't look like the type for jewellery."

Damen, smiling a little, said, "No. Thank you."

"Is there something else I can offer you?"

He thought about it. There was something he wanted, very badly. It was dangerous to ask. The grain of the table was dark, and only the edge was carved; the rest was a smooth plain surface.

"You were in Akielos. You were there after the funeral ceremonies?"

"Yes, that's right."

"What happened to the Prince's household—after his death?"

"I assume it was disbanded. I did hear that his personal slaves slit their own throats from grief. I don't know anything more."

"From grief," said Damen, remembering the ringing of swords, and his own surprise—the surprise that had meant he had not understood what was happening until it was too late.

"Kastor was furious. The Keeper of the Royal Slaves was executed for letting it happen. And several of the guard."

Yes. He had warned Adrastus. Kastor would have wanted the evidence of what he had done blotted out. Adrastus, the guards, probably even the yellow-haired slave who had tended him in the baths. Everyone who knew the truth, systematically, would have been killed.

Almost everyone. Damen took a steadying breath. He

knew with every locked-down particle in his body that he shouldn't let himself ask, and yet he couldn't help it.

"And Jokaste?" Damen said.

He said her name as he would have said it to her, without a title. Torveld gazed at him speculatively.

"Kastor's mistress? She was in good health. The pregnancy is proceeding without incident . . . You didn't know? She carries Kastor's child. Whether there will be a wedding or not is still in question, but certainly it's in Kastor's interests to secure the succession. He gives every indication that he will raise the child as—"

"His heir," said Damen.

It would have been her price. He remembered every perfect coil of her hair, like winding silk. Close those doors.

He looked up. And suddenly he was aware, from the way Torveld was looking back at him, that he had lingered on this topic too long.

"You know," said Torveld, slowly, "you resemble Kastor a little. It's something in the eyes. In the shape of the face. The more I look at you—"

No.

"—the more I see it. Has anyone ever—"

No.

"—remarked on it before? I'm sure Laurent would—"

"*No,*" said Damen. "I—"

It came out sounding too loud and too urgent. His heartbeat was loud in his chest, as he was dragged from thoughts of home back to this—deception. He knew that the only thing standing between himself and discovery at this moment was the sheer audacity of what Kastor had done. A right-minded man like Torveld would never guess at this kind of brazen, inventive treachery.

"Forgive me. I meant to say that—I hope you won't tell the Prince you think I look like Kastor. He wouldn't be pleased by the comparison at all." It wasn't a lie. Laurent's mind would have no trouble jumping from clue to answer. Laurent was too close to guessing the truth already. "He has no love for the Akielon royal family."

He should say something about being flattered to hear there was a likeness, but he knew he wasn't going to be able to get his mouth around the words.

For the moment at least, it distracted Torveld.

"Laurent's feelings about Akielos are too well-known," Torveld said, with a troubled look. "I've tried to talk to him about it. I'm not surprised he wanted those slaves gone from the palace—if I were Laurent, I'd be suspicious of any gift from Akielos. With conflict brewing among the kyroi, the last thing Kastor can afford is a hostile neighbour on his northern border. The Regent is open to friendship with Akielos, but Laurent . . . it would be in Kastor's interests to keep Laurent off the throne."

Trying to imagine Kastor plotting against Laurent was like trying to imagine a wolf plotting against a serpent.

"I think the Prince can hold his own," said Damen, dryly.

"Yes. You could be right. He has a rare mind." Torveld rose as he spoke, indicating that the interview was done. In the same moment, Damen became aware that there were signs of stirring from the bed. "I'm looking forward to a renewed relationship with Vere, after his ascension."

Because he's bewitched you, Damen thought. *Because you're moonstruck and you have no idea of his nature.*

"You can tell him I said that if you like. Oh, and tell him I'm looking forward to beating him to the mark today," said Torveld with a grin, as Damen made his way out.

◆ ◆ ◆

Damen, thankfully for his sense of self-preservation, had no chance to tell Laurent anything of the kind, but instead was thrust into a change of clothing. He was to be taken out to accompany the Prince. He didn't have to ask, "Accompany him where?" It was Torveld's last day, and Torveld was well-known for his enjoyment of the hunt.

The real sport was in Chastillon, but it was too far to go in a day, and there were some reasonable runs in the lightly wooded lands around Arles. So—only slightly the worse for wine the night before—half the court picked itself up around mid-morning and moved outside.

Damen was transported, ridiculously, on a litter, as were Erasmus and a few of the wispier pets. Their role was not to participate, but to attend their masters after the sport was done. Damen and Erasmus both were bound for the royal tent. Until the Patran delegation departed, Damen was unable to attempt escape. He couldn't even use the outing as a chance to see the city of Arles and its environs. The litter was covered. He did have a very good view of a series of figures copulating, which was the scene embroidered on the inside of the silk cover.

The nobility were hunting boar, which the Veretians called sanglier, a northern breed that was larger, with longer tusks on the male. A stream of servants, up before dawn—or perhaps even working through the night—had brought all of the opulence of the palace outside, erecting tented pavilions, richly coloured and covered in pennants and flags. There were a great deal of refreshments served by attractive pages. The horses were beribboned and their saddles encrusted with precious stones. This was hunting with every leather exquisitely polished, every pillow plumped, and every need met. But despite all the luxury, it was still a dangerous sport. A boar was more intelligent than a deer or even a hare, which would run until it escaped or was overcome. A boar, fearsome, furious and aggressive, would occasionally turn and fight.

They arrived, rested, lunched. The party mounted. The beaters fanned out. To Damen's surprise, there were one or two pets among the riders milling about; he saw Talik on a horse alongside Vannes, and riding very neatly indeed on a pretty strawberry roan was Ancel, accompanying his master Berenger.

Inside the tent, there was no sign whatsoever of Nicaise. The Regent was riding, but the child pet had been left behind.

Laurent's words last night had been a shock. It was hard to reconcile what he now knew with the manner and the bearing of the man. The Regent gave no sign of his—tastes. Damen might almost have thought Laurent was lying.

Except he could see in Nicaise's actions all the ways it was true. Who but the Regent's pet would behave as brazenly as Nicaise did in the company of princes?

Considering Nicaise's loyalties, it was strange that Laurent had seemed drawn to him—had seemed even oddly to like him—but who knew what went on in that maze of a mind?

There was nothing to do but watch while the riders mounted and waited for the first signal of game. Damen wandered over to the mouth of the tent and looked out.

The hunting party, sunlit, spanned the hill, flashing with jewels and polished saddlery. The two princes were mounted alongside one another, close by the tent. Torveld looked powerful and competent. Laurent dressed in black hunting leathers was an even more austere sight than normal. He was riding a bay mare. She was a beautiful mount, with perfectly balanced proportions and long hips made for hunting, but she was fractious and difficult, already covered in a thin sheen of sweat. It gave Laurent, controlling her under a light rein, a chance to show off his seat, which was excellent. But it was show without substance. The hunt, like the art of war, required strength, stamina, and skill with a weapon. But more important than all three was a calm horse.

Dogs wove their way through the legs of the horses. They were trained to be calm around large animals, trained to ignore hares and foxes and deer, and focus on nothing but sanglier.

Laurent's fussy horse began acting out again, and he leaned forward in the saddle, murmuring something as he stroked her neck in an uncharacteristically gentle gesture to quiet her. Then he looked up at Damen.

It was wasteful of nature to have bestowed those looks on one whose character was so unpleasant. Laurent's fair skin and blue eyes were a combination that was rare in Patras, rarer in Akielos, and a particular weakness of Damen's. The golden hair made it worse.

"Can't afford a good horse?" said Damen.

"Try to keep up," said Laurent.

He said it to Torveld, after a chilly look at Damen. A touch of his heels, and his mount moved out like she was part of him. Torveld, who was grinning, followed.

In the distance, a horn blew, announcing game. The riders kicked their mounts, and the whole party streamed towards the sound of the horn. Hooves thundered after the baying of hounds. The terrain was only lightly wooded, with trees scattered here and there. A large party could canter. There was a clear view of the dogs and the front-runners, who were approaching a more heavily wooded area. The boar was somewhere under the cover. It was not long before the party was out of sight, through the trees, over the crest of a hill.

◆ ◆ ◆

Inside the royal tent, servants were clearing away the last of the luncheon, which had been eaten reclining on strewn cushions, the occasional hound wandering in only to be pushed good-naturedly off the cloths.

Erasmus was like an exotic ornament, kneeling obediently on a cushion the colour of yellow apples. He had done a beautifully unobtrusive job of serving Torveld at lunch, and later in arranging his riding leathers. He was wearing a short tunic in Patran style that exposed his arms and legs, yet was long enough to cover his scarring. Re-entering the tent, Damen looked nowhere else.

Erasmus looked down and tried not to smile, and instead blushed, slowly and thoroughly.

"Hello," said Damen.

"I know that you have somehow arranged this," said Erasmus. He was incapable of hiding what he felt and just seemed to radiate embarrassed happiness. "You kept your promise. You and your master. I told you he was kind," Erasmus said.

"You did," said Damen.

He was pleased to see Erasmus happy. Whatever Erasmus believed about Laurent, Damen wasn't going to dissuade him.

"He's even nicer in person. Did you know he came and talked to me?" said Erasmus.

"—He did?" said Damen. It was something he couldn't imagine.

"He asked about . . . what happened in the gardens. Then he warned me. About last night."

"He warned you," said Damen.

"He said that Nicaise would make me perform before the court, and it would be awful, but that if I was brave, something good might come at the end of it." Erasmus looked up at Damen curiously. "Why do you look surprised?"

"I don't know. I shouldn't be. He likes to plan things in advance," said Damen.

"He wouldn't have even known about someone like me if you hadn't asked him to help me," said Erasmus. "He's a prince, his life is so important, so many people must want him to do things for them. I'm glad I have this chance to say thank you. If there is a way to repay you, I will find it. I swear that I will."

"There's no need. Your happiness is repayment enough."

"And what about you?" said Erasmus. "Won't you be lonely, all by yourself?"

"I have a kind master," said Damen.

He did pretty well in getting the words out, all things considered. Erasmus bit his lip, and all his burnished curls fell over his forehead. "You're—in love with him?"

"Not quite," said Damen.

There was a moment of silence. It was Erasmus who broke it.

"I . . . was always taught that a slave's duty was sacred, that we honoured our masters through submission and they honoured us in return. And I believed that. But when you said that you were sent here as punishment, I understood that for men here, there is no honour in obedience, and it is shameful to be a slave. Perhaps I had already started to understand that—even before you spoke to me. I tried to tell myself that it was an even greater submission, to become nothing, to have no value, but—I couldn't—I think it is in my nature to submit, as it is not in yours, but I need someone—to belong to."

"You have someone," said Damen. "Slaves are prized in Patras, and Torveld is smitten with you."

"I like him," said Erasmus, shyly, blushing. "I like his eyes. I think he's handsome." And then he blushed again at his own boldness.

"More handsome than the Prince of Akielos?" Damen teased.

"Well, I never saw him, but I really don't think he could be more handsome than my master," said Erasmus.

"Torveld wouldn't tell you this himself, but he's a great man," said Damen, smiling. "Even among princes. He spent most of his life in the north, fighting on the border with Vask. He's the man who finally brokered the peace between Vask and Patras. He's King Torgeir's most loyal servant, as well as his brother."

"Another kingdom . . . In Akielos, none of us thought we'd ever leave the palace."

"I'm sorry that you'll have to be uprooted again. But it won't be like last time. You can look forward to the journey."

"Yes. That is—I . . . I will be a little frightened, but so obedient," said Erasmus. And blushed again.

◆ ◆ ◆

The first to return were the foot-huntsmen and the dog handlers from the first station, who were bringing back a set of exhausted hounds, having released a second fresh set as the riders swept past. To them also fell the job of destroying any dogs that were wounded past recovery by the sharp-tusked boar.

There was a strange atmosphere among them, not only the heavy, tongue-lolling fatigue of the hounds. It was something in the faces of the men. Damen felt a twist of unease. Boar hunting was a dangerous sport. At the mouth of the tent, he called to one of them.

"Has something happened?"

The dogsman said, "Tread lightly. Your master's in a vicious mood."

Well, that was order restored.

"Let me guess. Someone else brought down the boar."

"No. He did," said the dogsman, a sour note in his voice. "He ruined his horse to do it—she never had a chance. Even before he rode her into the fight that shattered her rear ankle, she was blood from flank to shoulder from the spur." He pointed his chin at Damen's back. "You'd know something about that," he said.

Damen stared at him, suddenly feeling faintly nauseated.

"She was a brave goer," he said. "The other one—Prince Auguste—he was a great one with horses, he helped break her in as a filly."

It was as close as any man of his station would come to criticising a prince.

One of the other men, eyeing them, approached a moment later. "Don't mind Jean. He's in a foul mood. He was the one who had to stick a sword through the mare's throat and put her down. The Prince tore strips off him for not doing it fast enough."

When the riders returned, Laurent was riding a well-muscled grey gelding, which meant that somewhere in the hunting party, a courtier was riding double.

The Regent came first into the tent, stripping off his riding gloves, his weapon taken by a servant.

Outside, there was a sudden baying; the boar had arrived and was likely being stripped down, its belly skin cut open and all the internal organs taken out, the offal given to the dogs.

"Nephew," said the Regent.

Laurent had come with soft, padding grace into the tent. There was an aseptic lack of expression in the cool blue eyes, and it was very clear that *vicious mood* was an understatement.

The Regent said, "Your brother never had any difficulty running down a mark without slaughtering his horse. But we aren't going to talk about that."

"Aren't we?" said Laurent.

"Nicaise tells me you influenced Torveld to bargain for the slaves. Why do it in secret?" said the Regent. His gaze tracked over Laurent slowly and consideringly. "I suppose the real question is what motivated you to do it at all?"

"I thought it was terribly unfair of you," drawled Laurent, "to burn the skin of your slaves when you would not let me flay mine even a little."

Damen felt all the breath leave his body.

The Regent's expression changed. "I see you can't be talked to. I won't indulge your current mood. Petulance is ugly in a child and worse in a man. If you break your toys, it is no one's fault but your own."

The Regent left through the folded tent flaps that were held open by red silk ropes. From outside there came voices and the chink of saddlery and all the milling hubbub of a hunting party, and nearer to was the sound of the tent canvases flapping in the wind. Laurent's blue eyes were on him.

"Something to say?" said Laurent.

"I heard you killed your horse."

"It's just a horse," said Laurent. "I'll have my uncle buy me a new one."

These words seemed savagely to amuse him; there was a jagged, private edge to his voice. Damen thought, Tomorrow morning Torveld departs, and I am once again free to try and leave this sickening, treacherous, overripe place however I can.

❖ ❖ ❖

The chance came two nights later, though not in any way that he had anticipated.

Woken in the dead of night, torches flaring and the doors to his room flung open. He was expecting it to be Laurent—when it came to these nocturnal visits, these abrupt awakenings, it was always Laurent—but he saw only two men in livery, the Prince's livery. He didn't recognise the men.

"You've been sent for," one said, unlocking his chain from the floor and giving it a tug.

"Sent where?"

"The Prince," said the one, "wants you in his bed."

"What?" said Damen, bringing up short, so that the chain pulled taut.

He felt a sharp push from behind. "Get a move on. Don't want to keep him waiting."

"But—" Digging his heels in after the push.

"Move it."

He took a step forward, still resisting. Another. It was going to be a slow journey.

The man behind him swore. "Half the guard is hot to fuck him. You think you'd be happier about the idea."

"The Prince doesn't want me to *fuck him*," said Damen.

"Will you *move it*," the man behind him said, and Damen felt the prick of a knife point behind him, and he let himself be taken out of the room.

CHAPTER TEN

DAMEN HAD SURVIVED summonses from Laurent before. He had no reason for the tension across his shoulders, the anxiety in his stomach, curled and hot.

His journey was made in total privacy, giving the false outward impression of a secret rendezvous. But whatever this looked like, whatever it *felt* like—whatever he'd been told—was wrong. If he thought about it too much, hysteria threatened: Laurent was not the type to smuggle men into his rooms for midnight assignations.

That wasn't what this was.

It didn't make sense, but Laurent was impossible to second-guess. Damen's eyes raked the passageway and found another inconsistency. Where were the guards who had held position all along these corridors the last time Damen had walked them? Did they stand down at night? Or had they been cleared out for a reason?

"Did he use those words—'his bed'? What else did he say?" Damen asked and received no answer.

The knife at his back pricked him forward. There was nothing to do but continue along the corridor. With every step he took, the tension tightened, the uneasiness increased. The grilled windows along the passage threw squares of moonlight that passed over the faces of his escort. No sound but their footsteps.

There was a thin line of light under the doors of Laurent's room.

There was only one guard at the door, a dark-haired man wearing the Prince's livery and, at his hip, a sword. He nodded at his two fellows and said, briefly, "He's inside."

They stopped long enough at the door to unlock the chain and free Damen completely. The chain dropped in a heavy coil and was simply left there on the floor. Maybe he knew then.

The doors were pushed open.

Laurent was on the reclining couch, his feet tucked up under him in a relaxed, boyish posture. A book of scroll-worked pages was open before him. There was a goblet on the small table beside him. At some point during the night, a servant must have spent the requisite half hour unlacing his austere outer garments, for Laurent wore only pants and a white shirt, the material so fine it did not require embroidery to declaim its expense. The room was lamp lit. Laurent's body was a series of graceful lines under the shirt's soft folds. Damen's eyes lifted to the white column of his throat, and above that the golden hair, parting around the shell cup of an unjewelled ear. The image was damascened, as beaten metal. He was reading.

He looked up when the doors opened.

And blinked, as though refocusing his blue eyes was difficult. Damen looked again at the goblet and recalled that he had seen Laurent once before with his senses blurred by alcohol.

It might have prolonged the illusion of an assignation a few seconds longer because Laurent drunk was surely capable of all kinds of mad demands and unpredictable behaviour. Except that it was perfectly clear from the first moment he looked up that Laurent was not expecting company. And that Laurent did not recognise the guards either.

Laurent carefully closed the book.

And rose. "Couldn't sleep?" said Laurent.

As he spoke, he came to stand before the open archway of the loggia. Damen wasn't sure that a straight two-storey drop into unlit gardens could be counted as an escape route. But certainly otherwise—with the three shallow steps leading up to where he stood, the small finely carved table and decorative objects all providing a series of obstacles—it was, tactically, the best position in the room.

Laurent knew what was happening. Damen, who had seen the long, empty corridor, dark and quiet and absent of men, knew also. The guard at the door had entered behind them; there were three men, all armed.

"I don't think the Prince is in an amorous mood," said Damen, neutrally.

"I take a while to warm up," said Laurent.

And then it was happening. As though on cue, the sound of a sword being unsheathed to his left.

Later, he'd wonder what it was that caused him to react as he did. He had no love for Laurent. Given time to think, he would surely have said, in a hardened voice, that the internal politics of Vere weren't his business, and that whatever acts of violence Laurent had brought down upon himself were thoroughly deserved.

Maybe it was bizarre empathy, because he'd lived through something like this, the betrayal of it, violence in a place he'd thought was safe. Maybe it was a way of reliving those moments, of repairing his failure because he had not reacted as quickly as he should have, then.

It must have been that. It must have been the echo of that night, all the chaos and the emotion of it that he had locked up behind closed doors.

The three men split their attention: two of them moved towards Laurent, while the third remained with a knife, guarding Damen. He obviously expected no trouble. His grip on the knife was slack and casual.

After days, weeks spent waiting for an opportunity, it felt good to have one, and to take it. To feel the heavy, satisfying impact of flesh on flesh in the blow that numbed the man's arm and caused him to drop the knife.

The man was wearing livery and not armour, a blunder. His whole body curved around Damen's fist as it drove into his abdomen, and he made a guttural sound that was half a choke for air, half a response to pain.

The second of the three men, swearing, turned back—

presumably deciding that one man was enough to dispatch the Prince, and that his attention was better spent subduing the unexpectedly troublesome barbarian.

Unfortunately for him, he thought just having a sword would be enough. He came in fast, rather than approaching cautiously. His two-handed sword, with its large grip, could cleave into a man's side and go some way towards cutting him in half, but Damen was already inside his guard and in grappling distance.

There was a crash on the far side of the room, but Damen was only distantly aware of it, all his attention on the task of immobilising the second of his assailants, no thought to spare on the third man and Laurent.

The swordsman in his grip gasped out, *"He's the Prince's bitch. Kill him,"* which was all the warning Damen needed to move. He swung his entire body weight against the swordsman, reversing their positions.

And the knife stroke meant for him ran into the swordsman's unarmoured sternum.

The man with the knife had pulled himself up and recovered his weapon; he was agile, with a scar running down his cheek under the beard, a survivor. Not someone Damen wanted darting around him with a knife. Damen didn't let him pull his knife from its grisly sheath, but pushed forward, so that the man stumbled backwards, his fingers opening. Then he simply took hold of the man at hip and shoulder and swung his body hard into the wall.

It was enough to leave him dazed, his features slackened, unable to muster any initial resistance when Damen restrained him in a hold.

This done, Damen looked over, half-expecting to see Laurent struggling, or overcome. He was surprised to see instead that Laurent was alive and intact, having dispatched his opponent, and was rising from a position bent over the third man's still form, relieving his dead fingers of a knife.

He supposed that Laurent had possessed, at the very least, the wits to utilise his surroundings.

Damen's eyes caught on the knife.

His gaze swung down to the dead swordsman. There, too, a knife. A serrated blade-edge finished with the characteristic fretted hilt design of Sicyon, one of the northern provinces of Akielos.

The knife Laurent held was of the same design. It was bloody up to the hilt, he saw, as Laurent descended the shallow steps. It looked incongruous in his hand, since his fine white shirt had survived the struggle in immaculate condition, and the lamplight was just as flattering to him as it had been before.

Damen recognised Laurent's cold, strapped-down expression. He didn't envy the man he held the interrogation that was coming.

"What do you want me to do with him?"

"Hold him still," said Laurent.

He came forward. Damen did as he was told. He felt the man make a renewed attempt to free himself; Damen simply tightened his grip, aborting the ripple of struggle.

Laurent lifted the serrated knife, and, calmly as a butcher, sliced open the man's bearded throat.

Damen heard the choked sound and felt the first spasms of the body within his grip. He let go, partly out of surprise, and the man's hands came up to his own throat in a hopeless, instinctive gesture, too late. The thin red crescent drawn across his throat widened. He toppled.

Damen didn't even think before he reacted—as Laurent slanted a look at him, changing his grip on the knife—he moved instinctively to neutralise the threat.

Body collided hard with body. Damen's grip closed on the fine bones of Laurent's wrist, but instead of having things immediately his own way, he was surprised to encounter a moment of muscled resistance. He applied greater pressure. He felt the resistance in Laurent's body pushed to its limit, though he was still far from his own.

"Let go of my arm," said Laurent, in a controlled voice.

"Drop the knife," said Damen.

"If you do not let go of my arm," said Laurent, "it will not go easily for you."

Damen pushed just slightly harder, and felt the resistance shudder and give way; the knife clattered to the ground. As soon as it did, he let Laurent go. In the same motion, Damen stepped backwards out of range. Instead of following him, Laurent also took two steps backwards, widening the distance between himself and Damen.

They stared at one another over the wreckage of the room.

The knife lay between them. The man with the slit throat was dead or dying, his body gone still and his head turned sideways. The blood had soaked through the livery he wore, blotting out the starburst device of gold on blue.

Laurent's struggles had not been as contained as Damen's; the table was knocked over, the shattered pieces of a fine ceramic were strewn across the floor, and the goblet rolled on the tile. A wall hanging had been partly torn down. And there was a great deal of blood. Laurent's first kill of the night had been even messier than his second.

Laurent's breathing was shallow with exertion. So was Damen's. Into the tense, wary moment, Laurent said, steadily:

"You seem to vacillate between assistance and assault. Which is it?"

"I'm not surprised you've driven three men to try and kill you, I'm only surprised there weren't more," said Damen, bluntly.

"There were," said Laurent, "more."

Understanding his meaning, Damen flushed. "I didn't volunteer. I was brought here. I don't know why."

"To cooperate," said Laurent.

"Cooperate?" said Damen, with complete disgust. "You were unarmed." Damen remembered the lax way that man had held a knife on him; they had indeed expected him to cooperate, or at the very least, stand by and watch. He frowned at the closest of the still faces. He disliked the idea that anyone at all believed him capable of cutting down an unarmed man, four on one. Even if that man was Laurent.

Laurent stared at him.

"Like the man you just killed," said Damen, looking back at him.

"In my part of the fight, the men were not helpfully killing each other," Laurent said.

Damen opened his mouth. Before he could speak, there was a sound from the corridor. They both instinctively squared off towards the bronze doors. The sound became the clatter of light armour and weaponry, and soldiers in the Regent's livery were pouring into the room—two—five—seven—the odds started to become daunting. But—

"Your Highness, are you hurt?"

"No," said Laurent.

The soldier in charge gestured to his men to secure the room, then to check the three lifeless bodies.

"A servant found two of your men dead at the perimeter of your apartments. He ran immediately to the Regent's Guard. Your own men have yet to be informed."

"I gathered that," said Laurent.

They were rougher with Damen, manhandling him into a restraining grip like the ones he remembered from the early days of his capture. He surrendered to it, because what else could he do? He felt his hands pulled behind his back. A meaty hand clasped the back of his neck.

"Take him," said the soldier.

Laurent spoke very calmly. "May I ask why you are arresting my servant?"

The soldier in charge gave him an uncomprehending look.

"Your Highness—there was an attack—"

"Not by him."

"The weapons are Akielon," said one of the men.

"Your Highness, if there's been an Akielon attack against you, you can bet this one's in on it."

It was too neat by half. It was, Damen realised, exactly why the three assailants had brought him here: to be blamed.

Of course, they would have expected to survive the encounter, but their intentions held all the same. And Laurent, who spent his every waking moment searching for ways to have Damen humiliated, hurt or killed, had just been given the excuse he needed handed to him on a platter.

He could see—he could *feel*—that Laurent knew it. He could feel too how badly Laurent wanted it, wanted to see him taken, wanted to trump both Damen and his uncle. He bitterly regretted the impulse that had led him to save Laurent's life.

"You're misinformed," said Laurent. He sounded like he was tasting something unpleasant. "There has been no attack against me. These three men attacked the slave, claiming some sort of barbarian dispute."

Damen blinked.

"They attacked—the slave?" said the soldier, who was apparently having almost as much difficulty digesting this information as Damen.

"Release him, soldier," Laurent said.

But the hands on him didn't let go. The Regent's men didn't take orders from Laurent. The soldier in charge actually shook his head slightly at the man holding Damen, negating Laurent's order.

"Forgive me, Your Highness, but until we can be sure of your safety, I would be negligent if I didn't—"

"You've been negligent," said Laurent.

This statement, calmly delivered, caused a silence, which the soldier in charge weathered, flinching only a little. It was probably why he was in charge. The grip on Damen slackened noticeably.

Laurent said, "You've arrived late and manhandled my property. By all means, compound your faults by arresting the goodwill gift of the King of Akielos. Against my orders."

The hands on Damen lifted. Laurent didn't wait for an acknowledgement from the soldier in charge.

"I require a moment of privacy. You can use the time until dawn to clear my apartments and inform my own men of the attack. I'll send for one of them when I'm ready."

"Yes, Your Highness," said the soldier in charge. "As you wish. We'll leave you to your rooms."

As the soldiers made the first movements towards leaving, Laurent said, "I assume I am to drag these three derelicts out myself?"

The soldier in charge flushed. "We'll remove them. Of course. Is there anything else you require from us?"

"Haste," said Laurent.

The men complied. It was not long before the table was righted, the goblet returned to its place. The pieces of fine ceramic were swept into a neat pile. The bodies were removed, and the blood was mopped at, in most cases ineffectually.

Damen had never before seen half a dozen soldiers reduced to compliant housekeeping by the sheer force of one man's personal arrogance. It was almost instructive.

Halfway through the proceedings, Laurent stepped back to lean his shoulders against the wall.

Finally, the men were gone.

The room had been superficially righted, but had not been returned to its former tranquil beauty. It had the air of a sanctuary disturbed, but it was not only the atmosphere that was disrupted; there were tangible blots on the landscape, too. The men were soldiers, not house servants. They had missed more than one spot.

Damen could feel the beat of his pulse, but he could not make sense of his own feelings, let alone of what had happened. The violence, the killing and the bizarre lies that had followed had been too sudden. His eyes scrolled around the room, surveying the damage.

His gaze snagged on Laurent, who was watching him in return rather warily.

Asking to be left alone for the rest of the night really didn't make much sense.

Nothing that had happened tonight made any sense, but there was one thing that, while the soldiers performed their work, Damen had come slowly to realise. Laurent's posture was perhaps slightly more exaggerated than his usual insouciant lean. Damen tipped his head to one side and gave Laurent a long, scrutinising look all the way down to his boots, then back up again.

"You're wounded."

"No."

Damen didn't remove his gaze. Any man but Laurent would have flushed or looked away or given some sign that he was lying. Damen half-expected it, even from Laurent.

Laurent returned the look, and then some. "If you mean excluding your attempt to break my arm."

"I mean excluding my attempt to break your arm," said Damen.

Laurent was not, as Damen had first thought, drunk. But

if you looked closely, he was controlling his breathing, and there was a faint, slightly febrile look in his eyes.

Damen took a step forward. He stopped when he ran into a blue-eyed look like a wall.

"I would prefer you to stand further away," said Laurent, each word finely chiselled, as though in marble.

Damen swung his gaze over to the goblet that had been knocked over during the fight, its contents spilt; the Regent's men, unthinkingly, had righted it. When he looked back, he knew from Laurent's expression that he was right.

"Not wounded. Poisoned," said Damen.

"You can restrain your delight. I am not going to die from it," said Laurent.

"How do you know that?"

But Laurent, delivering him a killing look, refused to elaborate.

He told himself, feeling oddly detached, that it was no more than justice: Damen perfectly recalled the experience of being doused with a drug then thrown into a fight. He wondered if the drug was chalis. Could it be drunk as well as inhaled? It explained why the three men had been so casually assured of their own success in tackling Laurent.

It also lay the blame all the more firmly at his own feet, Damen realised. It was sordidly believable that he would revenge himself on Laurent with the same tactics that Laurent had thrown at him.

This place sickened him. Anywhere else, you simply killed your enemy with a sword. Or poisoned him, if you had the honourless instincts of an assassin. Here, it was layer upon layer of constructed double-dealing, dark, polished and unpleasant. He would have assumed tonight the product of Laurent's own mind, if Laurent were not so clearly the victim.

What was really going on?

Damen went over to the goblet and lifted it. A shallow slide of liquid remained in the cup. It was water, surprisingly, not wine. That was why the thin rim of pinked colour on the inside of the cup was visible. It was the distinctive mark of a drug Damen knew well.

"It's an Akielon drug," said Damen. "It's given to pleasure slaves, during training. It makes them—"

"I am aware of the effect of the drug," Laurent said, in a voice like cut glass.

Damen looked at Laurent with new eyes. The drug, in his own country, was infamous. He had sampled it himself, once, as a curious sixteen-year-old. He had taken only a fraction of a normal dose, and it had provided him with an embarrassment of virility for several hours, exhausting three cheerfully tumbled partners. He had not bothered with it since. A stronger dose led from virility to abandonment. To leave residue in the goblet, the amount had been generous, even if Laurent had taken only a mouthful.

Laurent was hardly abandoned. He was not speaking with his usual ease, and his breathing was shallow, but these were the only signs.

Damen realised, suddenly, that what he was witnessing was an exercise in sheer iron-willed self-control.

"It wears off," said Damen. Adding, because he was not

above enjoying the truth as a form of minor sadism, "After a few hours."

He could see in the look Laurent levelled at him that Laurent would rather have cut off his own arm than have anyone know about his condition; and further, that he was the last person Laurent wished to know, or be left alone with. Damen was not above enjoying that fact either.

"Think I'm going to take advantage of the situation?" said Damen.

Because the one thing that emerged clearly from whatever tangled Veretian plot had unfolded this evening was the fact that he was free of restraints, free of obligations, and unguarded for the first time since his arrival in this country.

"I am. It was good of you to clear your apartments," said Damen. "I thought I'd never have the chance to get out of here."

He turned. Behind him, Laurent swore. Damen was halfway to the door before Laurent's voice turned him back.

"Wait," said Laurent, as though he forced the word out, and hated saying it. "It's too dangerous. Leaving now would be seen as an admission of guilt. The Regent's Guard wouldn't hesitate to have you killed. I can't . . . protect you, as I am now."

"Protect me," said Damen, flat incredulity in his voice.

"I am aware that you saved my life."

Damen just stared at him.

Laurent said: "I dislike feeling indebted to you. Trust that, if you don't trust me."

"Trust you?" said Damen. "You flayed the skin from my back. I have seen you do nothing but cheat and lie to every person you've encountered. You use anything and anyone to further your own ends. You are the last person I would ever trust."

Laurent's head tipped backwards against the wall. His eyelids had dropped to half-mast, so that he regarded Damen through two golden-lashed slits. Damen was half-expecting a denial, or an argument. But Laurent's only reply was a breath of laughter, which strangely showed more than anything else how close to the edge he was.

"Go, then."

Damen looked again at the door.

With the Regent's men on heightened alert, there was real danger, but escape would always mean risking everything. If he hesitated now and waited for another chance . . . if he managed to find a way out of the perpetual restraints, if he killed his guard or got past them some other way . . .

Right now Laurent's apartments were empty. He had a head start. He knew a way out of the palace. A chance like this one might not come again for weeks, or months, or at all.

Laurent would be left alone and vulnerable in the aftermath of an attempt on his life.

But the immediate danger was past, and Laurent had lived through it. Others had not. Damen had killed tonight, and witnessed killing. Damen set his jaw. Whatever debt was between them had been paid. He thought, I don't owe him anything.

The door opened beneath his hand, and the corridor was empty.

He went.

CHAPTER ELEVEN

H E KNEW OF only one sure way out, and that was through the courtyard from the first-floor training arena.

He forced himself to walk calmly and purposefully, like a servant who has been sent on an errand for his master. His mind was full of slit throats and close fighting and knives. He pushed all of that down and thought instead about his path through the palace. The passage was empty at first.

Passing his own room was strange. It had surprised him from the moment he'd been moved there how close his room was to Laurent's, nestled inside Laurent's own apartments. The doors were slightly ajar, as they had been left by the three men who now lay dead. It looked—empty and wrong. Out of some instinct, perhaps an instinct to hide the telltale signs of his own escape, Damen stopped to close them. When he turned, there was someone watching him.

Nicaise was standing in the middle of the passage, as though brought up short on his way to Laurent's bedchamber.

Somewhere distant, the urge to laugh accompanied a spill of tight, ridiculous panic. If Nicaise reached it—if he sounded the alarm—

Damen had prepared himself for fighting men, not small boys with frothy silken over-robes thrown on top of bedshirts.

"What are you doing here?" said Damen, since one of them was going to say it.

"I was sleeping. Someone came and woke us up. They told the Regent there had been an attack," said Nicaise.

Us, thought Damen, sickly.

Nicaise took a step forward. Damen's stomach lurched and he stepped forward into the corridor, blocking Nicaise's path. He felt absurd. He said, "He ordered everyone out of his apartments. I wouldn't try to see him."

"Why not?" Nicaise said. He looked past Damen towards Laurent's chamber. "What happened? Is he all right?"

Damen thought of the most dissuasive argument he could make. "He's in a foul mood," he said, briefly. If nothing else, it was accurate.

"Oh," said Nicaise. And then, "I don't care. I just wanted to . . ." But then he lapsed into a weird silence, just staring at Damen without trying to get past him. What was he doing here? Every moment Damen spent with Nicaise was a moment in which Laurent could emerge from his chambers, or the guard could return. He felt the seconds of his life ticking past.

Nicaise lifted his chin and announced: "I don't care. I'm going back to bed." Except that he was just standing there, all brown curls and blue eyes, light from the occasional torches falling on every perfect plane of his face.

"Well? Go on," said Damen.

More silence. There was obviously something on Nicaise's mind, and he wouldn't leave until he said it. Eventually:

"Don't tell him I came."

"I won't," said Damen, with complete truthfulness. Once out of the palace, he didn't intend to see Laurent ever again.

More silence. Nicaise's smooth brow corrugated. Finally, he turned, and disappeared back down the passage.

◆ ◆ ◆

Then—

"You," came the command. "Stop."

He stopped. Laurent had ordered that his apartments be left empty, but Damen had reached the perimeter now, and faced the Regent's Guard.

He said, as calmly as he could, "The Prince sent me to fetch two men of his own guard to him. I assume they've been alerted."

So much could go wrong. Even if they did not stop him, they could send an escort with him. A hint of suspicion was all it would take.

The guard said, "Our orders are no one in or out."

"You can tell the Prince that," said Damen, "after you tell him you let through the Regent's pet."

That got a flicker of reaction. Invoking Laurent's bad mood was like a magical key, unlocking the most forbidding doors.

"Get on with it," said the guard.

Damen nodded, and walked away at a normal pace, feeling their eyes on his back. He couldn't relax, even when he got out of sight. He was continually aware of the palace activity around him as he walked. He passed two servants, who ignored him. He prayed that the training hall would be as he remembered it, remote, unguarded and empty.

◆ ◆ ◆

It was. He felt a rush of relief when he saw it, with its older fittings and sawdust scattered across the floor. In the centre stood the cross, a dark, solid bulk. Damen felt an aversion to going near it, his instinct to skirt around the periphery of the room rather than walk across it openly.

Disliking this reaction so much in himself, he deliberately took a precious few moments to walk over to the cross, to place a hand on the solid centre beam. He felt the immovable wood beneath his hand. He had somehow expected to see the quilted covering, darkened by sweat or blood—some sign of what had happened—but there was nothing. He looked up at the place where Laurent had stood and watched him.

There was no reason to have laced Laurent's drink with that particular drug if the intent had been only to incapacitate. Rape, therefore, was to have preceded murder. Damen had no idea whether he'd been intended as a participant or merely an observer. Both ideas sickened him. His own fate, as the supposed perpetrator, would probably have been even more drawn out than Laurent's, a long, lingering execution before crowds.

Drugs, and a trio of assailants. A scapegoat, brought in for the sacrifice. A servant running to inform the Regent's Guard at just the right time. It was a thorough plan, rendered shoddy by a failure to predict how Damen himself would react. And by underestimating Laurent's adamantine will resisting the drug.

And by being overly elaborate, but that was a common failing of the Veretian mind.

Damen told himself that Laurent's current predicament was not so terrible. In a court like this, Laurent could simply summon a pet to help relieve him of his difficulties. It was stubbornness if he didn't.

He didn't have time for this.

He left the cross. On the sidelines of the training area, close to one of the benches, there were a few mismatched pieces of armour, and a few pieces of old, discarded clothing. He was glad they were here as he had remembered, because outside the palace he would not go unnoticed in flimsy slave garments. Thanks to his close instruction in the baths, he was familiar with the foolish idiosyncrasies of Veretian clothing and could dress quickly. The pants were very old, and the fawn-coloured fabric was worn threadbare in places, but they fit. The ties were two long, thin strips of softened leather. He looked down while hurriedly tying and tightening them; they served both to close the open V and to create an external criss-cross of ornamentation.

The shirt didn't fit. But since it was in an even worse state of disrepair than the pants, with one of the sleeve seams already coming open along the join between sleeve and shoulder, it was easy to quickly tear the arms off, then tear a split in the collar, until it did fit. It was otherwise loose enough; it would cover the telltale scars on his back. He discarded his slave garments, hiding them out of the way behind the bench. The armour pieces were uniformly useless, consisting as they did of a helm, a rusted breastplate, a single shoulder guard and a few belts and buckles. A leather vambrace would have helped to hide his gold cuffs. It was a shame there weren't any. It was a shame there were no weapons.

He couldn't afford to look for other armaments; too much time had passed already. He headed for the roof.

◆ ◆ ◆

The palace did not make things easy for him.

There was no friendly route up and over, leading to a painless first-storey descent. The courtyard was surrounded by higher edifices that must be climbed.

Still, he was lucky this was not the palace at Ios, or any Akielon stronghold. Ios was a fortification, built on the cliffs, designed to repel intruders. There was no unguarded way down, excluding a beetling vertical drop of smooth white stone.

The Veretian palace, afroth with ornament, paid only lip service to defence. The parapets were purposeless curving decorative spires. The slippery domes that he skirted would be a nightmare in an attack, hiding one part of the roof from the other. Once, Damen used a machicolation as a handhold, but it seemed to have no function besides ornament. This was a place of residence, not a fort or a castle built to resist an army. Vere had fought its share of wars, its borders drawn and redrawn, but for two hundred years there had been no foreign army in the capital. The old defensive keep at Chastillon had been replaced, the court moving north to this new nest of luxury.

At the first sound of voices, he flattened himself against a parapet and thought, *Only two*, judging from the sounds of their feet and the voices. Only two meant he could still succeed, if he could do it quietly, if they did not sound an alarm. His pulse quickened. Their voices seemed casual, as though they were here for some routine reason, rather than part of a search party hunting down a lost prisoner. Damen waited, tense, and their voices grew distant.

The moon was up. To the right, the river Seraine, which oriented him: west. The town was a series of dark shapes with edges picked out in moonlight; sloping rooves and gables, balconies and gutters met one another in a chaotic, shadowed jumble. Behind him, the far-flung darkness of what must be the great northern forests. And to the south . . . to the south, past the dark shapes of the city, past the lightly wooded hills and rich central provinces of Vere, lay the border, prickling with true castles, Ravenel, Fortaine, Marlas . . . and across the border Delpha, and home.

Home.

Home, though the Akielos he had left behind him was not the Akielos he would return to. His father's reign was ended, and it was Kastor who at this moment lay sleeping in the King's chamber—with Jokaste beside him, if she had not yet begun her lying-in. Jokaste, her waist thickening with Kastor's child.

He took a steadying breath. His luck held. There was no sound of alarm from the palace, no search party on the roof or on the streets. His escape was unnoticed. And there was a way down, if you were prepared to climb.

It would feel good to test his physicality, to pit himself against an arduous challenge. When he had first arrived in Vere, he had been in peak condition, and staying fight-ready was something that he had worked at during long hours of confinement in which there was little else to do. But several weeks of slow recuperation from the lash had taken a toll. Tussling with two men of mediocre training was one thing, scaling a wall was something else altogether, a feat of stamina that drew continually on upper-arm strength and the muscles of the back.

His back, his weakness, newly healed and untested. He was unsure how much continual strain it could stand before muscle strength gave out. One way to find out.

Night would provide a cover for descent, but after that—night was not a good time to move through the streets of a city. Perhaps there was a curfew, or perhaps it was simply the custom here, but the streets of Arles looked empty and silent. One man creeping around at street level would stand out. By contrast, the grey light of dawn, with its accompanying bustle of activity, would be a perfect time for him to find his way out of the city. Perhaps he could even move earlier. An hour or so before dawn was an active time in any town.

But he had to get down first. After that, a darkened corner of the town—an alleyway or (back permitting) a rooftop—would be an ideal place to wait until the bustle of morning came. He was thankful that the men on the palace rooves were gone, and the patrols were not yet out.

* * *

The patrols were out.

The Regent's Guard burst out of the palace, mounted and carrying torches, only minutes after Damen's feet first touched the ground. Two dozen men on horses, split into two groups: exactly the right amount to wake a town. Hooves struck the cobblestones, lamps lit up, shutters banged open. Complaining shouts could be heard. Faces appeared at windows until, grumbling sleepily, they disappeared again.

Damen wondered who had finally sounded the alarm. Had Nicaise put two and two together? Had Laurent, emerging from his drugged stupor, decided he wanted his pet back? Had it been the Regent's Guard?

It didn't matter. The patrols were out, but they were loud and easy to avoid. It was not long before he was neatly ensconced on a rooftop, hidden between sloping tiles and chimney.

He looked at the sky and judged it would be another hour, perhaps.

* * *

The hour passed. One patrol was out of sight and earshot, the other was a few streets away, but retreating.

Dawn began threatening from the wings; the sky was no longer perfectly black. Damen couldn't stay where he was, crouched like a gargoyle, waiting while the light slowly exposed him like a curtain rising on an unexpected tableau. Around him, the town was waking. It was time to get down.

The alley was darker than the rooftop. He could make out several doorways of different shapes, the wood old, the stone mouldings crumbling. Other than that, it had only a dead end, piled with refuse. He preferred to get out of it.

One of the doors opened. He smelled a waft of perfume and stale beer. There was a woman in the doorway. She had curly brown hair, and a prettyish face from what he could see in the dark, and an ample chest, partially exposed.

Damen blinked. Behind her the shadowy shape of a man, and behind that, warm light from red-covered lamps, a particular atmosphere and faint sounds that were unmistakable.

Brothel. No hint of it on the outside, not even light coming from the shuttered windows, but if this act was a social taboo between unmarried men and women, it was understandable that a brothel be discreet, tucked out of sight.

The man didn't seem to have any self-consciousness about what he'd been doing, exiting with the heavy body language of one recently sated, hefting his pants. When he saw Damen, he stopped and gave him a look of impersonal territorialism. And then he really stopped, and the look changed.

And Damen's luck, which had so far held, deserted him in a rush.

Govart said, "Let me guess, I fucked one of yours, so you've come here to fuck one of mine."

The distant sound of hooves on the cobblestones was followed by the sound of voices coming from the same direction, the cries that had woken the town a complaining hour ahead of schedule.

"Or," said Govart, in the slow voice of one who nevertheless gets there in the end, "are *you* the reason the Guard's out?"

Damen avoided the first swing, and the second. He kept a distance between their bodies, remembering Govart's bearlike holds. The night was becoming an obstacle course of outlandish challenges. Stop an assassination. Scale a wall. Fight Govart. What else?

The woman, with her impressive, half-unclothed lung capacity, opened her mouth and screamed.

After that, things happened very quickly.

Three streets away, shouts and the clatter of hooves as the nearer patrol wheeled and made for the scream at full pelt. His only chance then was that they would miss the narrow opening of the alley. The woman realised this, too, and screamed again, then ducked inside. The brothel door slammed, and was bolted.

The alley was narrow and could not comfortably manage three horses abreast, but two was enough. As well as horses and torches, the patrol had crossbows. He couldn't resist, unless he wished to commit suicide.

Beside him, Govart was looking smug. He perhaps hadn't realised that if the guard fired on Damen, he was going to be collateral damage.

Somewhere behind the two horses, a man dismounted and came forward. It was the same soldier who had been in charge of the Regent's Guard in Laurent's apartments. More smugness. From the look on his face, being proven right about Damen had him extremely gratified.

"On your knees," said the soldier in charge.

Were they going to kill him here? If so, he would fight, though he knew, against this many men with crossbows, how the fight would end. Behind the soldier in charge, the mouth of the alley bristled like a pine with crossbow bolts. Whether they planned to do it or not, they would certainly kill him here if given a single reasonable excuse.

Damen went, slowly, to his knees.

It was dawn. The air had that still, translucent quality that came with sunrise, even in a town. He looked around himself. It wasn't a very pleasant alley. The horses didn't like it, more fastidious than the humans who lived there. He let a breath out.

"I arrest you for high treason," said the soldier. "for your part in the plot to assassinate the Crown Prince. Your life is forfeit to the Crown. The Council has spoken."

He had taken his chance, and it had led him here. He felt not fear but the hard tangled sensation between his ribs of freedom dangled before him then snatched from his grasp. What rankled the most was that Laurent had been right.

"Tie his hands," said the soldier in charge, tossing a piece of thin rope to Govart. Then he moved to one side, sword at Damen's neck, giving the men in range a clear shot with the bow.

"Move and die," said the soldier in charge. Which was an apt summary.

Govart caught the rope. If Damen was going to fight, he would have to do it now, before his hands were tied. He knew that, even as his mind, trained to fighting, saw the clear line to the crossbows and the twelve men on horseback, and returned with no tactic that would do more than make a commotion and a dent. Perhaps a few dents.

"The punishment for treason is death," said the soldier.

In the moments before his sword lifted, before Damen moved, before the last, desperate act played out in the filthy alley, there was another burst of hooves, and Damen had to force down a breath of disbelieving laughter, remembering the second half of the patrol. Arriving now, like an unnecessary flourish. Really, even Kastor hadn't sent as many men against him as this.

"Hold!" called a voice.

And in the dawn light, he saw that the men reining in their horses were not wearing the red cloaks of the Regent's Guard, but instead were turned out in blue and gold.

"It's the bitch's pups," said the soldier in charge, with total contempt.

Three of the Prince's Guard had forced their horses past the impromptu blockade and into the cramped space of the alley. Damen even recognised two of them, Jord in front on a bay gelding, and behind him the larger figure of Orlant.

"You've got something of ours," said Jord.

"The traitor?" said the soldier in charge. "You've no rights here. Leave now, and I'll let you go peacefully back."

"We're not the peaceful sort," said Jord. His sword was unsheathed. "We don't leave without the slave."

"You'd defy Council orders?" said the soldier in charge.

The soldier in charge, on foot, was left in the unenviable

position of facing down three riders. It was a small alley. And Jord had his sword out. Behind him, the reds and the blues were about equal in numbers. But the soldier in charge didn't seem fazed.

He said, "Drawing on the Regent's Guard is an act of treason."

In answer, with casual contempt, Orlant drew his sword. Instantly, metal flashed all along the ranks behind him. Crossbows bristled on both sides. Nobody breathed.

Jord said, "The Prince is before the Council. Your orders are an hour old. Kill the slave, and you'll be the next one with your head on the block."

"That's a lie," said the soldier in charge.

Jord pulled something out of a fold in his uniform, and dangled it. It was a councillor's medallion. It swung on its chain in the torchlight, glinting gold as a starburst.

Into the silence, Jord said, "Want to bet?"

✦ ✦ ✦

"You must be the fuck of a lifetime," said Orlant, just before he shoved Damen into the audience chamber where Laurent stood alone, in front of the Regent and Council.

It was the same diorama as last time, with the Regent enthroned and the Council in full dress, formidably arrayed alongside him, except that there were no courtiers thronging the chamber. It was just Laurent, alone, facing them. Damen immediately looked to see which councillor was missing his medallion. It was Herode.

Another shove. Damen's knees hit the carpet, which was

red like the cloaks of the Regent's Guard. He was right near a part of the tapestry where a boar was speared under a tree heavy with pomegranates.

He looked up.

"My nephew has argued for you very persuasively," said the Regent. And then, oddly echoing Orlant's words, "You must have hidden charm. Maybe it's your physique he finds so appealing. Or do you have other talents?"

Laurent's cold, calm voice: "Do you imply I take the slave into my bed? What a revolting suggestion. He's a brute soldier from Kastor's army."

Laurent had assumed, once again, the intolerable self-possession, and was dressed for a formal audience. He was not, as Damen had last seen him, languid and somnolent-eyed, head tipped back against a wall. The handful of hours that had passed since Damen's escape was enough time for the drug to have passed from his system. Probably. Though of course there was no way of telling how long Laurent had been in this room, arguing with the Council.

"Only a soldier? And yet, you've described the bizarre circumstance in which three men broke into your chambers in order to attack him," said the Regent. He regarded Damen briefly. "If he doesn't lie with you, what was he doing in your private space so late at night?"

The temperature, already cool, dropped sharply. "I don't lie in the cloying sweat of men from Akielos," said Laurent.

"Laurent. If there has been an Akielon attack against you that you are concealing for some reason, we must and will know about it. The question is serious."

"So was my answer. I don't know how this interrogation found its way into my bed. May I ask where I can expect it to travel next?"

The heavy folds of a state robe swathed the throne on which the Regent sat. With the curve of a finger, he stroked the line of his bearded jaw. He looked again at Damen, before returning his attention to his nephew.

"You wouldn't be the first young man to find himself at the mercy of a flush of new infatuation. Inexperience often confuses bedding with love. The slave could have convinced you to lie to us for him, having taken advantage of your innocence."

"Taken advantage of my innocence," said Laurent.

"We've all seen you favour him. Seated beside you at table. Fed by your own hand. Indeed, you've barely been seen without him, the last few days."

"Yesterday I brutalised him. Today I am swooning into his arms. I would prefer the charges against me to be consistent. Pick one."

"I don't need to pick one, nephew, you have a full range of vices, and inconsistency is the cap."

"Yes, apparently I have fucked my enemy, conspired against my future interests, and colluded in my own murder. I can't wait to see what feats I will perform next."

It was only by looking at the councillors that you could see this interview had been going on a long time. Older men, dragged out of their beds, they were all showing signs of weariness.

"And yet, the slave ran," said the Regent.

"Are we back to this?" said Laurent. "There was no assault against me. If I'd been attacked by four armed men, do you really think I would have survived, killing three? The slave ran for no more sinister reason than that he is difficult and rebellious. I believe I have mentioned his intractable nature to you— all of you—before. You chose to disbelieve me then also."

"It isn't a question of belief. This defence of the slave bothers me. It isn't like you. It speaks to an uncharacteristic attachment. If he has led you to sympathise with forces outside your own country—"

"Sympathise with *Akielos*?"

The cold disgust with which Laurent said these words was more persuasive than any hot burst of outrage. One or two of the councillors shifted in place.

Herode said, awkwardly, "I hardly think he could be accused of that, not when his father—and brother—"

"No one," said Laurent, "has more reason to oppose Akielos than I have. If Kastor's gift-slave had attacked me, it would be grounds for war. I would be overjoyed. I stand here for one reason only: the truth. You have heard it. I will not argue further. The slave is innocent or he is guilty. Decide."

"Before we decide," said the Regent. "You will answer this: If your opposition towards Akielos is genuine, as you maintain, if there is not some collusion, why do you continually refuse to do service on the border at Delfeur? I think, if you were as loyal as you claim, you would pick up your sword, gather what little there is of your honour, and do your duty."

"I," said Laurent.

The Regent sat back on the throne, spread his hands palm

down on the dark, carved wood of the curled armrests, and waited.

"I—don't see why that should be—"

It was Audin who said, "It *is* a contradiction."

"But one that's easily resolved," said Guion. Behind him, there were one or two murmurs of assent. Councillor Herode slowly nodded.

Laurent passed his gaze over each member of the Council.

Anyone appraising the situation at that moment would have seen how precarious it was. The councillors were weary of this argument and ready to accept any solution that the Regent was offering, however artificial it might seem.

Laurent had only two options: earn himself their censure by continuing a beleaguered wrangle mired in accusations and failure, or agree to border duty and get what he wanted.

More than that, it was late, and human nature being what it was, if Laurent did not agree to his uncle's offer, the councillors might turn on him simply for drawing this out further. And Laurent's loyalty was in question now, too.

Laurent said, "You're right, uncle. Avoiding my responsibilities has led you understandably to doubt my word. I will ride to Delfeur and fulfil my duty on the border. I dislike the idea that there are questions about my loyalty."

The Regent spread his hands in a pleased gesture.

"That answer must satisfy everyone," said the Regent. He received his agreement from the Council, five verbal affirmations, given one after the other, after which he looked at Damen, and said, "I believe we can acquit the slave, with no more questions about loyalty."

"I humbly submit to your judgement, uncle," said Laurent, "and to the judgement of the Council."

"Release the slave," the Regent ordered.

Damen felt hands at his wrists, unbinding the rope. It was Orlant, who had been standing behind him, this whole time. The motions were short jerks.

"There. It is done. Come," said the Regent to Laurent, extending his right hand. On the smallest finger was his ring of office, gold, capped with a red stone: ruby, or garnet.

Laurent came forward, and knelt before him gracefully, a single kneecap to the floor.

"Kiss it," said the Regent, and Laurent lowered his head in obedience to kiss his uncle's signet ring.

His body language was calm and respectful; the fall of his golden hair hid his expression. His lips touched the hard red kernel of the gem without haste, then parted from it. He did not rise. The Regent gazed down at him.

After a moment, Damen saw the Regent's hand lift again to rest in Laurent's hair and stroke it with slow, familiar affection. Laurent remained quite still, head bowed, as strands of fine gold were pushed back from his face by the Regent's heavy, ringed fingers.

"Laurent. Why must you always defy me? I hate it when we are at odds, yet you force me to chastise you. You seem determined to wreck everything in your path. Blessed with gifts, you squander them. Given opportunities, you waste them. I hate to see you grown up like this," said the Regent, "when you were such a lovely boy."

CHAPTER TWELVE

THE RARE MOMENT of avuncular affection ended the meeting, and the Regent and Council left the chamber. Laurent remained, rising from where he knelt, watching his uncle and the councillors file out. Orlant, who had bowed his way out after releasing Damen from his bonds, was gone also. They were alone.

Damen rose without thinking. He remembered after a second or two that he was supposed to wait for some sort of order from Laurent, but by then it was too late: He was on his feet and the words were out of his mouth.

"You lied to your uncle to protect me," he said.

Six feet of tapestried carpet lay between them. He didn't mean it the way it sounded. Or maybe he did. Laurent's eyes narrowed.

"Have I once again offended your high-minded principles?

Perhaps you can suggest a more wholesome détente. I seem to recall telling you not to wander off."

Damen could hear, distantly, the shock in his own voice. "I don't understand why you would do that to help me, when telling the truth would have served you far better."

"If you don't mind, I think I've heard enough said about my character for one night, or am I to go twelve rounds with you, too? I will."

"No, I—didn't mean—" What did he mean? He knew what he was supposed to say: gratitude from the rescued slave. It wasn't how he felt. He'd been so close. The only reason he'd been discovered at all was because of Govart, who would not be his enemy if not for Laurent. *Thank you*, meant thank you for being dragged back to be shackled and tied up inside this cage of a palace. Again.

Yet, unequivocally, Laurent had saved his life. Laurent and his uncle were close to being a match when it came to bloodless verbal brutality. Damen had felt exhausted just listening to it. He wondered exactly how long Laurent had stood his ground before he had been brought in.

I can't protect you as I am now, Laurent had said. Damen hadn't thought about what protection might entail, but he would never have imagined that Laurent would step into the ring on his behalf. And stay in it.

"I meant—that I am gratef—"

Laurent cut him off. "There is nothing further between us, certainly not *thanks*. Expect no future niceties from me. Our debt is clear."

But the slight frown with which Laurent regarded Damen

was not wholly one of hostility; it accompanied a long, searching look. After a moment:

"I meant it when I said I disliked feeling indebted to you." And then: "You had far less reason to help me than I did to help you."

"That's certainly true."

"You don't prettify what you think, do you?" said Laurent, still frowning. "A more artful man would. An artful man would have stayed put and won advantage by fostering the sense of obligation and guilt in his master."

"I didn't realise you had a sense of guilt," said Damen, bluntly.

An apostrophe appeared at one corner of Laurent's lips. He moved a few steps away from Damen, touching the worked armrest of the throne with his fingertips. And then, in a sprawling, relaxed posture, he sat down on it. "Well, take heart. I am riding to Delfeur, and we will be rid of each other."

"Why does the idea of border duty bother you so much?"

"I'm a coward, remember?"

Damen thought about that. "Are you? I don't think I've ever seen you shy away from a fight. More like the opposite."

The apostrophe deepened. "True."

"Then—"

Laurent said, "It doesn't concern you."

Another pause. Laurent's relaxed sprawl on the throne had a boneless quality, and Damen wondered, as Laurent continued to gaze at him, whether the drug still lingered in his veins. When Laurent spoke, the tone was conversational.

"How far did you get?"

"Not far. A brothel somewhere in the southern quarter."

"Had it really been that long since Ancel?"

The gaze had taken on a lazy quality. Damen flushed.

"I wasn't there for pleasure. I did have one or two other things on my mind."

"Pity," said Laurent, in an indulgent tone. "You should have taken your pleasure while you had the chance. I am going to lock you up so tightly you won't be able to breathe, let alone inconvenience me like this again."

"Of course," said Damen, in a different voice.

"I told you you shouldn't thank me," said Laurent.

◆ ◆ ◆

And so they took him back into his small, familiar, over-decorated room.

It had been a long, sleepless night, and he had a pallet and cushions on which to rest, but there was a feeling in his chest that prevented sleeping. As he looked around the room, the feeling intensified. There were two arched windows along the wall to his left, with low wide sills, each covered with patterned grilles. They looked out on the same gardens as Laurent's loggia, which he knew from the position of his room in Laurent's apartments, not from personal observation. His chain would not stretch far enough to give him a view. He could imagine below the tumbled water and cool greenery that characterised Veretian interior courtyards. But he could not see them.

What he could see, he knew. He knew every inch of this

room, every curl of the ceiling, every frond-curve of the window grille. He knew the opposite wall. He knew the unmovable iron link in the floor, and the drag of the chain, and its weight. He knew the twelfth tile that marked the limit of his movements when the chain pulled taut. It had all been exactly the same each and every day since his arrival, with a change only in the colour of the cushions on the pallet, which were whisked in and out as though from some inexhaustible supply.

Around mid-morning, a servant entered, bearing the morning meal, left him with it, and hastened away. The doors closed.

He was alone. The delicate platter contained cheeses, warm flaking breads, a handful of wild cherries in their own shallow silver dish, a pastry artfully shaped. Each item was considered, designed, so that the display of food, like everything else, was beautiful.

He threw it across the room in an expression of total violent impotent rage.

◆ ◆ ◆

He regretted this almost as soon as he'd done it. When the servant reentered later, and white-faced with nerves, began creeping around the edges of the room picking up cheese, he felt ridiculous.

Then, of course, Radel had to enter and view the disorder, fixing Damen with a familiar look.

"Throw as much food as you like. Nothing will change. For the duration of the Prince's stay at the border, you will not leave this room. The Prince's orders. You will wash here, and dress here, and remain here. The excursions you have enjoyed to banquets, to hunts and to the baths are ended. You will not be let off that chain."

For the duration of the Prince's stay at the border. Damen closed his eyes briefly.

"When does he leave?"

"Two days hence."

"How long will he be gone?"

"Several months."

It was incidental information to Radel, who spoke the words oblivious to their effect on Damen. Radel dropped a small pile of clothing onto the ground.

"Change."

Damen must have shown some reaction in his expression, because Radel continued: "The Prince dislikes you in Veretian clothing. He ordered the offense remedied. They are clothes for civilised men."

He changed. He picked up the clothes Radel had dropped from their little folded pile, not that there was much fabric to fold. It was back to slave garments. The Veretian clothing in which he'd escaped was removed by the servants as though it had never been.

Time, excruciatingly, passed.

That one brief glimpse of freedom made him ache for the world outside this palace. He was aware, too, of an illogical frustration: Escape, he had thought, would end in freedom or death—but whatever the outcome, it would make some kind of difference. Except now he was *back here*.

How was it possible that all the fantastical events of last night had affected no change in his circumstances at all?

The idea of being trapped inside this room for several months—

Perhaps it was natural, trapped like a fly in this filigree web, that his mind should fixate on Laurent, with his spider's brain under the yellow hair. Last night, Damen had not given much thought to Laurent or the plot that centred on him: His mind had been filled with thoughts of escape; he'd had neither the time nor the inclination to muse on Veretian treachery.

But now he was alone with nothing to think about except the strange, bloody attack.

And so, as the sun climbed its way from morning to afternoon, he found himself remembering the three men, with their Veretian voices and Akielon knives. *These three men attacked the slave,* Laurent had said. Laurent needed no reason to lie, but why deny he'd been attacked at all? It helped the perpetrator.

He remembered Laurent's calculating cut with the knife, and the struggle after, Laurent's body hard with resistance, the breath in his chest drug-quickened. There were easier ways to kill a prince.

Three men, armed with weapons from Sicyon. The Akielon gift-slave brought in to be blamed. The drug, the planned rape. And Laurent, winnowing around talking. And lying. And killing.

He understood.

He felt, momentarily, as though the floor was sliding out from under him, the world rearranging itself.

It was simple and obvious. It was something he should have seen straight away—would have seen, if he had not been blinded by the need to escape. It lay before him, dark and consummate in design and intent.

There was no way out of this room, so he had to wait, and wait, and wait, until the next gorgeous platter. He gave all his thanks that the silent servant was accompanied by Radel.

He said, "I have to talk to the Prince."

◆ ◆ ◆

The last time he had made a request like this Laurent had appeared promptly, in court clothes, with brushed hair. Damen expected no less now, in these urgent circumstances, and he scrambled up from the pallet when the door was pushed open no more than an hour later.

Into his room, alone, dismissing the guards, came the Regent.

He entered with the slow strolling walk of a lord touring his lands. This time there were no councillors, no retinue, no ceremony. The overwhelming impression remained one of authority; the Regent had an imposing physical presence, and his shoulders wore the robes well. The silver shot through his dark hair and beard spoke to his experience. He was not Laurent, lounging idly on the throne. He was to his nephew as a warhorse to a show pony.

Damen made his obeisance.

"Your Highness," he said.

"You're a man. Stand," said the Regent.

He did so, slowly.

"You must be relieved that my nephew is leaving," said the Regent. It was not a good question to answer.

"I'm sure he'll do honour to his country," said Damen.

The Regent gazed at him. "You are quite diplomatic. For a soldier."

Damen took a steadying breath. This high, the air was thin.

"Your Highness," he said, submissively.

"I wait for a real answer," said the Regent.

Damen made the attempt. "I'm—glad he does his duty. A prince should learn how to lead men before he becomes a king."

The Regent considered his words. "My nephew is a difficult case. Most men would think that leadership was a quality that ran naturally in the blood of a king's heir—not something that must be forced on him against his own flawed nature. But then, Laurent was born a second son."

So were you, came the thought, unbidden. The Regent made Laurent feel like a warm-up. He was not here for an exchange of views, whatever it might look like. For a man of his status to visit a slave at all was unlikely and bizarre.

"Why don't you tell me what happened last night?" said the Regent.

"Your Highness. You already have the story from your nephew."

"Perhaps, in the confusion, there was something my nephew misunderstood, or left out," said the Regent. "He is not used to fighting, as you are."

Damen was silent, though the urge to speak dragged at him like an undertow.

"I know your first instinct is to honesty," said the Regent. "You will not be penalised for it."

"I—" said Damen.

There was movement in the doorway. Damen shifted his gaze, almost with a guilty start.

"Uncle," said Laurent.

"Laurent," said the Regent.

"Did you have some business with my slave?"

"Not business," said the Regent. "Curiosity."

Laurent came forward with the twinned deliberation and disinterest of a cat. It was impossible to tell how much he had overheard.

"He isn't my lover," said Laurent.

"I'm not curious about what you do in bed," said the Regent. "I'm curious about what happened in your rooms last night."

"Hadn't we settled that?"

"Half-settled. We never heard the slave's account."

"Surely," said Laurent, "you wouldn't value a slave's word over mine?"

"Wouldn't I?" said the Regent. "Even your tone of surprise is feigned. Your brother could be trusted. Your word is a tarnished rag. But you can rest easy. The slave's account matches yours, as far as it goes."

"Did you think there was some deeper plot here?" said Laurent.

They gazed at each other. The Regent said, "I only hope

your time on the border will improve and focus you. I hope
you will learn what you need as the leader of other men. I
don't know what else I can teach you."

"You keep offering me all these chances to improve
myself," said Laurent. "Teach me how to thank you."

Damen expected the Regent to reply, but he was silent,
his eyes on his nephew.

Laurent said, "Will you come to see me off tomorrow,
uncle?"

"Laurent. You know I will," said the Regent.

◆ ◆ ◆

"Well?" said Laurent when his uncle had left. The steady
blue gaze was on him. "If you ask me to rescue a kitten from
a tree, I'm going to refuse."

"I don't have a petition. I just wanted to speak with you."

"Fond goodbyes?"

"I know what happened last night," said Damen.

Laurent said, "Do you?"

It was the tone he used with his uncle. Damen drew a
breath.

"So do you. You killed the survivor before he could be
interrogated," said Damen.

Laurent moved to the window and sat, arranging himself
on the sill. His pose was side-saddle. The fingers of one hand
slid idly into the ornate grillework that covered the window.
The last of the day's sunlight lay on his hair and face like
bright coins, shaped by the fretted openings. He gazed at
Damen.

"Yes," Laurent said.

"You killed him because you didn't want him interrogated. You knew what he was going to say. You didn't want him to say it."

After a moment: "Yes."

"I assume he was to say that Kastor sent him."

The scapegoat was Akielon, and the weapons were Akielon: Every detail had been carefully arranged to throw the blame southward. For verisimilitude, the assassins would also have been told they were agents of Akielos.

"Better for Kastor to have friend uncle on the throne than nephew prince who hates Akielos," said Laurent.

"Except that Kastor can't afford war now, not with dissent among the kyroi. If he wanted you dead, he'd do it secretly. He'd never send assassins like this: crudely armed with Akielon weapons, announcing their provenance. Kastor didn't hire those men."

"No," agreed Laurent.

He'd known, but to hear it was another matter, and the confirmation sent a shock down into him. In the warmth of the late afternoon, he felt himself turn cold.

"Then . . . war was the aim," he said. "A confession like that—if your uncle heard it, he would have no choice but to retaliate. If you'd been found—" Raped by an Akielon slave. Murdered by Akielon knives. "Someone is trying to provoke war between Akielos and Vere."

"You have to admire it," said Laurent, in a detached voice. "It's the perfect time to attack Akielos. Kastor is dealing with factional problems from the kyroi. Damianos, who turned the tide at Marlas, is dead. And the whole of Vere would rise up against a bastard, especially one who had cut down a Veretian prince. If only my murder weren't the catalyst, it's a scheme I would wholeheartedly support."

Damen stared at him, his stomach churning in distaste at the casual words. He ignored them; ignored the final honeyed tones of regret.

Because Laurent was right: the timing was perfect. Pit a galvanised Vere against a fractured, feuding Akielos, and his country would fall. Worse, it was the northern provinces that were unstable—Delpha, Sicyon—the very provinces that lay closest to the Veretian border. Akielos was a powerful military force when the kyroi were united under a single king, but if that bond dissolved, it was no more than a collection of city states with provincial armies, none of which could stand against a Veretian attack.

In his mind's eye he saw the future: the long train of Veretian troops moving southward, the provinces of Akielos falling one by one. He saw Veretian soldiers streaming through the palace at Ios, Veretian voices echoing in his father's hall.

He looked at Laurent.

"Your welfare hinges on this plot. If only for your own sake, don't you want it stopped?"

"I have stopped it," said Laurent. The astringent blue gaze was resting on him.

"I meant," said Damen, "can't you put aside whatever family quarrel you have and speak honestly to your uncle?"

He felt Laurent's surprise, transmitting itself through the air. Outside, the light was just beginning to turn orange.

"I don't think that would be wise," said Laurent.

"Why not?"

"Because," said Laurent, "the murderer is my uncle."

CHAPTER THIRTEEN

B UT, IF THAT'S true—" Damen began.

It was true; it was somehow not even a surprise, more like a truth that had grown for some time on the edge of his awareness, now brought into sharp relief. He thought: two thrones for the price of a few hired swords and a dose of pleasure drug. He remembered Nicaise, appearing in the hallway with his huge blue eyes, wearing bed clothes.

"You can't go to Delfeur," Damen said. "It's a death trap."

The moment he said it, he understood that Laurent had always known this. He recalled Laurent avoiding border duty again, and again, and again.

"You'll forgive me if I don't take tactical advice from a slave, scant moments after he is dragged back from a failed attempt to escape."

"You can't go. It isn't just a matter of staying alive. You forfeit the throne as soon as you set foot outside the city. Your uncle will hold the capital. He has already—" Casting his mind back over the Regent's actions, Damen saw the series of moves that had led to this, each one played out precisely, and far in advance. "He has already cut off your supply lines through Varenne and Marche. You don't have finances or troops."

The words were an unfolding realisation. It was clear now why Laurent had worked to exonerate his slave and obfuscate the attack. If war was declared, Laurent's life expectancy would be even shorter than it was going to be in Delfeur. To actually ride out to the border with a company of his uncle's men was madness.

"Why are you doing this? Is it a forced move? You can't think of a way around it?" Damen searched Laurent's face. "Is your reputation so far in the dirt that you think the Council will choose your uncle for the throne anyway, unless you prove yourself?"

"You are right on the edge of what I will allow from you," said Laurent.

"Take me with you to Delfeur," said Damen.

"No."

"Akielos is my country. Do you think I want her overrun by your uncle's troops? I will do anything in my power to prevent war. Take me with you. You will need someone you can trust."

Speaking those last words, he almost winced, immediately regretting them. Laurent had asked him for trust last night, and he had thrown the words back in his face. He would receive the same treatment.

Laurent just gave him a blankly curious look. "Why would I need that?"

Damen stared at him, suddenly aware that if he asked, "Do you think you can juggle attempts on your life, military command, and your uncle's tricks and traps by yourself?" The answer was going to be: Yes.

"I would have thought," said Laurent, "that a soldier like you would be quite happy to see Kastor dethroned, after all he's done to you. Why not side with the Regency against him—and against me? I'm sure my uncle has approached you to spy for him, on very generous terms."

"He has." Remembering the banquet: "He asked me to bed you, then report back to him." Damen was forthright. "Not in those words."

"And your answer?"

That, unreasonably, annoyed him. "If I'd bedded you, you'd know it."

There was a dangerous, narrow-eyed pause. Eventually: "Yes. Your style of grabbing your partner and kicking their legs open does stand out in the memory."

"That isn't—" Damen set his jaw, in no mood to get drawn into one of Laurent's infuriating exchanges. "I'm an asset. I know the region. I will do whatever it takes to stop your uncle." He looked into the impersonal blue gaze. "I've helped you before. I can again. Use me however you will. Just—take me with you."

"You're hot to help me? The fact that we ride towards Akielos factors in your request not at all?"

Damen flushed. "You will have one more person standing between you and your uncle. Isn't that what you want?"

"My dear brute," said Laurent, "I want you to rot here."

Damen heard the metallic sound of the chain links before he realised that he had jerked against his restraints. They were Laurent's parting words, spoken with relish. Laurent had turned for the door.

"You can't *leave me here* while you ride off into your uncle's trap. There's more than your life at stake." The words were harsh with frustration.

They had no effect; he could not prevent Laurent leaving. Damen swore.

"Are you that sure of yourself?" Damen called after him. "I think if you could beat your uncle on your own, you would have done it already."

Laurent stopped in the doorway. Damen saw the cupped yellow of his head, the straight line of his back and shoulders. But Laurent didn't turn back to face him; the hesitation only lasted for a moment before he continued out the door.

Damen was left to jerk once more, painfully, at the chains, alone.

◆ ◆ ◆

Laurent's apartments filled with the sounds of preparation, the hallways busy, men tramping to and fro in the delicate garden below. It was no small task to arrange an armed expedition in two days. Everywhere, there was activity.

Everywhere except here, in Damen's rooms, where the only knowledge of the mission came from the sounds outside.

Laurent was leaving tomorrow. Laurent, infuriating, intolerable Laurent, was pursuing the worst possible course, and there was nothing Damen could do to stop him.

The Regent's plans were impossible to guess. Damen had frankly no idea why he had waited as long as he had to move against his nephew. Was Laurent simply lucky that the Regent's ambitions spanned two kingdoms? The Regent could have dispensed with his nephew years ago, with little fuss. It was easier to blame the death of a boy on mischance than that of a young man about to ascend to the throne. Damen could see no reason why boy-Laurent should have escaped that fate. Perhaps familial loyalty had held the Regent back . . . until Laurent had blossomed into poisonous maturity, sly-natured and unfit to rule. If that was the case, Damen felt a certain amount of empathy with the man: Laurent could inspire homicidal tendencies simply by breathing.

It was a family of vipers. Kastor, he thought, had no idea what lay across the border. Kastor had embraced an alliance with Vere. He was vulnerable, ill-equipped to fight a war, the bonds within his own country showing cracks to which a foreign power had only to apply pressure.

The Regent must be stopped, Akielos must be rallied, and for that, Laurent must survive. It was impossible. Stuck here, Damen was powerless to act. And whatever cunning Laurent possessed was neutralised by the arrogance that prevented him from grasping how completely his uncle had him outmatched, once he left the capital to go traipsing across the countryside.

Did Laurent really believe he could do this alone?

Laurent would need every weapon at his disposal in order to navigate this course alive. Yet Damen had not been able to persuade him of that. He was aware, not for the first time, of a fundamental inability to communicate with Laurent. It was not only that he was navigating a foreign language. It was as though Laurent was an entirely other species of animal. He had nothing but the stupid hope that somehow Laurent would change his mind.

The sun slid slowly across the sky outside, and in Damen's locked chamber the shadows cast by the furniture moved in a dawdling semicircle.

It happened in the hours before dawn the next morning. He woke to find servants in his room, and Radel, the overseer who never slept.

"What is it? Is there some word from the Prince?"

He pushed himself up, one arm braced among the cushions, hand fisting in silk. He felt himself being manhandled before he was fully upright, the hands of the servants on him, and instinct almost shrugged them off, until he realised they were unlocking his restraints. The chain ends fell with a muffled chink into the cushions.

"Yes. Change," said Radel, and dropped a bundle unceremoniously down onto the floor beside him, much as he had done the night before.

Damen felt the thudding of his heart as he looked down at it.

Veretian clothing.

It was a clear message. The long, drawn-out frustration of the last day meant that he almost couldn't absorb it, couldn't trust it. He bent slowly to pick the clothes up. The pants resembled those he had found in the training arena, but were very soft and very fine, of a quality well beyond that of the threadbare pair he had hurried into that night. The shirt was made to fit. The boots looked like riding boots.

He looked back at Radel.

"Well? Change," said Radel.

He put a hand to the fastening at his waist, and felt a bemused curve tug at his mouth as Radel somewhat awkwardly averted his eyes.

Radel only interrupted once, "No, not like that," and shooed his hands away, gesturing for a servant to step forward and retie some idiotic piece of lacing.

"Are we—?" Damen began, as the last lace was tied to Radel's satisfaction.

"The Prince ordered you brought down into the courtyard, dressed to ride. You'll be fitted for the rest there."

"The rest?" Dryly. He looked down at himself. It was already more clothing than he had worn at any one time since his capture in Akielos.

Radel didn't answer, just made a sharp gesture for him to follow.

After a moment, Damen did, feeling a strange awareness of the lack of restraints.

The rest? he'd asked. He did not think much about that, as they wound their way through the palace to emerge in an outer courtyard near the stables. Even if he had, he would not have come up with the answer. It was so unlikely that it simply didn't occur to him—until he saw with his own eyes—and even then, he almost didn't believe it. He almost laughed aloud. The servant who came forward to meet them had his arms full of leather, straps and buckles, and some larger, hardened leather pieces, the largest with chest mouldings.

It was armour.

◆ ◆ ◆

The courtyard by the stables was filled with the activity of servants and armourers, stableboys and pages, the shout of orders, the chinking sounds of saddlery. Punctuating these was the discharge of breath through equine nostrils, and the occasional strike of a hoof against paving.

Damen recognised several faces. There were the men who had guarded him in stony-faced twos throughout his confinement. There was the physician who had tended his back, now out of his floor-length robes and dressed for riding. There was Jord who had waved Herode's medallion in the alleyway and saved his life. He saw a familiar servant ducking riskily under the belly of one of the horses on some errand, and across the courtyard he caught a glimpse of a man with a black moustache who he knew from the hunt as a horse-master.

The predawn air was cool, but soon it would warm. The season was ripening from spring into summer: a good time for a campaign. In the south, of course, it would be hotter. He flexed his fingers and deliberately straightened his back, let the feeling of freedom sink down into him, a powerful physical sensation. He was not particularly thinking of escape. He would, after all, be riding with a contingent of heavily armed men, and besides, there was now another urgent priority. For now it was enough that he was unshackled and outside in the open air, and that very soon the sun would rise, warming leather and skin, and they would mount up, and ride.

It was light riding armour, with enough nonessential decoration that he took it to be parade armour. The servant told him, yes, they would properly equip at Chastillon. His fitting took place by the stable doors, near to a water pump.

The last buckle was tightened. Then, startlingly, he was given a sword belt. Even more startlingly, he was given a sword to put in it.

It was a good sword. Under the decoration, it was good armour, though not what he was used to. It felt . . . foreign. He touched the starburst pattern at his shoulder. He was dressed in Laurent's colours, and bearing his insignia. That was a strange feeling. He had never thought he would ride out under a Veretian banner.

Radel, who had departed on some errand, now returned, to give him a list of duties.

Damen listened with part of his mind. He was to be a functional member of the company, he would report to his ranking senior, who would report to the Captain of the Guard, who in turn would report to the Prince. He was to serve and obey, as any man. He would also have the additional duties of attendant. In that capacity, he would report directly to the Prince. The duties described to him seemed to be a mixture of man-at-arms, adjutant and bed slave—ensuring the Prince's safety, attending to his personal comfort, sleeping in his tent— Damen's whole attention swung back to Radel.

"Sleeping in his *tent*?"

"Where else?"

He passed a hand over his face. Laurent had agreed to this?

The list continued. Sleeping in his tent, carrying his messages, attending to his needs. He would be paying for any relative freedom with a period of enforced proximity to Laurent.

With the other part of his mind, Damen surveyed the activity in the courtyard. It was not a large group. When you looked past the ruckus, it was the supplies for perhaps fifty men, armed to the teeth. At most, seventy-five, more lightly armed.

Those he recognised were Prince's Guard. The majority of them, at least, would be loyal. Not all of them. This was Vere. Damen drew in a breath and let it out, looking at each of the faces and wondering which of them had been coaxed or coerced into the employ of the Regent.

How the taint of this place had sunk down into his bones: He was certain betrayal would come; he was only unsure from where.

He thought logistically about what it would take to ambush and slaughter this number of men. It would not be discreet, but it would also not be difficult. At all.

"This can't be everyone," said Damen.

He spoke to Jord, who had come to splash his face with some water from the nearby pump. It was his first concern: too few men.

"It isn't. We ride to Chastillon and form up with the

Regent's men stationed there," said Jord, adding, "Don't get your hopes up. It's hardly much more than this."

"Not enough to make a dent in a real battle. Enough for the Regent's men to outnumber the Prince's several to one," was Damen's guess.

"Yes," said Jord, shortly.

He looked at Jord's dripping face, the set of his shoulders. He wondered if the Prince's Guard knew what they were facing: outright treachery at worst, and at best, months on the road, subject to the rule of the Regent's men. The thin line of Jord's mouth suggested that they did.

Damen said, "I owe you my thanks for the other night."

Jord gave him a steady look. "I was following orders. The Prince wanted you back alive, like he wants you here. I just hope he knows what he's doing with you and that he's not like the Regent says, distracted by his first taste of cock."

After a long moment, Damen said, "Whatever else you think, I don't share his bed."

It was not a new insinuation. Damen wasn't sure why it rankled so much now. Perhaps because of the uncanny speed with which the Regent's speculations had spread from the audience chamber to the guard. The rewording smacked of Orlant.

"However you've turned his head, he sent us right to you."

"I won't ask how he knew where to find me."

"I didn't send them after you," said the cool, familiar voice. "I sent them after the Regent's Guard, who were making enough racket to raise the dead, the drunk, and those without ears."

"Your Highness," said Jord, red. Damen turned.

"If I'd sent them after you," said Laurent, "I would have told them you went out the only way you knew, through the courtyard off the northern training arena. Did you?"

"Yes," said Damen.

The predawn light bleached Laurent's hair from gold to something paler and finer; the bones of his face appeared as delicate as the calamus of a feather. He was relaxed against the doorway of the stables as though he'd been there quite a while, which would explain the colour of Jord's face. He must have come not indolently from the direction of the palace, but from the stables, long up, attending to some other matter. He was dressed for the day in riding leathers, the severity of which ruthlessly cancelled out any effect of the fragile light.

Damen had half-expected a gaudy parade costume, but Laurent had always defined himself against the opulence of the court. And he did not need gilt to be recognised under a parade standard, only the uncovered bright of his hair.

Laurent paced forward. His eyes passed over Damen in turn, displaying jagged distaste. Seeing him in armour seemed to have drawn something unpleasant from the depths.

"Too civilised?"

"Hardly," said Laurent.

About to speak, Damen caught sight of Govart's familiar form. Immediately, he stiffened.

"What is he doing here?"

"Captaining the Guard."

"What?"

"Yes, it's an interesting arrangement, isn't it?" said Laurent.

"You should throw him a pet to keep him off the men," said Jord.

"No," said Laurent, after a moment. He said it thoughtfully.

"I'll tell the servants to sleep with their legs closed," said Jord.

"And Aimeric," said Laurent.

Jord gave a snort. Damen, who didn't know the man in question, followed Jord's eyes to one of the soldiers on the far side of the courtyard. Brown hair, reasonably young, reasonably attractive. Aimeric.

"Speaking of pets," said Laurent in a different voice.

Jord bowed his head and moved off, his part done. Laurent had noticed the small figure on the periphery of the activity. Nicaise, wearing a simple white tunic, his face free of paint, had come out into the courtyard. His arms and legs were bare, his feet in sandals. He picked his way towards them, until he faced Laurent, and then he just stood there, looking up. His hair was a careless tumble. Under his eyes were the faintest shadows, mark of a sleepless night.

Laurent said, "Come to see me off?"

"No," said Nicaise.

He held out something to Laurent, the gesture peremptory and full of repugnance.

"I don't want it. It makes me think of you."

Blue, limpid, twin sapphires dangled from his fingers. It

was the earring he'd worn to the banquet. And which he'd lost, spectacularly, in a bet. Nicaise held it away from himself as though it was made of something fetid.

Laurent took it without saying anything. He tucked it carefully into a fold of his riding clothes. Then after a moment, he reached out, and touched Nicaise's chin with one knuckle.

"You look better without all the paint," said Laurent.

It was true. Without the paint, Nicaise's beauty was like an arrow-shaft to the heart. He had something of that in common with Laurent, but Laurent possessed the confident, developed looks of a young man entering his prime, while Nicaise's was the epicene beauty peculiar to young boys of a certain age, short-lived, unlikely to survive adolescence.

"Do you think a compliment will impress me?" said Nicaise. "It won't. I get them all the time."

"I know you do," said Laurent.

"I remember the offer you made me. Everything you said then was a lie. I knew it was," said Nicaise. "You're leaving."

"I'm coming back," said Laurent.

"Is that what you think?"

Damen felt the hair rise all over his body. He remembered again Nicaise in the hallway after the attempt on Laurent's life. He resisted with difficulty the urge to crack Nicaise open and spill all his secrets out from inside.

"I'm coming back," said Laurent.

"To keep me as a pet?" said Nicaise. "You'd love that. To make me your servant."

Dawn passed over the courtyard. Colours changed. A

sparrow landed on one of the stable posts close by him but lifted off again at the sound of one of the men dropping an armful of tack.

"I would never ask you to do anything you found distasteful," said Laurent.

"Looking at you is distasteful," said Nicaise.

♦ ♦ ♦

There was no loving goodbye between uncle and nephew, only the impersonal ritual of public ceremony.

It was a spectacle. The Regent was in full robes of state, and Laurent's men were turned out with perfect discipline. Lined and polished, they stood arrayed in the outer court-yard, while the Regent at the top of wide steps received his nephew. It was a morning of warm, breathless weather. The Regent pinned some sort of jewelled badge of office to Laurent's shoulder, then urged him to rise, and kissed him calmly on both cheeks. When Laurent turned back to face his men, the clasp on his shoulder winked in the sunlight. Damen felt almost dizzy as the full sense memory of a long-ago fight took him: Auguste had worn that same badge on the field.

Laurent mounted. Banners furled out around him in a series of starbursts, blue and gold. Trumpets blared and Govart's horse kicked, despite its training. It was not only courtiers who were here to watch, but commoners, crowding near the gate. The scores of people who had turned out to see their Prince made a wall of approving sound. It didn't surprise Damen that Laurent was popular with the townspeople. He looked the part, all bright hair and astonishing profile. A golden prince was easy to love if you did not have to watch him picking wings off flies. Straight-backed and effortless in the saddle, he had an exquisite seat, when he was not killing his horse.

Damen, who had been given a horse as good as his sword and a place in the formation close by Laurent, kept his place as they rode out. But as they passed beyond the inner walls, he could not resist turning in his seat and looking back at the palace that had been his prison.

It was beautiful, the tall doors, the domes and towers, and the endless, intricate, interwoven patterns carved into the creamy stone. Alight with marble and polished metal, stretching themselves up to the sky were the curving roof spires that had hidden him from the sight of guards during his attempt to escape.

He was not insensible to the irony of his situation, riding out to protect the man who had done all he could to grind him under his heel. Laurent was his jailor, dangerous and malicious. Laurent was as likely to rake Akielos with his claws as his uncle. None of that mattered before the urgency of stopping the machinery of the Regent's plans. If it was the only way to prevent war, or postpone it, then Damen would do whatever was necessary to keep Laurent safe. He had meant that.

But having passed out of the walls of the Veretian palace, he knew one thing more. Whatever he had promised, he was leaving the palace behind him, and he did not intend, ever, to come back.

He returned his eyes to the road, and the first part of his journey. South, and home.

ACKNOWLEDGMENTS

This book was born in a series of Monday-night phone conversations with Kate Ramsay, who said, at one point, "I think this story is going to be bigger than you realise." Thank you, Kate, for being a great friend when I needed it most. I will always remember the sound of the wonky old phone ringing in my tiny Tokyo apartment.

I owe an enormous debt of thanks to Kirstie Innes-Will, my incredible friend and editor, who read countless drafts and spent tireless hours making the story better. I can't put into words how much that help has meant to me.

Anna Cowan is not only one of my favourite writers, she helped me so much on this story with her amazing brainstorming sessions and insightful feedback. Thank you so much, Anna. This story wouldn't be what it is without you.

All my thanks to my writing group—Isilya, Kaneko and Tevere—for all your ideas, feedback, suggestions and support.

I feel so lucky to have wonderful writer-friends like you in my life.

Finally, to everyone who has been part of the *Captive Prince* online experience, thank you all for your generosity and your enthusiasm, and for giving me the chance to make a book like this.

THE TRAINING
OF ERASMUS

A Captive Prince
Short Story

THE MORNING THAT he woke to feel the sheets sticky beneath him, Erasmus did not understand at first what had happened. The dream faded slowly, leaving an impression of warmth; he stirred, sleepily, his limbs heavy with pleasure that lingered. The cosy bedding felt good against his skin.

It was Pylaeus who drew back the bedding and knew the signs, and sent Delos to ring the bell and a boy runner to the palace, the bottoms of his feet flashing over the marble.

Erasmus scrambled up, dropped, knelt, his forehead pressed against the stone. He didn't dare to believe, yet his chest filled with hope. With every mote of his body he was aware that the sheets were being taken from the bed, wrapped with great care, and tied with a ribbon of gold thread to signify what—at last, oh please, at long last—had happened.

The body won't be rushed, old Pylaeus had said to him once,

kindly. Erasmus had flushed at the thought that he might
have shown his yearning on his face; yet every night he had
wished for it, wished that it would come before the sun rose
and he was another day older. The yearning had in those later
days taken on a new quality, a physical note that hummed
through his body like the quivering of a plucked string.

The bell started to clang through the gardens of Nereus as
Delos heaved on the rope, and Erasmus rose, his chest filled
with heartbeats, to follow Pylaeus to the baths. He felt gan-
gly and over-tall. He was old for it. He was older by three
years than the oldest to take training silks before him, despite all his fervent wishes that his body would offer up what
was needed to show him ready.

In the baths, the steam jets were turned on, and the air in
the room grew heavy. He soaked first, then he was laid out
on the white marble and his skin was steamed until it seemed
to throb with the perfumes of the air. He lay in the submissive posture with his wrists crossed above his head, which,
some nights, he had practiced alone in his own room, as if in
practicing he could conjure this very moment into being. His
limbs grew pliant against the smooth stone beneath him.

He had imagined it. At first excitedly, and then tenderly,
and then, as years passed, achingly. How he would lie still
for the ministrations, how he would lie perfectly still. How,
at the end of the day's rituals, the gold ribbon from the sheets
would be tied around his wrists, and he would be arranged
just so on the cushioned litter, the ribbon's ties so very fine,
so that a single breath might cause the knot to slither open,

and he must lie so still as the litter was carried out of the gates to begin his training in the palace. He had practiced that, too, wrists and ankles pressed together.

He emerged from the baths heat-dazed and yielding, so that when he knelt in the ritual pose, it felt natural, his limbs pliant and willing. Nereus, the owner of the gardens, flung out the sheets, and everyone admired the stains, and the younger boys clustered around, and while he knelt, gave him touches and happy tributes, kisses on the cheek, a garland of white morning glory dropped around his neck, chamomile flowers tucked behind his ear.

When he had imagined it, Erasmus had not imagined that he would feel so affectionate towards each moment, the shy little proffering of flowers from Delos, the shaking voice of old Pylaeus as he said the ritual words, the fact of parting making everything suddenly very dear. He felt, with a sudden swell, that he didn't want to stay where he knelt; he wanted to rise, to give Delos a fierce goodbye hug. To rush out to the narrow bedroom he would leave behind forever, the bare bed, his little relics that he must leave also, the spray of magnolia blossom in the vase on the sill.

He thought of the day the bell had rung for Kallias, the long embrace as they clung to each other at parting. *The bell will ring for you soon, I know it,* Kallias had said. *I know it, Erasmus.* That had been three summers ago.

It had taken so long, but suddenly it was too soon that boys were sent out, and the bolts on the doors were being thrown open.

And that was when the man came into the hallway.

Erasmus did not realise that he had fallen to his knees until he felt the cool marble against his forehead. The obliterating image of the man silhouetted in the doorway had struck him down. It beat inside Erasmus, dark hair framing a commanding face, features indomitable as the eagle. The power of him, the hard curve of a biceps where a leather strap gripped it, the muscles of a bronzed thigh between knee sandal and leather skirt. He wanted to look again, and did not dare lift his gaze from the stone.

Pylaeus addressed the man with the grace of his long-ago palace career, but Erasmus was barely aware of him, his skin hot. He didn't take in the words that Pylaeus and the man spoke to each other. He didn't know how much time passed after the man left before Pylaeus was coaxing him to look up.

Pylaeus said, "You're trembling."

He heard the soft, stunned quality of his voice.

"That . . . was a master from the palace?"

"A master?" Pylaeus's voice was not unkind. "That was a soldier of your retinue, sent to protect your litter. He is to your master as a single droplet to the great storm that comes from the ocean and splits open the sky."

♦ ♦ ♦

It was hot in summer.

Under the relentless blue sky, the walls, the steps and the paths heated steadily, so that by the time night fell, the marble gave off heat, like a warming brick taken straight from the fire. The ocean, which could be seen from the courtyard, seemed to withdraw from dry rocks each time it rolled back from the cliffs.

Palace slaves-in-training did what they could to keep cool: they kept to the shade; they practiced the art of the fan; they slipped in and out of the refreshing waters of the baths; they lay, sprawled like starfish beside the outdoor pools, the smooth stone hot beneath them, a friend propped up beside them, perhaps, drizzling cool water over their skin.

Erasmus liked it. He liked the extra strain that heat brought to his training, the extra effort of concentration that was required. It was right that training here in the palace should be more arduous than in the gardens of Nereus. It was befitting of the golden ribbon around his neck, a symbol of the golden collar he would earn when his three years as a palace slave-in-training were done. It was befitting of the golden pin he wore, a little weight at his shoulder that made his heart pound every time he thought of it, carved as it was with a tiny lion's head, the device of his future master.

He took his morning lessons with Tarchon in one of the small marble training rooms filled with accoutrements that he did not use, because from dawn until the sun reached the middle of the sky, it was the three forms, over and over and over again. Tarchon gave impassive corrections that Erasmus struggled to perform. At the end of each sequence, "Again." Then, when his muscles were aching, when his hair was drenched in the heat and his limbs slippery with sweat from holding a pose, Tarchon would tell him curtly, "Again."

"So Nereus's prize flower has finally blossomed," Tarchon had said on the day of his arrival. His inspection had been systematic and thorough. Tarchon was First Trainer. He had spoken inflectionlessly:

"Your looks are exceptional. This is an accident of birth for which you are not entitled to praise. You are training now for the royal household, and looks are not enough to earn you a place there. And you are old. You are older than the oldest I have worked with. Nereus hopes to have one of his slaves chosen to train for a First Night, but in twenty-seven years he has produced only one hopeful, the rest bath boys, table attendants."

Erasmus had not known what to do, or say. Arriving in the stifled dark of the litter, he had tried with each painful heartbeat to hold himself still. A fine sheen of sweat had broken out over him at the terror of being *outside*. Outside the gardens of Nereus, the calming, comforting gardens that contained all that he knew of life. He had been glad of the litter's coverings, the thick fabric that was dropped down to snuff out the light. There to protect him from the debasing stares of outside eyes, it had been all that had stood between him and vast, unknown space, the muffled unfamiliar sounds, clatters and shouts, the blinding light as the litter's coverings were thrown back.

But now the palace paths were as familiar as the palace routines, and when the noontime bell rang, he touched his forehead to the marble and said the ritual words of thanks, his limbs trembling with exhaustion, then he stumbled out to his afternoon lessons: languages, etiquette, ceremonies, massage, recitation, singing and the kithara—

Shock stopped him when he stepped out into the courtyard, and he stood, numb.

A spray of hair, a body limp. Blood on Iphegin's face where he lay on the shallow marble steps, a trainer supporting his head, two others kneeling in concern. Coloured silk bent over him like exotic feeding birds.

Slaves-in-training were gathering around him, a semicircle of onlookers.

"What happened?"

"Iphegin slipped on the stairs." And then, "You think Aden pushed him?"

The joke was awful. There were dozens of male slaves-in-training, but only four wore a golden pin, and Aden and Iphegin were the only two who wore the pin of the King. A voice at his elbow.

"Come away, Erasmus."

Iphegin was breathing. His chest was rising and falling. Blood down Iphegin's chin had stained the front of his training silks. He would have been on his way to a kithara lesson.

"Erasmus, come away."

Distantly, Erasmus felt a hand on his arm. He looked around blindly and saw Kallias. Trainers were lifting Iphegin and carrying him indoors. In the palace, he would be tended by concerned trainers and palace physicians.

"He'll be all right, won't he?"

"No," said Kallias. "It will scar."

◆ ◆ ◆

Erasmus would never forget how it had felt to see him again: a slave-in-training rising from a prostration to his trainer, heart-wrenchingly lovely, with a tumble of dark brown curls and wide-set blue eyes. There had always been something untouchable about his beauty, his eyes like the unreachable blue sky. Nereus had always said of him, *A man only has to look at him to want to possess him.*

Aden's mouth had turned down. "Kallias. You can moon over him all you want, everyone does. He won't look twice at you. He thinks he's better than everyone else."

"Erasmus?" Kallias had said, stopping as Erasmus had stopped, staring as Erasmus was staring, and in the next moment, Kallias was throwing his arms around Erasmus, holding him tight, pressing his cheek to Erasmus's cheek, the highest intimacy allowed to those who were forbidden to kiss.

Aden was staring at them, open-mouthed.

"You're here," said Kallias. "And you're for the Prince."

Erasmus saw that Kallias also wore a pin, but that it was plain gold, without a lion's head.

"I'm for the other Prince," said Kallias. "Kastor."

◆ ◆ ◆

They were inseparable, close as they had been in the gardens of Nereus, as though the three years of separation had never been. *Close as brothers,* the trainers said, smiling because this was a charming conceit, young slaves echoing the relationship of their princely masters.

In the evenings, and in the moments snatched around training, they spilled out their words and seemed to talk about everything. Kallias talked in his quiet, serious voice about vast, wide-ranging topics: politics, art, mythology, and he always knew the best of the palace gossip. Erasmus talked hesitatingly and for the first time about his most private feelings, his responsiveness to his training, his eagerness to please.

All of this with a new consciousness of Kallias's beauty. Of how far beyond him Kallias seemed.

Of course, Kallias was three years ahead of him in training, although they were the same age. That was because the age at which one took training silks differed and was not marked in years. *The body knows when it is ready.*

But Kallias was ahead of everyone. The slaves-in-training who weren't jealous hero-worshipped him. Yet there was a distance between Kallias and the others. He wasn't conceited. He often offered help to the younger boys, who blushed and grew awkward and flustered. But he never really talked to them, beyond politeness. Erasmus didn't know why Kallias singled him out, glad of it though he was. When Iphegin's room was cleared out and his kithara given to one of the new boys, all Kallias had said was, "He was named for Iphegenia, the most loyal. But they don't remember your name if you fall." Erasmus had said, meaning it. "You won't fall."

That afternoon, Kallias flung himself down in the shade and let his head rest in Erasmus's lap, his legs tumbled out on the soft grass. His eyes were closed, dark lashes resting against his cheeks. Erasmus barely moved at all, not wanting to disturb him, over-conscious of his heartbeats, of the weight of Kallias's head against his thigh, unsure of what to do with his hands. Kallias's un-self-conscious ease made Erasmus feel happy and very shy.

"I wish we could stay like this forever," he said, softly.

And then flushed. A curl of hair lay across Kallias's smooth forehead. Erasmus wanted to reach out and touch it, but he wasn't brave enough. Instead, this daring had blurted out of his mouth.

The garden was drenched with the heat of summer, the piping of a bird, the slow buzzing of an insect. He watched a dragonfly land on a pepperstalk. The slow movement only made him more conscious of Kallias.

After a moment, "I've started training for my First Night."

Kallias didn't open his eyes. It was Erasmus's heart that was suddenly beating too fast.

"When?"

"I'm to be Kastor's welcome when he returns from Delpha."

He said Kastor's name with its honorific, as all slaves did when they spoke of those above them, *Kastor-exalted*.

It had never made sense that Kallias was being trained for Kastor. Yet for some reason the Keeper of the Royal Slaves had decreed that his finest slave-in-training should go not to the heir or the King, but to Kastor.

"Do you ever wish for a lion pin? You're the finest slave in the palace. If anyone deserves to be in the retinue of the future King, it's you."

"Damianos doesn't take male slaves."

"Sometimes he—"

"I don't have your colouring," Kallias said, and he opened his eyes, reaching up to put his finger around a curl of Erasmus's hair.

◆ ◆ ◆

His colouring, if truth were told, had been carefully cultivated to the Prince's taste. His hair was daily rinsed with chamomile, so that it brightened and improved in lustre, and his skin kept from the sun until it changed from the golden cream of his early boyhood in the gardens of Nereus to a milky white.

"It's the cheapest way to get noticed," Aden said, his eyes displeased as he stared at Erasmus's hair. "A slave with real form doesn't draw attention to himself."

Kallias said later, "Aden would give his arm for fair hair. He wants a Prince's pin more than anything."

"He doesn't need a Prince's pin. He's training for the King."

"But the King is sick," said Kallias.

◆ ◆ ◆

The Prince's taste was for songs and verses of battle, which were more difficult to remember than the love poetry Erasmus preferred, and longer. A full performance of *The Fall of Inachtos* was four hours, and the *Hypenor* was six, so that every spare moment was spent in internal recitation. *Cut off from his brothers, he strikes too short at Nisos*, and *Held steady in single purpose, twelve thousand men*, and, *In relentless victory cleaves Lamakos with his sword*. He fell asleep murmuring the long heroic genealogies, the lists of weapons and of deeds that Isagoras wrote into his epics.

But that night, he let his mind drift to other poems, *In the long night, I wait*, Laechthon's yearning for Arsaces, as he unpinned his silks and felt the evening air against his skin.

Everyone whispered about First Night.

It was rare for boys to wear the pin. The pin meant a permanent place in the retinue of a member of the royal family. The pin meant more than that. Of course, any slave might be called on to serve in private, if the royal eye fell on him. But the pin meant the certainty of a First Night, in which the slave was presented to the royal bed.

Those who wore a pin received the best rooms, the strictest training and first privileges. Those without, dreamed of acquiring one and worked day and night in the attempt to prove worthy. In the male gardens, Aden said with a flick of his shiny brown hair, that was almost impossible. In the female gardens, of course, pins were more common. The tastes of the King and his two sons ran along predictable lines.

And since the birth of Damianos, there was no queen to select slaves for her own retinue. The King's permanent mistress Hypermenestra had full rights and kept slaves as befitted her status, but was too politic to take any but the King into her bed, said Aden. Aden was nineteen and in the last year of his training, and spoke about First Night with sophistication.

Laying himself down on the bedsheets, Erasmus was aware of the lingering responsiveness of his body, which he could not touch himself. Only those with special dispensation were allowed to handle him there, to wash him in the baths. Some days he liked it. He liked the ache of it. He liked the feeling that he was denying himself something to please his Prince. It felt strict, virtuous. Some days he just wanted, beyond reason, and it made the feeling of self-denial, of obedience, stronger, wanting it yet wanting to do as he was told, until he was all confusion. The idea of lying untouched on a bed and the Prince entering the room. . . It was an obliterating thought that overwhelmed him.

As yet untutored, he had no idea how it would be. He knew what the Prince liked, of course. He knew his favourite foods, those that might be selected for him at table. He knew his morning routine, the way he liked to have his hair brushed, his preferred style of massage.

He knew . . . he knew the Prince had many slaves. The attendants spoke of this with approval. The Prince had healthy appetites and took lovers frequently, slaves and nobles, too, when the need was on him. That was good. He was liberal with his affections, and a King should always have a large retinue.

He knew the Prince's eye tended to roam, that he was always pleased by something new, that his slaves were looked after, kept in permanent style, while his eye, roaming, frequently fell on new conquests.

He knew that when he wanted men, the Prince rarely took slaves. He was more likely to come from the arena with his blood up and pick out some display fighter. There was a gladiator from Isthima who had lasted in the arena for twelve minutes against the Prince before he'd fallen to him, and who had spent six hours in the Prince's chambers, after. He was told those stories, too.

And of course he only had to choose a fighter and they would yield to him as any slave, for he was the son of the King. Erasmus remembered the soldier he had seen in the gardens of Nereus, and the idea of the Prince mounting him was a stunning image in his mind. He could not imagine that power, and then he thought, *But he will take me like that*, and the deep shiver went all the way through his body.

He shifted his legs together. What would it be like, to be the receptacle for the Prince's pleasure? He lifted a hand to his own cheek and it felt hot, flushed as he lay back on the bed, exposed. The air felt like silk, his curls trailing like fronds across his forehead. He drew his hand to his forehead and pushed the curls back and even that gesture felt over-sensual, the slow motion of one underwater. He raised his wrists above his head and imagined the ribbon binding them, his body the Prince's to touch. His eyes closed. He thought of weight, dipping the mattress, an unformed image of the soldier he had seen silhouetted above him, the words of a poem, *Arsaces, undone*.

◆ ◆ ◆

The night of the fire festival, Kallias sang the ballad of Iphegenia, who had loved her master so much that she waited for him, though she knew what it meant to do so, and Erasmus felt the tears well up in his throat. He left the recital and walked out into the dark gardens, where the breeze was cool

in the scented trees. He did not care that the music was growing distant behind him, needing suddenly to see the ocean.

In the moonlight it was different, dark and unknowable,
but he felt it before him nonetheless, felt its vast openness.
He looked out from the stone balustrade in the courtyard
and felt the reckless wind against his face, the ocean like a
part of himself. He could hear the waves, imagined them
splashing his body, filling his sandals, the foaming water
swirling around him.

He'd never felt it before, that yearning, tossed feeling,
and he became aware that the familiar shape of Kallias was
coming up behind him. He spoke the words swelling up
inside him for the first time.

"I want to be taken across the ocean. I want to see other
lands. I want to see Isthima and Cortoza, I want to see the
place where Iphegenia waited, the great palace where Arsaces
gave himself to a lover," he said, recklessly. The yearning
inside him crested. "I want—to feel what it is to—"

"Live in the world," said Kallias.

It wasn't what he had meant to say, and he stared at Kallias and felt himself flush. And he was aware of something
different in Kallias, too, as Kallias drew alongside him, and
leaned on the stone balustrade, his eyes on the ocean.

"What is it?"

"Kastor has returned from Delpha early. Tomorrow will
be my First Night."

He looked at Kallias, saw that distant expression on his
face as he gazed out at the water, looking out to a world
Erasmus couldn't imagine.

"I'll work hard," Erasmus heard himself saying, the words a tumble. "I'll work so hard to catch up with you. You promised me in the gardens of Nereus that we'd see each other again, and I promise you now. I'll come to the palace, and you'll be a fêted slave, you'll perform on the kithara at the King's table every night, and Kastor will never be without you. You'll be magnificent. Nisos will write songs about you, and every man in the palace will look at you and envy Kastor."

Kallias didn't say anything, and the silence stretched out until Erasmus grew self-conscious of the words he had spoken. And then Kallias spoke in a raw little voice.

"I wish you could be my first."

He felt the words in his body, little explosions. It was as if he lay uncovered on the pallet as he had done in his small room, offering up his longing. His own lips parted without sound.

Kallias said, "Would you . . . would you put your arms around my neck?"

His heart beat painfully. He nodded, then wanted to hide his head. He felt lightheaded with daring. He slid his arms around Kallias's neck, feeling the smooth skin of his neck. His eyes closed to just feel. Snippets of verse floated through his mind.

In the columned halls, we embrace
His cheek rests against mine
Happiness like this comes once in a thousand years

He put his forehead against Kallias's.
"Erasmus," said Kallias, unsteadily.

"It's all right. It's all right as long as we don't—"

He felt Kallias's fingers on his hips. It was a delicate, helpless touch that preserved the space between their bodies. But it was as if he had completed a circle, Erasmus's arms around Kallias's neck, Kallias's fingers at his hips. The space between their bodies felt clouded and hot. He understood why those three places on his body were forbidden to him, because all of them began to ache.

He couldn't open his eyes, as he felt the embrace tighten, their cheeks pressing against one another, rubbing together, blindly, lost to the sensation, and just for a moment he felt—

"We *can't*!"

It was Kallias who pushed him away with a strangled cry. Kallias was panting, two feet away, his body curved around itself, as a breeze lifted the leaves of the tree, and they swayed back and forth, as the ocean swelled far below.

◆ ◆ ◆

On the morning of Kallias's First Night ceremony, he ate apricots.

Little round halves, ripened just past their early tang to perfect sweetness. Apricots, figs stuffed with a paste of almonds and honey, slices of salty cheese that crumbled against the tongue. Festival food for everyone: The ceremonies of First Night eclipsed anything he had seen in the gardens of Nereus, the height of a slave's career. And at the centre of it all, Kallias, paint on his face, the gold collar around his neck. Erasmus looked at him from a distance, holding on to the promise he had made to Kallias, tightly.

Kallias performed his role in the ceremony with perfect form. He never once looked at Erasmus.

Tarchon said, "He is fit for a King. I always questioned Adrastus's decision to send him to Kastor." *Your friend is a triumph,* the attendants whispered to him the next morning. And in the weeks after that, *He is the jewel of Kastor's household. He performs on kithara every night at table, displacing Ianessa. The King would covet him, if he weren't sick.*

◆ ◆ ◆

Aden was shaking him awake.

"What is it?" He rubbed his eyes sleepily. Aden was kneeling next to his narrow bed.

"Kallias is here. He had an errand for Kastor. He wants to see you."

It was like a dream, but he hurried to put on his silks, pinning them as best he could. "Come quickly," Aden said. "He's waiting."

He stepped out into the garden, following Aden out, past the courtyard to the paths winding through the trees. It was past midnight, and the gardens were so quiet that he could hear the sounds of the ocean, a soft murmur. He felt the paths under his bare feet. In the moonlight, he saw a slender, familiar figure gazing out at the water beyond the high cliffs.

He was barely aware of Aden retreating. Kallias's cheeks were brushed with paint, his lashes heavy with it. There was a single beauty mark high on his cheekbone that drew the gaze to his wide blue eyes. Painted like that, he had come from entertainments in the palace, or from his place in Kastor's household, at Kastor's side.

He had never looked so beautiful, the moon above him, the gleaming stars falling slowly into the sea.

"I'm so glad to see you, so glad you've come," said Erasmus, feeling happy but suddenly shy. "I am forever asking my attendants for stories of you, and saving stories of my own, thinking this or that I must tell Kallias."

"Are you?" said Kallias. "Glad to see me?" There was something strange about his voice.

"I missed you," said Erasmus. "We haven't talked to each other since—that night." He could hear the sounds of the water. "When you—"

"Tried to dine from a prince's table?"

"Kallias?" said Erasmus.

Kallias laughed, the sound uneven. "Tell me again that we'll be together. That you'll serve the Prince and I'll serve his brother. Tell me how it will be."

"I don't understand."

"Then I will teach you," said Kallias, and kissed him.

Shock, Kallias's painted lips against his, the hard press of teeth, Kallias's tongue in his mouth. His body was yielding, but his mind was clamouring, his heart felt that it was going to burst.

He was dazed, reeling, clutching his tunic to himself, to keep it from falling. Standing two paces away, Kallias was holding Erasmus's golden pin in his hand where he'd torn it from the silk.

And then the first real understanding of what they had done, the bruised throb of his lips, the stunned feeling of the ground opening up beneath his feet. He was staring at Kallias.

"You can't serve the Prince now, you're tainted." The words were sharp, jagged. "You're tainted. You could scrub at it for hours and you'd never wash it off."

"What is the meaning of this?" Tarchon's voice. Aden was suddenly there with Tarchon in tow, and Kallias was saying, *"He kissed me."*

"Is this true?" Tarchon took hold of his arm roughly, the grip painful.

I don't understand, he had said, and still he didn't understand it, even when he heard Aden saying, "It's true, Kallias even tried to push him away."

"Kallias," he gasped, but Tarchon was tipping his face up into the moonlight, and the evidence was smeared all over his lips, Kallias's red paint.

Kallias said, "He told me he couldn't stop thinking about me. That he wanted to be with me, not with the Prince. I told him it was wrong. He said he didn't care."

"Kallias," he said.

Tarchon was shaking him. "How could you do this? Were you trying to lose him his position? It is you who have wrecked yourself. You have thrown away everything that you have been given, the work of dozens, the time and attention that has been lavished on you. You will never serve inside these walls."

His eyes, desperately searching found Kallias's gaze, cool and untouchable.

"You said you wanted to cross the ocean," said Kallias.

◆ ◆ ◆

Three days of confinement, while trainers came in and out and spoke about his fate. And then the unthinkable.

There weren't witnesses. There wasn't a ceremony. They put a gold collar around his neck and dressed him in slave silks that he hadn't earned, that he didn't yet deserve.

He was a full slave, two years early, and they were sending him away.

He didn't start shaking until he was brought into a white marble room in an unknown part of the palace. The sounds were strange echoes, as though it was a vast cavern containing water. He tried to look around himself but the figures wavered like the flame of a candle behind warped glass.

He could still feel the kiss, the violence of it, his lips felt swollen.

But slowly he was becoming aware that the activity in this room was to some larger purpose. There were other slaves-in-training in the room with him. He recognised Narsis and Astacos. Narsis was about nineteen years of age, with a simple but sweet temperament. He would never wear a pin, but he would make an excellent table attendant, and perhaps a trainer himself one day, patient with the younger boys.

There was a strange atmosphere, bursts of sound here and there from outside. The rise and fall of voices were the voices of free men, masters, in whose presence he had never been allowed before.

Narsis whispered, "It's been like that all morning. No one knows what's happening. There are rumours—there have been soldiers in the palace. Astacos said he saw soldiers speaking with Adrastus, asking for the names of all the slaves who belonged to Damianos. Everyone wearing a lion pin was taken away. That's where we thought you'd be. Not here with us."

"But where are we? Why have we—why have we been brought here?"

"You don't know? We're being sent across the water. There are twelve of us, and twelve from the female training quarters."

"To Isthima?"

"No, along the coast, to Vere."

For a moment it seemed that the outside sounds grew louder. There was a distant metallic clash that he couldn't interpret. Another. He looked for answers to Narsis and saw his confused expression. It occurred to him, stupidly, that Kallias would know what was happening, that he should ask Kallias, and that was when the screams began.

KEEP READING FOR AN EXCERPT
FROM THE SECOND BOOK IN
THE CAPTIVE PRINCE TRILOGY
BY C. S. PACAT

PRINCE'S GAMBIT

AVAILABLE NOW FROM BERKLEY

◆ ◆ ◆

THE SHADOWS WERE long with sunset when they rode up, and the horizon was red. Chastillon was a single jutting tower, a dark round bulk against the sky. It was huge and old, like the castles far to the south, Ravenel and Fortaine, built to withstand battering siege. Damen gazed at the view, unsettled. He found it impossible to look at the approach without seeing the castle at Marlas, that distant tower flanked by long red fields.

"It's hunting country," said Orlant, mistaking the nature of his gaze. "Dare you to make a run for it."

He said nothing. He was not here to run. It was a strange feeling to be unchained and riding with a group of Veretian soldiers of his own free will.

A day's ride, even at the slow pace of wagons through pleasant countryside in late spring, was enough by which to judge the quality of a company. Govart did very little but sit, an impersonal shape above the swishing tail of his muscled horse, but whoever had captained these men previously had drilled them to maintain immaculate formation over the long course of a ride. The discipline was a little surprising. Damen wondered if they could hold their lines in a fight.

If they could, there was some cause for hope, though in truth, his wellspring of good mood had more to do with the outdoors, the sunshine and the illusion of freedom that came with being given a horse and a sword. Even the weight of the gold collar and cuffs on his throat and wrists could not diminish it.

The household servants had turned out to meet them, arraying themselves as they would for the arrival of any significant party. The Regent's men, who were supposedly stationed at Chastillon awaiting the Prince's arrival, were nowhere to be seen.

There were fifty horses to be stabled, fifty sets of armour and tack to be unstrapped, and fifty places to be readied in the barracks—and that was only the men-at-arms, not the servants and wagons. But in the enormous courtyard the Prince's party looked small, insignificant. Chastillon was large enough to swallow fifty men as though the number were nothing.

No one was pitching tents. The men would sleep in the barracks; Laurent would sleep in the keep.

Laurent swung out of the saddle, peeled off his riding gloves, tucking them into his belt, and gave his attention to the castellan. Govart barked a few orders, and Damen found himself occupied with armour, detailing and care of his horse.

Across the courtyard, a couple of alaunt hounds came bounding down the stone stairs to throw themselves ecstatically at Laurent, who indulged one of them with a rub behind the ears, causing a spasm of jealousy in the other.

Orlant broke Damen's attention. "Physician wants you," he said, pointing with his chin to an awning at the far end of the courtyard, under which could be glimpsed a familiar grey head. Damen put down the breastplate he was holding and went.

"Sit," said the physician.

Damen did so, rather gingerly, on the only available seat, a small three-legged stool. The physician began to unbuckle a worked leather satchel.

"Show me your back."

"It's fine."

"After a day in the saddle? In armour?" said the physician.

"It's fine," said Damen.

The physician said, "Take off your shirt."

The physician's gaze was implacable. After a long moment, Damen reached behind himself and drew his shirt off, exposing the breadth of his shoulders to the physician.

It was fine. His back had healed enough that new scars had replaced new wounds. Damen craned for a glimpse but, not being an owl, saw almost nothing. He stopped before he got a crick in his neck.

The physician rummaged in the satchel and produced one of his endless ointments.

"A massage?"

"These are healing salves. It should be done every night. It will help the scarring to fade a little, in time."

That was really too much. "It's cosmetic?"

The physician said, "I was told you would be difficult. Very well. The better it heals, the less your back will trouble you with stiffness, both now and later in life, so that you will be better able to swing a sword around, killing a great many people. I was told you would be responsive to that argument."

"The Prince," said Damen. But of course. All this tender care of his back, like soothing with a kiss the reddened cheek you have slapped.

But he was, infuriatingly, right. Damen needed to be able to fight.

The ointment was cool, and scented, and it worked on the effect of a long day's ride. One by one, Damen's muscles unlocked. His neck bent forward, his hair falling a little about his face. His breathing eased. The physician worked with impersonal hands.

"I don't know your name," Damen admitted.

"You don't remember my name. You were in and out of consciousness the night we met. A lash or two more, you might not have seen morning."

Damen snorted. "It wasn't that bad."

The physician gave him an odd look. "My name is Paschal," was all he said.

"Paschal," said Damen. "It's your first time to ride with troops on campaign?"

"No. I was the King's physician. I tended the fallen at Marlas and at Sanpelier."

There was a silence. Damen had meant to ask Paschal what he knew of the Regent's men, but now he said nothing, just held his bunched shirt in his hands. The work on his back continued, slow and methodical.

"I fought at Marlas," said Damen.

"I assumed you had."

Another silence. Damen had a view of the ground under the awning, packed earth instead of stone. He looked down at a scuff mark, the torn edge of a dry leaf. The hands on his back eventually lifted and were done.

Outside, the courtyard was clearing; Laurent's men were efficient. Damen stood, shook out his shirt.

"If you served the King," said Damen, "how is it you now find yourself in the Prince's household and not his uncle's?"

"Men find themselves in the places they put themselves," Paschal said, closing his satchel with a snap.

◆ ◆ ◆

Returning to the courtyard, he couldn't report to Govart, who had vanished, but he did find Jord, directing traffic.

"Can you read and write?" Jord asked him.

"Yes, of course," said Damen. Then stopped.

Jord didn't notice. "Almost nothing's been done to prepare for tomorrow. The Prince says we're not leaving without a full arsenal. He also says we're not delaying departure. Go to the western armoury, take an inventory, and give it to that man." Pointing. "Rochert."

Since taking a full inventory was a task that would take all night, Damen assumed what he was to do was check the existing inventory, which he found in a series of leather-bound books. He opened the first of them, searching for the correct pages, and felt a strange sensation pass over him when he realised that he was looking at a seven-year-old list of hunting weaponry made for the Crown Prince Auguste.

Prepared for His Highness the Crown Prince Auguste, garniture of hunter's cutlery, one staff, eight tipped spearheads, bow and strings.

He was not alone in the armoury. From somewhere behind shelves came the cultured voice of a young male courtier saying, "You've heard your orders. They come from the Prince."

"Why should I believe that? You his pet?" said a coarser voice.

And another: "I'd pay to watch that."

And another: "The Prince has got ice in his veins. He doesn't fuck. We'll take orders when the Captain comes and tells us them himself."

"How dare you speak about your Prince like that. Choose your weapon. I said choose your weapon. Now."

"You're going to get hurt, pup."

"If you're too much of a coward to—" said the courtier, and before he was even halfway through that sentence, Damen was folding his grip around one of the swords and walking out.

He rounded the corner just in time to see one of three men in the Regent's livery draw back, swing, and punch the courtier hard in the face.

The courtier wasn't a courtier. It was the young soldier whose name Laurent had dryly mentioned to Jord. *Tell the servants to sleep with their legs closed. And Aimeric.*

Aimeric staggered backwards and hit the wall, sliding halfway down its length as he opened and closed his eyes with stupefied blinks. Blood poured from his nose.

The three men had seen Damen.

"That's shut him up," said Damen, equitably. "Why don't you leave it at that, and I'll take him back to the barracks."

It wasn't Damen's size that stopped them. It wasn't the sword he held casually in his hand. If these men really wanted to make a fight of it, there were enough swords, flingable armour pieces, and teetering shelves to turn this into something long and ludicrous. It was only when the leader of the men saw Damen's gold collar that he shoved out an arm, holding the others back.

And Damen understood, in that moment, exactly how things were going to be on this campaign: the Regent's men in ascendancy. Aimeric and the Prince's men were targets because they had no one to complain to except Govart, who would slap them back down. Govart, the Regent's favourite thug, brought here to keep the Prince's men in check. But Damen was different. Damen was untouchable because Damen had a direct line of reportage to the Prince.

He waited. The men, unwilling to openly defy the Prince, decided on discretion; the man who had laid out Aimeric nodded slowly, and the three moved off and out, Damen watching them go.

He turned to Aimeric, noting his fine skin and elegant wrists. It wasn't unheard of for younger sons of the highborn to seek out a position in the royal guard, making what name for themselves they could. But as far as Damen had seen, Laurent's men were of a rougher sort. Aimeric was probably exactly as out of place among them as he looked.

Damen held out his hand, which Aimeric ignored, pushing himself up.

"How old are you? Eighteen?"

"Nineteen," said Aimeric.

Around the smashed nose, he had a fine-boned aristocratic face, beautifully shaped dark brows, long dark lashes. He was more attractive up close. You noticed things like his pretty mouth, even dripping with nosebleed.

Damen said, "It's never a good idea to start a fight. Particularly against three men when you're the type who goes down with one punch."

"If I go down, I stand back up. I'm not afraid to be hit," said Aimeric.

"Well, good, because if you insist on provoking the Regent's men, it's going to happen a lot. Tip your head back."

Aimeric stared at him, hand clasped to his nose, holding a fistful of blood. "You're the Prince's pet. I've heard all about you."

Damen said, "If you're not going to tip your head back, why don't we go find Paschal? He can give you a scented ointment."

Aimeric didn't budge. "You couldn't take a flogging like a man. You opened your mouth and squealed to the Regent. You laid hands on him. You spat on his reputation. Then you tried to escape, and he still intervened for you because he'd never abandon a member of his household to the Regency. Not even someone like you."

Damen had gone very still. He looked at the boy's young, bloody face, and reminded himself that Aimeric had been willing to take a beating from three men in defence of his Prince's honor. He'd call it misguided puppy love, except that he'd seen the glint of something similar in Jord, in Orlant, and even, in his own quiet way, in Paschal.

Damen thought of the ivory-and-gold casing that held a creature duplicitous, self-serving and untrustworthy.

"You're so loyal to him. Why is that?"

"I'm not a turncoat Akielon dog," said Aimeric.

◆ ◆ ◆

Damen delivered the inventory to Rochert, and the Prince's Guard began the task of preparing arms, armour and wagons for their departure the following morning. It was work that should have been done before their arrival, by the Regent's men. But of the hundred and fifty Regent's men set to ride out with the Prince, fewer than two dozen had turned out to help them.

Damen joined the work, where he was the only man to smell, expensively, of ointments and cinnamon. The sole knot remaining in Damen's back concerned the fact that the castellan had ordered him to report to the keep when he was done.

After an hour or so, Jord approached him.

"Aimeric's young. He says it won't happen again," said Jord.

It will happen again, and once the two factions in this camp start retaliating against each other your campaign is over, he didn't say. He said, "Where's the Captain?"

"The Captain is in one of the horse stalls, up to his waist in the stableboy," said Jord. "The Prince has been waiting for him at the barracks. Actually . . . I was told to have you fetch him."

"From the stables," said Damen. He stared at Jord in disbelief.

"Better you than me," said Jord. "Look for him down the back. Oh, and when you're done, report to the keep."

It was a long walk across two courtyards from the barracks to the stables. Damen hoped that Govart would be finished by the time he arrived, but, of course, he wasn't. The stables contained all the quiet sounds of horses at night, yet even so, Damen heard it before he saw it: the soft rhythmic sounds coming, as Jord had accurately predicted, from the back.

Damen weighed Govart's reaction to an interruption against Laurent's to being kept waiting. He pushed open the stall door.

Inside, Govart was unambiguously fucking the stableboy against the far wall. The boy's pants were in a crumpled heap on the straw not far from Damen's feet. His bare legs were splayed wide, and his shirt was open and pushed up onto his back. His face was pressed to the rough wooden panelling and held in place by Govart's fist in his hair. Govart was dressed. He had unlaced his own pants only enough to take out his cock.

Govart stopped long enough to glance sideways and say, "What?" before, deliberately, continuing. The stableboy, seeing Damen, reacted differently, squirming.

"Stop," said the stableboy. "Stop. Not with someone watching—"

"Calm down. It's just the Prince's pet."

Govart jerked the stableboy's head back for emphasis.

Damen said, "The Prince wants you."

"He can wait," said Govart.

"No. He can't."

"He wants me to pull out on his order? Go visit him with a hard prick?" Govart bared his teeth in a grin. "You think that too-stuck-up-to-fuck stuff is just an act, and he's really just a tease who wants cock?"

Damen felt anger settle inside him, a tangible weight. He recognized an echo of the impotence Aimeric must have experienced in the armoury, except that he was not a green nineteen-year-old who had never seen a fight. His eyes passed impassively over the half-unclothed body of the stableboy. He realised that in a moment he was going to return to Govart in this small, dusty stall all that was owed for the rape of Erasmus.

He said, "Your Prince gave you an order."

Govart forestalled him, pushing the stableboy away in annoyance. "Fuck, I can't get off with all this—" Tucking himself back in. The stableboy stumbled a few steps, sucking in air.

"The barracks," said Damen, and weathered the impact of Govart's shoulder against his own as Govart strode out.

The stableboy stared at Damen, breathing hard. He was braced against the wall with one hand; the other was between his legs in furious modesty. Wordlessly, Damen picked up the boy's pants and tossed them at him.

"He was supposed to pay me a copper sol," said the stable-boy, sullenly.

Damen said, "I'll take it up with the Prince."

◆ ◆ ◆

And then it was time to report to the castellan, who led him up steps and all the way into the bedchamber.

It was not as ornate as the palace chambers in Arles. The walls were thick hewn stone. The windows were frosted glass, criss-crossed with lattice. With the darkness outside, they did not offer a view, but instead reflected the shadows of the room. A frieze of twining vine leaves ran around the room. There was a carved mantle and a banked fire; and lamps, and wall hangings, and the cushions and silks of a separate slave pallet, he noticed, with a feeling of relief. Dominating the room was the heavy opulence of the bed.

The walls around the bed were panelled in dark, carved wood, depicting a hunting scene in which a boar was held at the end of a spear, pierced through the neck. There was no sign of the blue and gold starburst. The draperies were blood red.

Damen said, "These are the Regent's chambers." There was something uneasily transgressive about the idea of sleeping in the place meant for Laurent's uncle. "The Prince stays here often?"

The castellan mistook him to mean the keep, not the rooms. "Not often. He and his uncle came here a great deal together, in the year or two after Marlas. As he grew older, the Prince lost his taste for the runs here. He now comes only rarely to Chastillon."

At the order of the castellan, servants brought him bread and meat, and he ate. They cleared away the plates and brought in a beautifully shaped pitcher and goblets, and left, perhaps by accident, the knife. Damen looked at the knife and thought about how much he would have given for an oversight like that when he was trussed up in Arles: a knife that he might take and use to prise his way out of the palace.

He sat himself down to wait.

On the table before him was a detailed map of Vere and Akielos, each hill and crest, each town and keep meticulously recorded. The river Seraine snaked its way south, but he already knew they were not following the river. He put his fingertip on Chastillon and traced one possible path to Delpha, south through Vere, until he reached the line that marked the edge of his own country, all the place-names written jarringly in Veretian: *Achelos, Delfeur.*

In Arles, the Regent had sent assassins to kill his nephew. It had been death at the bottom of a poisoned cup, at the end of a drawn sword. That was not what was happening here. Throw together two feuding companies, put them under a partisan, intolerant captain, and hand the result to a green commander-prince. This group was going to tear itself apart.

And likely there was nothing Damen could do to stop it happening. This was going to be a ride of disintegrating morale; the ambush that surely awaited them at the border would devastate a company already in disarray, ruined by infighting and negligent leadership. Laurent was the only counterweight against the Regent, and Damen would do all he had promised to keep him alive, but the stark truth of this ride to the border was that it felt like the last play in a game that was already over.

Whatever business Laurent had with Govart kept him deep into the night. The sounds from the keep grew quiet; the fluttering of the flames grew audible in the hearth.

Damen sat and waited, his hands loosely clasped. The feelings that freedom—the illusion of freedom—stirred in him were strange. He thought of Jord and Aimeric and all Laurent's men working through the night to prepare for an early departure. There were house servants in the keep, and he was not eager for Laurent's return. But as he waited in the empty rooms, the fire flickering in the hearth, his eyes passing over the careful lines of the map, he was conscious, as he had seldom been during his captivity, of being alone.

Laurent entered, and Damen rose from his seat. Orlant could be glimpsed in the doorway behind him.

"You can go. I don't need a guard on the door," said Laurent.

Orlant nodded. The door closed.

Laurent said, "I have saved you till last."

Damen said, "You owe the stableboy a copper sol."

"The stableboy should learn to demand payment before he bends over."

Laurent calmly helped himself to goblet and pitcher, pouring himself a drink. Damen couldn't help glancing at the goblet, remembering the last time they had been alone together in Laurent's rooms.

Pale brows arched a fraction. "Your virtue's safe. It's just water. Probably." Laurent took a sip, then lowered the goblet, holding it in refined fingers. He glanced at the chair, as a host might offering a seat, and said, as though the words amused him, "Make yourself comfortable. You are going to stay the night."

"No restraints?" said Damen. "You don't think I'll try to leave, pausing only to kill you on the way out?"

"Not until we get closer to the border," said Laurent. He returned Damen's gaze evenly. There was no sound but the crack and pop of the banked fire.

"You really do have ice in your veins, don't you?" said Damen.

Laurent placed the goblet carefully back on the table and picked up the knife.

It was a sharp knife, made for cutting meat. Damen felt his pulse quicken as Laurent came forward. Only a handful of nights ago, he had watched Laurent slit a man's throat, spilling blood as red as the silk that covered this room's bed. He felt shock as Laurent's fingers touched his, pressing the hilt of the knife into his hand. Laurent took hold of Damen's wrist below the gold cuff, firmed his grip, and drew the knife forward so that it was angled towards his own stomach. The tip of the blade pressed slightly into the dark blue of his prince's garment.

"You heard me tell Orlant to leave," said Laurent.

Damen felt Laurent's grip slide down his wrist to his fingers, and tighten.

Laurent said, "I am not going to waste time on posturing

and threats. Why don't we clear up any uncertainty about your intentions?"

It was well-placed, just below the rib cage. All he would have to do was push in, then angle up.

He was so infuriatingly sure of himself, proving a point. Damen felt desire come hard upon him: not wholly a desire for violence, but a desire to drive the knife into Laurent's composure, to force him to show something other than cool indifference.

He said: "I'm sure there are house servants still awake. How do I know you won't scream?"

"Do I seem like the type to scream?"

"I'm not going to use the knife," said Damen, "but if you're willing to put it in my hand, you underestimate how much I want to."

"No," said Laurent. "I know exactly what it is to want to kill a man, and to wait."

Damen stepped back and lowered the knife. His knuckles remained tight around it. They gazed at each other.

Laurent said, "When this campaign is over, I think—if you are a man and not a worm—you will attempt to gain retribution for what has happened to you. I expect it. On that day, we roll the dice and see how they fall. Until then, you serve me. Let me therefore make one thing above all clear to you: I expect your obedience. You are under my command. If you object to what you are told to do, I will hear reasoned arguments in private, but if you disobey an order once it is made, I will send you back to the flogging post."

"Have I disobeyed an order?" said Damen.

Laurent gave him another of those long, oddly searching looks. "No," said Laurent. "You have dragged Govart out of the stables to do his duty, and rescued Aimeric from a fight."

Damen said, "You have every other man working until dawn to prepare for tomorrow's departure. What am I doing here?"

Another pause, and then Laurent indicated the chair once again. This time Damen followed his prompt and sat. Laurent took the chair opposite. Between them, unfurled on the table, was all the intricate detail of the map.

"You said you knew the territory," Laurent said.

C. S. Pacat is the *New York Times* and *USA Today* bestselling author of the Captive Prince trilogy, *Dark Rise*, and the GLAAD-nominated graphic novel series Fence. Educated at the University of Melbourne, C. S. Pacat has lived in a number of cities, including Tokyo and Perugia, and currently resides and writes in Melbourne. You can find the author at CSPacat.com.